Murder at Thumb Butte

**Center Point
Large Print**

Also by James D. Best
and available from Center Point Large Print:

The Shopkeeper
Leadville

**This Large Print Book carries the
Seal of Approval of N.A.V.H.**

Murder at Thumb Butte

A Steve Dancy Tale

James D. Best

CENTER POINT PUBLISHING
THORNDIKE, MAINE

Library of Congress Cataloging-in-Publication Data

Best, James D., 1945–
    Murder at Thumb Butte : a Steve Dancy tale / James D. Best. — Center Point large print ed.
        p. cm.
    ISBN 978-1-61173-262-7 (library binding : alk. paper)
    1. Large type books. I. Title.
    PS3602.E785M87 2011
    813′.6—dc23
                                                        2011035314

For Luke, Charlotte, and Wyatt

Murder at Thumb Butte

Chapter 1

"Four."

"I'm impressed," Sharp said.

"Four thousand isn't that much," I said. "Mrs. Baker's done better with our store in Leadville."

"Yep, but she ain't gonna be a literary giant like you."

Jeff Sharp and I lounged on the porch of the St. Charles Hotel in Carson City, Nevada. While Sharp oversaw his mining operations in Belleville, I had spent the winter writing a novel about my adventures in the West. He had driven a buggy into town the previous evening, just in time to enjoy the first decent spring morning. It may have been the warmest day of 1880, but it remained chilly enough for us to wear heavy coats as we sipped our morning coffee.

I was pleased to see Sharp again, but not because we jointly owned a general store in Leadville, Colorado. The store was a minor investment, and Mrs. Baker ran it with very little direction from us. I was happy because Sharp's timing was perfect. I had mailed my manuscript to a publisher two days earlier, and after spending the winter indoors with fictional characters, I was eager to sit outside and talk to breathing human beings.

Sharp shook his head. "I can't believe they gave ya four grand, sight unseen."

"They saw six chapters before settling on the amount. Besides, they won't deposit the final part of the advance until they approve the complete manuscript."

Sharp grinned. "Am I in it?"

"Jeff, I didn't use real names . . . but you might recognize a gent named Jeffery Harper."

"Damn it, Steve, ya know I hate Jeffery."

Now I grinned. "I know."

"Ya use Steve Dancy?"

"Of course not. I'm the author. Besides, I thought Dancy sounded citified."

"What'd ya call yerself?"

"It's fictional."

"Okay, what'd ya call the hero?"

"Jeffery Harper."

"Bull."

I smiled. "Joseph Steele."

Sharp laughed. "I s'pose Mr. Steele rid the West of outlaws without any help from Mr. Harper."

I smiled. "It'll cost you two bits to find out."

"Whoa, ya gonna make me buy a copy?"

"No . . . I owe you more than a book, but I won't tell you about it." I threw Sharp a glance. "You're going to have to read it."

"Fair 'nough." Sharp sipped his coffee and surveyed the street. After a long silence, he asked, "Ever think 'bout Sam?"

"Every day. Probably should have changed hotels, but it seemed disrespectful to run from memories."

The previous summer, two hired killers had tried to ambush me in front of this very hotel. My quick-witted Pinkerton guards threw me to the boardwalk, and a gun battle raged for several minutes. Sam—a friend and a Pinkerton—had died from a shot to the gut. I had been the only one at his side in his last hours.

"Damn shame."

"Damn shame," I repeated.

"Too early for flowers. Like to stop by his grave, just the same."

"On occasion, I go up there and share a whiskey with him."

"Let's take a bottle out there this evening."

"He'd like that."

We drank our coffee and watched the traffic wheel by for a few minutes. Carson City was the capital of Nevada and close to Virginia City's Comstock Lode. The traffic in front of our hotel was dominated by politicians and silver barons—and the crafty who had grown wealthy supplying the needs of the other two. The exclusive St. Charles Hotel was only a few blocks away from the sandstone capitol, and the traffic this spring morning—whether on foot, hoof, or wheels—strutted like each and every one of them was the cock of the walk.

"The book's done." I shook my head at the parade in front of me. "I want to get out of here."

"I'm ready to git too. Been thinkin' 'bout returnin' to Leadville."

"Mrs. Baker's doing a fine job. I was thinking south."

"I like to check on my investments."

I laughed at Sharp's lame excuse. "Hell, that store's a small operation for you. You want to entice Mrs. Baker into your bed."

"Hadn't entered my mind, but I'll convey yer suggestion to her."

"Jeff, it's cold in Leadville. The town won't thaw for months. Let's go to Arizona. It's warm and there's plenty of silver."

"Ain't America."

"Hell, we own it."

"Things are different below the border. There ain't nothin' but Apaches an' outlaws down there . . . an' territorial law can't be trusted to protect ya."

"That's why I want to go to Prescott. John C. Frémont's the territorial governor. I can get him to grease wheels for us."

"Ya know him?"

I laughed. "Not really, but I've sat on his knee."

"Hope that weren't recent."

"Twenty-five years ago. I was six. Still too old to be bounced on someone's knee, but the ol' Pathfinder insisted."

"Ya think he'll remember yer bony derrière?"

"He'll remember how my family helped his bid

for the presidency. The Republican Party was new, and he needed New York money and publicity. Horace Greeley provided the ink, and my family showed him the money."

"I met Greeley in Colorado," Sharp mused. "Hated the little rooster. He said, 'Go west, young man,' but he wanted 'em to build some sort of Garden of Eden out of this wilderness. Don't 'xpect that's what Frémont's doin' in Arizona."

"Doubt it. Frémont was down to someone else's last dollar when he begged President Hayes for a position. Hayes knew he was a pain in the ass, so he gave Frémont a useless job as far away from the capital as he could send him."

"That man has failed at everything. What makes ya think he can help us?"

"Jeff, that's too harsh. He was a great explorer."

"Then maybe he belongs in a desert wilderness." Sharp waved at a passerby he recognized. "I say we head for Leadville. Lots of money to be made in that town. By the way, rail line's finished, so no need to ride horses."

"There's more opportunity in Arizona, and a man can move between buildings without taking fifteen minutes to bundle up."

"Steve, I set my mind on Leadville. I'm leavin' in a couple of days, an' I came to Carson City to fetch ya. Spring's the best time to find good claims." He turned his head to catch my eye. "Ya with me?"

I sipped the last remnants of my coffee to stall. I had grown up in New York City, and lived there until a little over a year ago, when I had sold my investments, including my gun shop, and ventured west to see and experience the frontier. Jeff and I had been in Leadville together last autumn. I wanted to see more of the West, not revisit places I had already been. Sharp was the biggest private mine operator in Nevada, and it appeared he wanted to extend his silver holdings to Colorado. I was tired of Carson City and wanted to venture away from Nevada. Damn. I couldn't imagine riding off into the wilderness without my friend.

I sighed and set my empty coffee mug down. "Will you go to Arizona with me after we explore investment opportunities?"

"Yep."

"Then I'll go with you, but I'm taking Liberty."

"Hell, yes, I'll take my horse as well. Transportin' our horses on the train'll be a lot cheaper than buyin' animals in Leadville." Something must have shown on my face, because he quickly added, "Steve, that buggy lets me carry a comfortable bedroll and food I don't need to gnaw a half hour before swallowin'. Must be gettin' old, 'cuz I'm gettin' to like them comforts. But don't get uppity, I still mainly ride a horse."

To disguise his embarrassment, Sharp picked up our coffee mugs to go inside for refills. He stopped at the door. "Steve, ya might as well know . . . I'm sellin' all of my silver interests in Nevada. That's why I'm goin' to Leadville. New start."

"Claims drying up?"

"Best to sell while they're still producin'. I don't like what's happenin' here. Lot of it yer fault."

"What're you talking about?"

"That whippersnapper ya put in charge of the bank in Pickhandle has turned greedier than Washburn ever was, and those dunderheads at the statehouse won't support free silver . . . and Richard's the worst of 'em."

Sharp disappeared into the hotel, apparently to give me time to ponder my sins.

The U.S. government had demonetized silver in 1873, and the Free Silver Movement wanted silver coinage reinstated. Silver men would grow richer, but I feared it would cause inflation that would erode my paper investments. Richard was my friend, one I had been proud to help elect to the state senate. Despite Sharp's criticism, I had no regrets on that score. The whippersnapper Sharp referred to was another matter altogether. Peter had been a skittish law clerk when I met him. I set him up as an assistant manager at a bank I had once owned in Pickhandle Gulch, Nevada. When I sold the bank to Commerce, he was made manager, and—away from the prying eyes of the parent bank—had built his deposits and profits using dubious means.

Something caught my attention in the street traffic. Speak of the devil. It was Richard hurrying directly toward me. What did he want?

He clambered up the porch steps and plopped into the seat Sharp had vacated. Without preamble, he blurted, "Steve, we need your help."

"Who's we, Senator?" I had no inclination to get involved in state politics.

"The Whist Club."

"I'm listening." These were people I cared about.

"Peter has taken over our hotel and Jeremiah's store."

"How?"

Jeremiah was another friend from my days in Pickhandle Gulch. When I left the mining encampment, I owned the sole hotel in town. In a gesture of friendship, I had deeded one quarter of the hotel to each of the members of our nightly whist club, which included a quarter share for me. The other partners were Richard, Jeremiah, and Dr. Dooley, who now resided in Glenwood Springs, Colorado. Since Jeremiah was the only one remaining in Pickhandle, he ran the hotel for us, along with his general store.

"Peter controls the county, and he boosted taxes on both properties . . . seven thousand a year for the hotel alone."

I almost jumped to my feet. "That's outrageous!"

"No, it's thievery."

"The town owns the hotel?"

"The county . . . and Peter is the county." With an embarrassed expression, he added, "You created this monster."

Because I was in a hurry, I had casually selected Peter to run my small bank. At the time, my main concern had been that he wasn't tough enough for a lawless outpost. I certainly never expected him to become a petty tyrant. I was wealthy, with most of my investments in Wall Street. I hadn't taken my small stake in this hotel seriously, except as a way of thanking my friends for helping me out of a tough situation.

"I'll talk to Commerce Bank," I said.

"No! You gotta go down there. I've already talked to Commerce. They said this is local politics and has nothing to do with them. They refuse to intervene."

"I can't go to Pickhandle. I promised Jeff to go with him to Leadville."

"That's right." I heard Sharp's voice behind me. "Nothin' Steve can do anyway."

I whipped my head around to see Sharp with a mug of coffee in each hand. "You know about this?" I asked.

"Yep. Reason I'm sellin'. This state's too corrupt. Knock down one crook, and another just pops up like those little creatures at a carnival shooting gallery."

"Why didn't you tell me?" I demanded.

Sharp smiled and waved his arm, encompassing the whole street. "Didn't want to spoil this gorgeous mornin'. Life's what it is down south. Nothin' gonna change for decades."

"You can change it, Steve," Richard insisted. "You can put Peter in his place."

Something occurred to me. "Is the sheriff part of this?"

"Clive? Of course. Peter couldn't handle this by himself. But Clive's been pushed aside. Now he's town marshal. There's a new sheriff, and I hear he makes Clive look like a schoolmarm."

I had been sympathetic up to this point, but now I had to bring this conversation to a halt. I was not going to get into another gun battle.

"Richard, I'm leaving for Colorado. Soon."

"It's your property they stole . . . and they beat the hell out of Jeremiah."

"What? How bad's he hurt?

"Not sure, but I heard he lost sight in one eye. Might be dead. Can't get a telegram out of that hellhole since the incident."

I gave Jeff an angry stare. "Didn't want to spoil a gorgeous morning, huh?"

Jeff shrugged. "Nothin' to be done 'bout it now."

I stood. "We'll see. I'm going to Pickhandle."

18

Chapter 2

Pickhandle Gulch hadn't changed. The stamp mill still spewed dust everywhere, and the miners' scattered rock hovels proved that only rough, untidy men resided in this woebegone encampment. The miner dwellings were made of rocks because trees were a long way off, and lumber that made it this far into the southern Nevada desert was more valuable shoring up mine tunnels. Leadville last autumn had been a beehive of frenzied construction, but I could see nothing new in Pickhandle. Materials were scarce, but more to the point, time was better spent clawing silver out of the ground.

Jeff Sharp rode beside me. He had suddenly claimed to have unfinished business at his mining headquarters in Belleville, twenty miles north of Pickhandle, but I suspected he felt guilty about convincing me to go to Leadville without telling me about Jeremiah. Whatever the reason, I welcomed his presence. I also welcomed the two guards he had picked up at his mining operation the night before. They were hard-looking men, which I liked. I'd much rather resolve this issue with intimidation than with guns.

I had renamed the Grand Hotel the Whist Hotel after I got full ownership, but as we approached, I noticed the sign over the porch once again read

Grand Hotel. Now I understood how a rancher felt when he discovered his cows with an altered brand.

I only knew the sheriff by the name of Clive. He was a big, heavy-gutted man who made a comfortable living as a bully. In fact, he had four thousand dollars of mine, money I had paid him for his half of the hotel. Come to think of it, he probably again owned the hotel that used to belong to my partners and me. Then I remembered that he had been booted out of the sheriff's job and was now town marshal. I found that disappointing. The new sheriff might not be as easy to handle.

We rode directly to the livery. Liberty had taken the four-day ride with ease. I cut him loose a few times, and he ran fast and with enormous enthusiasm. Even though I had owned this horse only a couple of months, we were getting used to each other, and I enjoyed riding him.

The liveryman recognized us but gave only a curt nod as he led the horses away for grooming and feed.

"The town doesn't feel friendly," I said.

"Yer trouble. They wanna stay clear." Sharp looked around. "What first?"

"Find Jeremiah. We'll start at his store. Why don't you let your men get a beer? It's been a long, dusty ride."

"Hell, they only rode from Belleville. I'm the

one could use a cold beer. That is, if Jeremiah still operates his icehouse."

"Let's find out if he operates anything."

Sharp nodded permission to his men to visit the saloon, and the two of us walked the fifty yards to the general store. Sharp carried his Winchester like always.

As soon as I stepped through the door, I knew Jeremiah wasn't running the shop. He kept things fastidiously neat, but the place had an unkempt look about it.

The shopkeeper saw us and then pretended to be busy with something on a lower shelf. I rapped hard on the counter to get his attention. I never saw a man rise more slowly.

"Yes, sir."

"Do you run this establishment?"

"I do."

"Where can I find Jeremiah?"

"Don't rightly know. Ain't been around in weeks."

"Do you know who I am?"

"Steve Dancy . . . and Jeff Sharp."

I made a point of looking around the empty store. "Then tell me where he is while I'm still calm."

Last summer, I had killed two gunmen in this town, and my reputation evidently still held sway. The shopkeeper's right cheek flinched twice before he glanced toward the door for help.

Deciding no one would come to his rescue, he

said simply, "He's got a shelter on the north side." I didn't say anything, so he added, "That's all I know."

"It's not, but that'll do for now." I slipped a ten-cent piece onto the counter. "Give me a bag of gingersnaps."

After he handed me a waxed-paper bag of the cookies, I nodded and we left.

We both looked across the street to the north side. Sharp asked, "How do ya 'xpect to find him? Those rock hovels don't have addresses."

"If we have to, we'll yell. Let's go."

Behind the single row of buildings, a ratty collection of rock structures crowded the relatively flat area. There must have been fifty of them. They were small and windowless, probably just big enough for a bedroll and a few personal belongings. Empty bean tins, cigar butts, and other trash had been tossed from inside to litter the front of each shelter. As we walked through them, I noticed burrows cut in the loose sand by piss. The foul smell led me to believe that these miners didn't bother to venture far to take care of other business.

A dirty, bearded man ducked out of a shelter, looking warily at us. His hand rested on the butt of a Civil War-era revolver tucked into his belt.

"What ya fellas doin'?"

"Looking for Jeremiah. He used to run the general store."

"Up thataway." He pointed up a scarred slope.

"Much obliged," Sharp answered.

"I guess we should tread lightly here," I said after we moved away.

"Noisily. Quiet men mean trouble."

Sharp knew miners, so I started whistling. Badly.

Laughing, Sharp said, "Steve, please stop before someone throws a blind shot out his hovel to shut that awful noise."

I dutifully quit. As we climbed up the easy slope, we saw no one else. It was eerily quiet. The men who slept in these rock enclosures were underground, swinging pickaxes. The bearded man was probably protecting their meager possessions. I glanced back, and sure enough, the unkempt ruffian was watching our every move.

"Jeremiah!" Sharp's voice was loud but not a yell.

We stopped and finally heard a muffled, "Here."

We marched toward his hail, but no one emerged from a shelter, so Sharp repeated, "Jeremiah."

"Is that you, Jeff?"

"And Steve. Come out."

From the next row of hovels emerged a man I barely recognized as my friend. The Jeremiah I knew was pudgy and neat. This man looked emaciated and as bedraggled as any of his neighbors. He wore a patch over his left eye, and his face had some ugly scars that would never disappear. This had been more than a beating.

We were stunned into silence, so Jeremiah said, "Glad to see you boys. Either of you got any food? Water?"

I stepped forward. "Damn. You look a mess." I held up the wax bag. "All I brought were gingersnaps. Let's go to the café."

Jeremiah took the bag, giving me a forlorn look. "They won't serve me. Do you have water?"

"They'll serve you with us. Remember, I'm a deadly gunfighter." I smiled to show I wasn't serious.

He looked at the small bag, and tears welled up. "Thanks for remembering that I love gingersnaps. Thoughtful, Steve." He sighed. "I haven't had a gingersnap since they took the store away from me, but I can't eat these without something to drink." He looked up from the bag. "They took all my money too. Not a penny for water, food, or a stage ticket out of here. They sent me here to die. Just punishment for my sins, in their eyes. More than that, I'm an example to anyone else that might be thinking about bucking town authority."

I put my arm on his thin shoulder. "Come on. You can tell us about it at Mary's."

He started down the hill on wobbly legs. "She's still there, but it ain't her café no more. They took her place too."

I looked at Sharp. "Is this why you're selling out?"

Sharp nodded. "They put a heavy use tax on the stamp mill. Ain't gonna work my butt off to make some politicians rich."

"Jeff, why didn't you tell me?"

"Only guns can fix this. No need for ya to get in another fight not yer doin'."

"Peter scares easy," I offered.

"Madison doesn't," Sharp said.

"Who's Madison?"

Jeremiah stopped me with a hand on my forearm. "The new sheriff. A tough man, and he's got two capable gun hands for deputies. Clive's still around too, but he's the town marshal." His voice was raspy.

"How long since you had water?" I asked.

"Last night . . . after dark. One of the miners I grubstaked a while back sneaks me a canteen."

"Let's get you watered and fed before you talk anymore."

We proceeded in silence down the slope and into town. When we emerged from between the buildings, I looked around but didn't spot anyone that looked dangerous. As we entered Mary's, I noticed that the new owners hadn't done anything to improve the dowdy café.

Mary spotted us immediately and approached with a worried expression. "Mr. Dancy, pleased to see you again." She gave Sharp a sly look. "You too, Jeffery."

"Mary, ya know . . . oh never mind. What've ya got in the kitchen?"

She wiped her hands on her apron, looking nervous. "You know I can't serve Jeremiah."

"Who owns this place?" I asked.

"The county got it for back taxes." Looking around, she said in a small voice, "I'm leaving as soon as I save enough for coach fare."

"Is Peter at the bank?"

She shrugged. "Probably."

"I'll go see him. In the meantime, get Jeremiah water and a meal."

"Will you save me from a beating?'

"I will."

"Then hurry. I want to see you back here before I serve food."

"Fair enough, but give him water now."

Sharp hoisted his rifle across his chest. "I'll stay with you."

She looked uneasy but nodded assent.

As I started to leave, Sharp grabbed my arm. "Be careful. People know we're in town."

Chapter 3

The foyer looked familiar from my days running this bank, but back then I had been on the other side of the cage. It being midday, the miners were underground, so the bank was empty. In fact, when I peered through the iron bars, I couldn't see Peter. I rapped hard to get his attention. Banging my knuckles on counters was becoming a habit.

Peter emerged from around the corner with a *how can I serve you* smile that faded when he recognized me.

"Hello, Peter." I kept my tone neutral.

"You may call me Mr. Humphrey."

"Got uppity since you made bank manager?"

"No, sir." There was a sarcastic note to his voice. "That happened when they put me on the board of Commerce Bank." He put his banker's smile back in place. "Thank you for giving me my first banking position. How can I help you?"

"I wish to speak to the county supervisor."

"I'd switch hats, but I'm not wearing one."

"Show me the tax statements for the hotel, the general store, and Mary's."

"I'm sorry, but you're not a lawful resident of Mineral County."

"I'm a property owner."

"No longer. The hotel was foreclosed. You have no standing."

I saw where this was going, and I didn't like it. I tried to look mean, which didn't work that well for me. "Back when I met you, I should've allowed my colleague to break your neck."

The previous summer in Carson City, Peter had been the assistant to a prominent lawyer. He had barred our access to his office, so I jokingly ordered Sharp to break his neck. Peter had jumped aside faster than a hare caught unawares by a coyote.

Unperturbed, Peter asked, "Do you have banking business?"

"No, but I want you to step over to Mary's with me and tell her she can serve Jeremiah a meal."

"I'm sorry, that's beyond my duties. Mary can serve anyone she likes. Unfortunately, she doesn't like Jeremiah."

I suppressed my first impulse, which was to reach through the bars and yank his head until it banged against the steel rods. "I'll be back shortly with a local citizen. Have the tax statements ready for us to review when I return."

"No."

"What do you mean, *no?*"

"Local citizens can only see their own tax records. We can't allow just anyone to rummage through the personal records of other people."

"Peter, do you remember who I am?"

"A rich man who resorts to guns to solve business issues, but you can't run roughshod over us. We have laws now, and deputies to make people like you behave properly."

Furious, I blurted out the first thing that came to mind. "I want my buckboard and horse. Are they at the livery?"

"What are you talking about?"

"You know exactly what I'm talking about. I loaned you a rig to drive from Carson City to Pickhandle. I said it was yours to use as long as you remained in my employ. Do you still work for me?"

"Absolutely not."

"Then I want my property." He looked confused, so I added, "I have the papers in my saddlebag if it comes to that." It was a bluff.

His expression changed to a smirk. "Not necessary. I'll tell the liveryman to turn the rig and horse over to you."

Winning my small victory, I stomped out of the bank with far too heavy a footfall.

Now what? My inclination was to throw Jeremiah onto my reacquired wagon and get the hell out of this sad encampment. My quarter share of the hotel wasn't important to me. Damn. I realized there was something that was important to me—my friends. Our common ownership in the hotel meant we wouldn't go our separate ways and forget about each other. Jeremiah had also lost his store, and as a shopkeeper in a prior life, I knew that store was worth more than the entire hotel. I wouldn't call Mary a friend, but we liked each other, and she had been kind to me last summer when I had some trouble in this town. She didn't deserve to have her café stolen by crooks that wielded ledgers instead of pistols.

I was still thinking about how to handle the situation when I stepped into Mary's café. The first person I saw was Clive, hovering over Sharp with what I thought was a menacing pose.

I kept my gun hand hanging loose at my side. "Good morning, Marshal."

Clive stood full height and faced me with an expression that conveyed no threat. "Mr. Dancy, I don't want trouble. Your beef is with the sheriff."

"Everybody in this town is pointing to someone else."

He shrugged. "Things ain't the same. I'm only town marshal now, so I don't got say anymore. Leastways, not where it's important. County has the power now."

I was angry and intent on provoking an argument. "Being the town authority and all, are you going to stop Mary from serving Jeremiah?"

He shrugged again. "No skin off my back."

"Clive ain't the problem," Sharp said.

"Fine." I sat down and waved Mary over. "Bring me steak, eggs, and lots of bread. I'm starving."

She looked hesitantly at Clive, and he actually winked at her.

"Be seein' you gents." Clive gave us a little farewell wave and walked out the door.

"What the hell's going on?" I asked Sharp.

"Clive's been shut outta the town graft by the new boys." Sharp chuckled. "He's a bit put out, but he still won't help us. Get anywhere with Peter?"

"No. I'm thinking the smart thing is to get the hell out of here. Take Jeremiah to Belleville until he's well enough to travel to Carson City." I glanced at Jeremiah to see how he took to the idea, but he looked resigned to whatever his fate might be.

Sharp leaned across the table to emphasize his point. "That's what I'm thinkin'. There ain't nothin' here for us 'cept trouble."

"Jeremiah?"

He looked furtively toward the kitchen. "I'm just hungry."

Before I made a decision, I needed to ask a question. "Jeff, is there anything else you're not telling me?"

"Nothin' that . . . oh hell, Steve, ya don't want to know."

"I do."

Sharp gave me a hard stare before saying, "Jenny's part of this."

"Jenny? How?"

"This is her doin'." Sharp leaned back and looked sad. "She might be tryin' to hurt ya by destroyin' yer friends, or she could just be takin' over the state. Ain't privy to her thinkin'.'"

Jenny Bolton had been an infatuation—one that had gotten me in real trouble. Escaping her charms had required me to see her for what she really was—a terribly disturbed woman who masked her emotional wounds with stunning good looks and girlish effervescence. I had broken it off last autumn and had seen her only from a distance during my long winter in Carson City.

"I don't understand. Why would she want to hurt me? She never cared about me."

"Maybe she did, maybe she didn't, but she sure as hell didn't like ya dumpin' her in front of her hands."

"Damn."

After a long silence, Sharp said, "Ya can't fight her."

Sharp looked at me with sympathy. Before I became too embarrassed, Mary brought over a huge plate of food, snapping it down directly in front of me. I stood and shoved the plate aside. "Not hungry anymore. Jeremiah, don't let my meal go to waste."

I bolted out of the café and raced after the marshal. I figured his heavy gut would have him breathing hard after a single flight of stairs, but I chased him all the way to his office before I caught up.

"Marshal, I want to talk in private," I said.

Clive nodded toward his office and bounded up the three steps with surprising agility.

Once inside, I decided not to waste time. "Clive, how would you like to run this town again?"

"Go on." He tried to sound indifferent, but I saw a light come into his eyes.

"This Sheriff Madison, he do anything wrong, anything you could arrest him for?"

"Me?"

"You, and a few friends."

I could see he liked the idea. "How many friends?"

"Four. Me, Sharp, and two of his toughest guards."

He rubbed his chin. "Five against three ain't bad, but they don't fight fair. One of the deputies always comes up from behind with a shotgun."

"Then we know how they work. But I want to arrest them for a legitimate crime, one that would put them behind bars for years."

"*You* want to arrest them? Who put you in charge?"

"You're the marshal, and we'll be your deputies, but if you ignore my counsel, we'll ride out of town and leave you to deal with this mess."

Clive casually leaned back in his swivel chair and rocked a bit. "Agreed." He didn't hesitate.

"With enough gun hands backin' me, there won't be any problem gettin' witnesses to extortion, larceny, assault, and possibly murder." He swung his chair up straight with a snap and leaned over his desk. "What do I get?"

"Everything you had before, except for the hotel."

He thought a second. "I want clear title to Ruby's."

"I thought you always had that."

"Nope. Washburn owned half. After you killed him, somehow that weasel banker got hold of his half. You want to set things right for your friends, then I want full ownership of that flea-infested whorehouse."

"How about Peter? Anything?"

"Malfeasance. But once we get him locked up, we can search his books for embezzlement."

I wasn't so sure about embezzlement, but malfeasance as county supervisor should keep him locked up for a couple of days, and it would certainly be sufficient to get him fired. Once he was dismissed, Commerce Bank would quickly sell their ownership in a whorehouse.

"Agreed." I held out my hand.

Clive leaped to his feet and shook my hand. "Glad to be on the same side this time. Get your boys in here, and I'll swear you all in as deputies."

"Not Sharp's men. Swear them in as deputies in

their room. Let's keep our superior numbers secret for now."

Clive laughed so hard, his ample belly bounced up and down against the desktop. "Yep, mighty glad to be on the same side this time."

Chapter 4

According to Clive, the sheriff and his deputies generally spent most of the night in saloons, so they were seldom seen before mid-afternoon. The three of them always moved around town together. When they entered a business—any business—the sheriff and one deputy came in the front, and a second deputy entered quietly from the back, carrying a shotgun. The shotgun was normally used to threaten but on occasion had been used to kill. One time, the shotgun had terminated negotiations with a stubborn business owner. That incident had stopped all further resistance by townsfolk.

After we stashed a satiated Jeremiah in a hotel room, Sharp and I waited in the lobby, while Clive worked to convince a few witnesses to lodge a complaint. Sharp had his ever-present Winchester leaning against a seat cushion by his left hand, and I had loaded my Colt with a sixth bullet in case of trouble.

I was reading *Roughing It*, by Mark Twain, when Sharp tapped my leg with the toe of his boot. I didn't turn to see who had entered the hotel because we had prearranged the silent signal that would tell me to put my attention on the back door.

I heard a voice behind me. "Mr. Sharp. What brings you to town?"

Sharp laid his newspaper beside him on the settee. "A friend needed help."

"What friend?" I heard wariness in the voice. "And who's this gent?"

I slowly stood and turned toward the voice. I saw a young man, probably about my age. He looked confident, not dangerous. In the West, however, I had learned that those two traits could be the same thing. He wore a Colt Army Model at his belly in a cross-draw holster and a large knife on his right hip. His shirt and pants were as dusty as everything else in Pickhandle, but they were nicely tailored, and his boots, belt, and hat were top-notch.

"I'm one of the marshal's new deputies. Jeff has been deputized, as well. Please tell your man to step out of the back hall and into the room. He makes me nervous, hiding back there."

Without flinching, Sheriff Madison sniffed. "Why the hell should I care if you're nervous?"

Where was Clive? Did the sheriff know about our scheme? And why wasn't he surprised that Clive had deputized us? I told myself to clear my mind and concentrate on the situation in the room.

"Since we're all lawmen, you don't need your man lurking around back there," I said.

"I do." He just stared at me like I was a curious specimen captured in a bottle.

"Steve, let 'im hang out in back if he wants."

Sharp picked up his newspaper and snapped it taut as he prepared to get back to reading.

I sat down with deliberation and followed Sharp's lead by picking up my book.

"What are you reading, Deputy?" The sheriff's tone was derisive.

"*Roughing It*," I answered without looking up.

"Good yarn, but exaggerated . . . for humor, I suppose."

"Did you laugh?"

"I did."

"Then the embroidery did its job."

So, the sheriff was not only literate but read books. I suspected this was not idle chatter. He probably wanted me to know I wasn't dealing with a dunderhead. I put the book down and swiveled to face him.

"Have you seen the marshal this afternoon?" I asked.

"Nope, but gonna look for him." The sheriff turned his attention to Sharp. "Why would a big mine operator take a deputy position?"

"I asked for his help," Clive barked. He stood behind the sheriff, aiming a rifle at his head. "George Madison, you're under arrest for extortion, assault, and accessory to murder. Your deputies are also under arrest on similar charges."

Sharp appeared to lay the newspaper back on the settee but used the motion to grab his Winchester by the barrel with his left hand and flip it up to his right shoulder. Before Clive had finished his first sentence, Sharp had the sheriff's deputy in his rifle sight. My task was to cover the deputy in back. I rose and my gun came smoothly out of my holster, but I realized we had made a mistake. Sharp's rifle would have been a better weapon to face a man hidden behind a wall. I slid to my left to get a better angle on the deputy but saw only part of his boot and the edge of his hat. Damn.

"Why, Marshal, you're just a town appointee. You can't arrest a duly elected official of Mineral County."

"Call your man out from the back," Clive commanded.

"Stay calm," the sheriff said evenly. Then he raised his voice almost to a yell. "Matt, did you take care of those men out back?"

"Yep," responded the deputy behind the wall.

I got a sick feeling. Sharp's two mine guards were supposed to come in behind the deputy. If they were covered, Madison had anticipated both our intent and strategy.

Then Peter Humphrey confirmed my fears when I heard him say, "I have a gun on Clive, Sheriff."

A quick glance confirmed that the bank manager had a rifle trained on the marshal. If the situation hadn't been potentially deadly, I would've laughed. The small hotel lobby was full of men getting the drop on other men who had the drop on still other men.

Clive sounded nervous when he said, "Looks to be a Mexican standoff."

"You're misreading the situation," Madison said as he slowly turned, using his left hand to lightly brush Clive's rifle away so it no longer pointed at him.

Clive's allowing that was a mistake. I realized that my life was not safe in his hands. Damn. What had I been thinking? I swung my gun around, aiming at the sheriff. "Sheriff Madison! Do not move!" Then I added quietly, "Because I *will* shoot you."

The face that turned in my direction was fierce. "Put that gun down, or my men will kill you."

"I prefer a Mexican standoff to being at your mercy."

After a hard stare, he smiled broadly. With a tip of the hat, he said, "You and Mr. Sharp may go." After a theatrical pause, he added more firmly, "But don't return to this town . . . either of you."

"The others?" I asked.

"I'm afraid townspeople must pay for their sins."

Sharp, having seen me abandon my target, shifted his aim away from the deputy in front to the deputy hiding behind the wall in the back of the room.

"My men?" Sharp asked, over his shoulder.

Madison grinned like a jack-o'-lantern. "Probably dead. I hired some wardens from the mines to split their skulls." He looked exceptionally pleased with himself.

"That's a shame," I said. "They were your only bargaining chip. Jeff, shoot that deputy behind the wall."

Three rapid reports from Sharp's Winchester rattled the glassware in the room. When the sheriff and his deputy went for their guns, I yelled, "Stop!" My ears were ringing and smoke stung my eyes, but I kept my sight on the sheriff. Suddenly, I caught movement out of the corner of my eye. I shifted aim and shot the second deputy just as he was raising his gun barrel in my direction. I had let the sheriff hold my attention with his eyes as his deputy smoothly slid his pistol out of his holster. My usual practice was to concentrate on the top dog, but in this instance, it almost got me killed.

The sheriff wasn't moving, so I glanced behind me and saw the first deputy stumble into view from around the corner and slump helplessly to the floor. Sharp's bullets had passed right through the thin layers of planking and severely wounded the man.

Everybody remained as still as an etching in a book. Finally Madison shrugged and said, "I guess we're even: your men for my men. Put your guns down and leave. We won't bother you."

"We still have the matter of my friends' safety. No . . . I think the best place for you is jail."

"Peter could kill the marshal."

"Jeff?"

"Already got 'im in my sights." Sharp had brought his gun around to take aim at the weaselly banker.

"Do we all start shooting again?" I asked.

After a slight hesitation, Humphrey yelled, "No!" The terrified banker snapped his rifle straight up and repeatedly shook his head. His face was as pale as a freshly washed bed sheet. Without the sheriff to give him courage, the Peter I had known had returned.

As I kept my aim on Madison, Sharp disarmed him. Clive wheeled around and snatched the rifle out of Humphrey's hands. After all the weapons clattered to the floor, I stepped around my chair and marched over to Peter. Without hesitation, I holstered my gun and hit him hard in the face, sending him slamming against the wall, then tumbling to the floor. I restrained an impulse to put my boot in the middle of his chest.

"If you'll excuse me, *Mr. Humphrey,* I need to go over to the telegraph office and get you fired."

Chapter 5

That evening, a meeting of townspeople elected a new sheriff of Mineral County. Much to his disappointment, it wasn't Clive. The town was done with lawlessness, at least for this one evening, and elected one of the more respected mine wardens. Due to his help in dispatching the sheriff and his deputies, Clive's continuing role as town marshal was not challenged.

All day, I had traded telegrams with officials in Carson City, and eventually everything had been worked out to my satisfaction. Humphrey was no longer employed, an almost-honest judge would be dispatched first thing in the morning, and Richard would send a capable prosecutor. It was agreed that beyond the criminal cases, the judge would also examine county tax assessments, and if deemed confiscatory, the property would be returned to the owners.

After a long, stressful day, the meeting had run late, but the outcomes pleased me. Things had been set about as right as possible for Pickhandle Gulch. As we stepped out of the meeting into the still night, Sharp ruined my good mood by asking, "What about Jenny?"

After a moment, I said, "I guess I'll ride up to Mason Valley to kill her . . . probably bury her next to her mother-in-law."

Instead of the rise I expected out of Sharp, he replied with all apparent seriousness, "A befittin' outcome, to be sure."

"Indeed?"

Sharp laughed in his unaffected manner and slapped me on the back. "Let's get a beer. Meetin's and politickin' parch me."

As we hurried ahead of the crowd toward the saloon, I wondered what I would do about Jenny. I couldn't believe she'd set these wheels in motion just to get even with me. Granted, a woman spurned could be treacherous, but her husband had been on a march to run just about everything in this state, and his mother—Jenny's tutor of sorts—had encouraged him. Jenny was probably following in their footsteps. Unlike her husband and mother-in-law, however, she was smart enough to make it happen.

Of course, I knew what I would do—nothing. I had been infatuated with Jenny since the first time I had seen her, but she had never allowed me to court her. After I realized that she was not the woman for me, I impolitely rode off without saying goodbye. She had been trained by her vicious mother-in-law to avenge any and all offenses. She might be seeking revenge, but the more I thought about it, the more certain I was that she was just extending her empire to the southern part of the state. If anything, she was killing two birds with one stone: getting control of Mineral County while sending a message to me. At least, that's what I hoped.

After we grabbed a couple of beers from the bar, we found a table toward the rear of the saloon. My beer was half gone with the first long swallow. After Sharp gulped an equal amount, I asked, "Jeff, have you ever read Powell's book about his adventures on the Colorado River?"

He looked at me askance but simply answered, "Yep."

"I want to see the Grand Canyon."

Sharp's expression turned from mild annoyance to anger. "Ya still wanna go south, don't ya?"

"I do. Let's go to Arizona. Together. Lots of new silver. Hell, Leadville can—"

"Damn it, Steve, despite what happened here, I'm still sellin' out my holdin's. Nevada's too corrupt, but it's heaven on earth compared to the Arizona Territory. I ain't sinkin' my fortune into that privy hole."

"I'm not asking you to invest."

"Ya just said there's lots of silver down there. Why the hell did ya bring it up if ya weren't suggestin' we invest?"

He was right, so I went in another direction. "Jeff, Leadville's frozen solid. It'll be three months before you can throw a pick into the ground. Besides, it's a four-day ride back to Carson City to catch the train. I want to see the Grand Canyon and Arizona. We can still be in Leadville by May."

"Nothin' to see in Arizona. It's a wilderness filled with Apaches, bandits, and poisonous creatures that bite ya for the fun of it. 'Sides, I already saw the Grand Canyon."

"Not worth seeing again?"

"Well, ya got me there." He tilted his mug high in the air and downed the last of his beer. "Let's get another beer an' I'll think about it."

"All I ask."

"No, it isn't." There was an edge to his voice.

Chapter 6

Sharp and I had been riding south for four days, and I couldn't spot anything out of the ordinary on the horizon. All I could see was flat landscape evenly broken by low scrub. Due to the lateness of the afternoon, we would have to make camp soon, and another day would be behind us.

In 1869 and 1872, Major John Wesley Powell had led river expeditions through the Grand Canyon. His published journal, *The Exploration of the Colorado River and Its Canyons*, was a remarkable tale, and I could look at the numerous illustrations over and over again. After studying the book for several years, I felt I knew the Grand Canyon. But where was it? Could Sharp be leading me astray because I coerced him into going to Arizona?

"How much further?" I asked.

"Just up ahead, greenhorn." The lilt in his voice told me he was kidding with the greenhorn crack.

"This is supposed to be one of the great wonders of the world." I stood in my stirrups. "I don't see anything."

"Damn it, Steve. It's a canyon, not a mountain."

"I thought by now I'd see some evidence of a monstrous gorge."

"What d'ya 'xpect, a signpost?"

"I don't know. Something. Powell's illustrations

showed soaring cliffs, huge monuments, and alcove gulches going off in every direction."

"You *are* a greenhorn." No lilt this time. "Powell was on the river . . . at the bottom. We're approaching the rim." Sharp shifted in his saddle to look at me. "Powell looked up at those soaring cliffs; we're gonna look down."

"I guess I hadn't thought this out." I felt disappointed. Powell's book had sparked my interest, and I wanted to see the canyon the way the book presented it. "Can we ride to the bottom?"

Sharp gave an exasperated sigh. "Ain't ridin' a horse down cliffs so steep a mule deer can lose its footin'. The only way ya can get to the bottom is to start in Utah and float the river down."

I was disheartened by my lack of imagination. I knew I was approaching the top, but I hadn't pictured how different that would make the experience. When I was little, my mother had paid William Page to give me art lessons. After three sessions, Page quit, telling my mother I had the visual ability of a one-eyed bookkeeper. Since that day, I've never had reason to question Page's judgment.

"What about when we go around the canyon to the east?"

"By the time we get to Lees Ferry, the deep part of the canyon will be to the west of us. Could we ride down next to the river from there? Yep, but it's dangerous. That canyon gets frightenin' narrow in parts, an' the river likes to wash everything out of its way all of a sudden-like. It may look real pretty, but that canyon's a killer."

Our conversation had distracted me. When I looked forward again, I gasped. Without warning, the canyon had suddenly come into view—and it was breathtaking. Never had I imagined color. My one-eyed bookkeeper's mind had projected the pencil etchings and photographs from Powell's book onto real life. Instead of the charcoal shades I had expected, a profusion of colors, predominantly beige, brown, and gold, washed the canyon. Pale green plants grew horizontally from vertical cliffs and then bent skyward. Remnants of pure-white snow that seemed to cling to every ledge and crevasse accented the whole landscape. Nor had anything prepared me for the size. A photograph in a book gave no indication of scale. It seemed over a mile to the far side.

I pulled Liberty up short, and as I gazed ahead, the setting sun caused the colors to pulse and slide across the far cliffs. Now gold sparkles danced where the sunlight hit the cliffs. I looked at Sharp, who sat there with both hands on his saddle horn, grinning at me.

"Why are you grinning?" I asked.

"It gets better."

"Better?"

"Yep."

With that, Sharp spurred his horse and galloped the last remaining yards to the edge of the canyon. He was right—it did get better. From the rim, I could see more than the far wall. Stunned, I dismounted and just stood there, holding Liberty's reins tight up against his chin. The expanse extended as far as the eye could see in both directions. Enormous outcroppings that plunged to a depth unreachable by a rifle shot serrated the entire canyon. Way below, like a thin pencil line, the Colorado River relentlessly toiled at cutting away even more earth. I could see why the canyon had so suddenly emerged before us: the northern rim was much higher than the southern rim, so until we got close, our line of sight just passed over the gaping hole to the horizon.

"Damn."

"Kinda makes ya feel small, don't it?" Despite having been here before, Sharp was as entranced as I. "Sure is pretty, but we gotta make camp 'fore dark."

"Fire?" I asked.

"Nothin' lyin' about burns long, so we're gonna need piles of dry scrub."

"I meant, are Indians a threat?"

"The Paiute mostly trade, but there ain't many around. Water an' game's better on the other side. If ya wanna worry, worry about rattlesnakes."

I had seen a rattlesnake or two, but so far I had avoided any formal introductions. Sharp's warning reminded me to use my rifle barrel to jiggle the brush as I gathered branches. I didn't want to surprise any creatures, especially poisonous ones. Fairly warned, snakes slither away. At least, that's what I had been told.

After we had groomed the horses, collected a huge stack of branches, and started supper, we moved our saddles close to the edge of the canyon to use as backrests while we watched the final setting of the sun. We sipped good whiskey, ate apples, and silently watched the last light play against the canyon cliffs.

At dusk, Sharp asked, "What're we doin' here?"

"I told you. We'll see Governor Frémont and look for investments."

"I'm not a prospector."

"Not what I had in mind." I stood and grabbed my saddle by the horn to carry it over to the fire. While we had watched the sun set, the fire had burned down to embers, which were better for cooking. Sharp had a tasty recipe for camp beans, and I used my knife to start opening a tin.

He plopped beside me and dug out the rest of the fixings from a saddlebag.

"What do ya have in mind?" he asked.

"A mine puts all your eggs in one basket." I slid my knife back in the sheath, and handed the open tin to Sharp. "I was thinking of providing something miners need, something they'll pay top dollar for. Let someone else take the big risk. We get rich no matter who finds the gold."

"I like takin' risks."

"No, you don't. You buy producing mines, and then you make them produce better."

"I'm a miner, not a lumberman."

"That's one option. Mines need protection, men, lumber, transport, food, tools, supplies, lodging, and diversions for the miners."

Sharp looked unhappy. "Steve, I ain't runnin' a whore- or boardinghouse, buyin' a saloon, or workin' with a bunch of guards that are a whisper away from bein' outlaws."

"Leaves lots of other options," I answered.

"Like what?"

"Beef, horses, shop keeping, ore hauling, and lumber, to name a few, but I'd like to figure out a way to make money from engineering."

"Engineerin'? How?"

"I have people in New York keeping an eye on things for me. I've got a couple of prospects but nothing firm yet. I'll know better after I talk to Frémont."

"Frémont? What the hell does that ol' codger know 'bout engineerin'?" Sharp had all of his ingredients in the beans and stirred the pot when it began to simmer.

"Nothing, but he still has connections in New York City."

Sharp stopped stirring and gave me a hard look. "Steve, yer not makin' sense. We're ridin' into a bleak desert territory to get connected to engineers in a bustlin' city thousands of miles away? Hell, we coulda rode to New York in a Pullman sippin' Champagne, eatin' good beef, and pinchin' cute derrières. What the hell are we doin' out here?"

"Fixing beans . . . and getting a look at Powell's canyon."

Sharp sputtered. "Steve, yer not tellin' me everything. There ain't nothin' we can do 'bout engineerin' in the territory that we couldn'a done better in Leadville."

I sat on my haunches and wondered what to say. "I've got an idea. It may be dumb, but I didn't want you squashing it without a fair hearing."

"What's Prescott got to do with this?"

"A man." I stood.

"Someone other than Frémont?"

"Yes." I hesitated. "What I told you about Frémont and the Dancy family is true. Frémont can help, but the real key is another man. I need to get to Prescott to find him.

"Who is he?"

"Jeff, I'd rather not say."

"Why the hell not?"

"Because it's someone you hate."

Chapter 7

We sat on our horses, looking down a rise to a rough encampment along the Colorado River. Actually, the Colorado looked less like a river than a relentless mud slide. We had spent three days slowly skirting the cliffs that descended into the Grand Canyon. I had enjoyed every minute, but Sharp had remained sullen ever since I refused to tell him who we were going to meet in Prescott.

"That's Lees Ferry," Sharp said. "The only means to cross the river for hundreds of miles in either direction."

"Looks desolate."

"Wait till ya get to the other side: empty land as far as ya can ride for days. I suggest ya stay on this side of the ferry until someone comes along headin' fer Prescott."

I turned in my saddle to look at Sharp. "That sounds like you're not coming with me."

"I'm not."

"Jeff—" I didn't have an argument.

"If I see Elisha Campbell, I might kill him. It's best we part ways right here."

He had figured it out. I shouldn't have been surprised. Sharp and I had spent untold hours talking about our respective histories, and despite his telling me about numerous bad characters in his life, there had been only one who had made his voice quiver in anger. Elisha Campbell had been Sharp's partner when he ran an import agency in New York City. While he was on a buying trip in South America, Campbell had exercised an innocuous turpitude clause that he had buried in a long partnership agreement. The clause protected each partner against grossly dishonest or immoral behavior on the part of the other partner. Campbell not only used it to take control of the partnership but had also besmirched Sharp's reputation to such an extent that he could no longer work in the import business or find himself welcomed in polite society.

I looked down at Lees Ferry. "What did he accuse you of?"

Sharp had never told me the specifics, and he hung fire for so long that I thought he still wouldn't.

Finally, he said, "He accused me of importin' young boys to satisfy rich old men with a taste for that kinda entertainment."

Keeping my voice even, I asked, "How did he make it stick?"

"He had a madam in the Bowery testify that she got her boys from me. The hearin's were in all the papers while I was out of the country an' couldn't defend myself." He shook his head. "Years later—after I had left New York—I discovered how Campbell happened on this way to grab control of our company."

"What do you mean?"

"I mean, unbeknownst to me, Campbell was supplyin' the whole East Coast with children for whorehouses. That's how he put together such a tight case against me. He had lawmen an' city officials in his pocket, an' no shortage of witnesses from the business . . . if ya're sick enough to call it that."

"Do you know how he got involved with Cornelius Vanderbilt?"

Sharp abruptly turned in his saddle to face me. "The Commodore?"

"No, his ne'er-do-well son, Corny."

"Campbell an' a Vanderbilt?" Sharp shook his head. "Sounds like him. He always sidled up to power."

"Odd choice of words."

"Why odd?'

"Power. This is about electricity. Through Vanderbilt, Campbell has become a shareholder in the Edison Electric Light Company."

"What's that got to do with . . . ?"

Sharp swung down from his saddle and led his horse over to some sparse grass. I followed suit, and for a long spell, the only sound on that barren ridge was the munching of horses, punctuated by an occasional snort or tail swish.

Sharp had been standing with his back to me,

and when he turned around, he wore the hugest grin I had ever seen on his face. "Does it work?" he asked.

"Yes. Well . . . soon. Last December, Edison showed off his invention by illuminating the Menlo Park buildings, but that test was only in a laboratory. He says he's close to taking his lighting scheme worldwide." I could see that Sharp had already grasped the significance, but I added, "Edison said he's going to make electricity so cheap, only the rich will burn candles."

"He built an electric motor too," Sharp said.

That took me aback. "You know about this?"

"Hell, I get newspapers in Belleville. Maybe not new, but not all that old . . . and I have friends that send me letters. I knew about it but thought people were exaggeratin'. That's been known to happen, ya know."

"I've got someone pretty close to Edison, and I've been trading telegraphs and letters all winter. It's true, all right . . . and everything's not been in the papers. Since December, he's found a better filament that'll last over a thousand hours. His laboratory has invented dynamos, conductors, fuses, insulators, sockets, and switches. This is moving fast. Jeff, I believe it will revolutionize hard-rock mining."

Sharp watched the ferry cross the muddy Colorado. "Steve, why didn't ya tell me about this?

"Because I was afraid when you heard the name Elisha Campbell, you would bolt."

"Still might. Why is Campbell in Prescott?"

"You're going to love this: Campbell's under investigation for securities fraud and possibly murder. Worse, for him, he's been ostracized by the smart set. He's hiding in Prescott and hopes to use Frémont to squash the inquiry before he's indicted."

"Frémont's a fool," Sharp snorted.

"I won't argue with you, but he's a legend in my family. Unfortunately, the 'ol Pathfinder seems lost when he leaves the wilderness. He was certainly misguided if he made friends with Campbell. I'll grant you that he may be a political fool, but he's still got powerful connections in New York City, connections Campbell hopes to tap so he can go home."

"Ya still haven't told me yer plan. What'd ya got in mind?"

"Right now, the only way to secure shares in Edison's company is to buy them from an investor who was part of the original Vanderbilt consortium. If we get clear title to the shares, perhaps we can get a license, and if we can get a license, we can change mining all over the world."

After a few moments, Sharp said, "How do ya plan to get him to sell the shares?"

"I'm not. I know the Vanderbilts, especially the

Commodore's son. Seems the son didn't inherit his father's business acumen. Cornelius issued a stock certificate to your dear friend, but Campbell fled before paying. Someone else has since paid Campbell's marker and is now the legal owner of those shares."

"Ya ol' scalawag. I'll bet I know who that is."

I merely smiled in response.

"Why do ya need to get the certificate from him?"

"I have a certificate in my name, but it'll be troublesome if Campbell returns to challenge my ownership. My lawyers say he could tie things up in court for years. They recommend I get hold of the document and destroy it so he doesn't have a leg to stand on."

"Steve, I know Campbell. He's clever as hell, an' not someone ya threaten with a gun. He fights in back rooms an' courts. How the hell do ya expect to get the certificate away from him?"

I tapped my coat pocket. "All the legal documents are right here. Cornelius got a judgment against Campbell and endorsed it over to me. The law will recover my property or provide me with a writ that says it's been destroyed."

Sharp paced in thought. "How long ya been plannin' this?"

"All winter."

"Do Vanderbilt or Edison know your full intentions?"

"No."

"Steve, ya got problems. Ownin' a small piece of Edison Electric Light Company don't mean you get an exclusive license to use the invention in mines." He stopped pacing and looked at me. A small grin grew until it took possession of his entire face. "*That's* why ya need me. I'm right, aren't I?"

"Yes."

"I'm the linchpin."

"Yes."

"Ya got people talkin' to Edison already, don't ya?"

"Yes."

He paced some more.

"Bright light in the depths of a mine. This is gonna be worth a lot of money . . . millions maybe."

"More. My engineers have already figured out how to use electricity generators to bring fresh air as well as light into the mines. Blasting and drilling efficiency will double."

"An' ya need a minin' expert to give the enterprise credibility."

"I do."

"But first, ya gotta get clear title to them shares."

"Legally, I've got title."

"But if Campbell gets back to New York, he can make big trouble for ya. Ya'd be forced to pay him off with big dollars. Best to find him out here—when he's desperate. That way, ya can get hold of that original certificate an' destroy it."

"That's my thinking. If someone else gets possession, they could also contest ownership, especially if they claim to be an innocent buyer."

Sharp paced some more before saying, "Tell me 'bout this murder investigation ya mentioned."

"Old lady, rich. He chiseled the demented woman, and when she started screaming about it, she turned up dead. Campbell has an alibi, but police suspect he hired someone to do the deed. They're not pursuing it very hard." I walked over and put a hand on Sharp's shoulder. "Jeff, I put Pinkertons on it. If I get proof, your old partner could swing from the gallows."

"If he returns to New York?"

"We'll figure out a way to lure him back." Now I slapped him on the back. "Hell, if we have to, we'll hogtie and ship him home."

Sharp nodded thanks. "By the way, how do ya intend to make electricity?"

"Steam engine. We'll roll a locomotive up the tracks to the mine head and use it to generate electricity. Or perhaps we drop off a boiler. Haven't figured it all out yet, but I have engineers working on it back east."

Sharp took a moment to rub his horse's forehead. "Let me see if I got this straight. Ya don't own this invention, ya want to cut a deal with a crook in some godforsaken territory, an' ya ain't figured out how to make electricity."

I laughed. "That pretty much covers it."

"And I thought I liked risk!"

"I saw you thinking. You know what this could be worth."

Sharp swung back into his saddle. "I do. That's why I'm ridin' with ya."

Chapter 8

Prescott made Carson City look cosmopolitan. At the town's center stood a two-story Victorian courthouse situated on a grass commons. The largest commercial building was the Palace, where we rented rooms behind the saloon. An outside staircase running along an extended arm of the building led to a covered walkway with access to rooms. The palace didn't offer suites, but our rooms were large and clean, with fresh bedding. It had been four weeks since we had left Carson City, so we drank a quick beer and then took a bottle of whiskey to a bathhouse. Within short order, we had boarded the horses, secured adequate rooms, taken baths, changed into clean clothes, and gotten a little drunk. I was getting this routine on entering a new town committed to memory.

The Palace saloon was grandiose. Shiny brass lamp fixtures accented the dark paneled walls, and mirrors the size of a bed reflected the light thrown from the hissing gas jets. Earlier in the afternoon, the saloon had been quiet, but by the time we returned, it had turned boisterous. My first thought was that I was going to like this place.

Sharp and I leaned against the bar and ordered beers. As we waited for the barkeep to draw our drinks, I listened to a woman singing near a window at the front of the saloon. Her lusty voice easily carried through the large room that held at least fifty animated men. I noticed her hair billowed a bit and saw that the window behind her was open. Then a couple of men yelled at her from the boardwalk. Without missing a note, she turned toward them with a seductive smile and a dip that exposed a generous amount of cleavage. Soon the men were inside admiring the songbird, swinging chilled beers in rhythm with the music.

I signaled the barkeep to come over. I wanted to know who ran this establishment so effectively.

"Whiskey?" he asked.

"Not yet. I'm Steve Dancy and this is Jeff Sharp."

He offered his hand. "Lew Davis. What can I do for you gentlemen?"

"Could you tell me who owns this establishment?"

"Bob Brow." The barkeep pointed. "He's over there, keeping an eye on the gaming tables." He gave me a curious but unchallenging look. "Complaint?"

"Not a one. I want to talk to him about business."

"Bob will talk your ear off about business—unless you want him to put money into some dumb scheme."

"Got my own money."

"Then sidle up to him. You'll find him agreeable."

Jeff and I waved thanks with our beer tankards and approached Brow, who stood behind a poker table, watching the play. I started to walk up to him, but Sharp put a restraining hand on my forearm.

"Don't walk behind the players. Ya might get yerself in a needless fight."

I caught Brow's eye and nodded in a friendly manner. "Mr. Brow, may we speak with you?"

He immediately came over, extending a hand. "I don't believe we've met."

"Steve Dancy from New York, and this is Jeff Sharp from Nevada." We shook all around, and I added, "We just arrived and settled into a couple of your rooms. You run a fine establishment."

"Thank you, and welcome to the Palace. What can I do for you gentlemen?"

"We were hoping that if we bought you a beer, you might advise us on doing business in Prescott."

"I might." He gave us an appraising look. "I prefer Irish whiskey."

"Then let's order a bottle of yer best," Sharp said with a huge grin.

"My best is expensive."

Sharp made an open-handed wave toward an empty table.

"Jameson!" Brow bellowed at the barkeep.

"The saints are with us," Sharp said, as we took seats around a square table in the middle of the room. "I feared that by crossin' the border, we had abandoned civilized comforts."

Jeff and I traded pleasantries with Brow until the bottle arrived. After glasses were filled, Brow asked, "What type of business?"

I took an appreciative sip and said, "We're looking—"

"Excuse me, gentlemen, Ah don't mean to be rude, but do Ah know you?"

The voice was deep and the accent from the Deep South. I turned to see a slender, well-tailored man looking directly at Sharp.

"Yes, I played your table in Dallas. Seems a long time ago." Sharp turned in his seat and nodded toward me. "This is Steve Dancy from New York City." Sharp gave me one of his wicked smiles. "Steve, I'd like to introduce Dr. John Holliday."

I gaped but recovered fast enough to hope I didn't look too foolish. I stood, extending my hand. "This is an honor."

He gave me a perfunctory shake and returned his attention to Sharp. "Ah seem to recall a closer relationship than playing cards."

Sharp looked nervous, an uncommon state for him. "I was a witness at your trial for knifing Mitchell."

Holliday gave Sharp an appraising stare. "In my defense, if Ah recall correctly."

Sharp shrugged. "I merely testified that he was cheating."

Holliday laughed. "In Texas, that's all the defense you need."

"Are ya runnin' faro here?" Sharp asked.

"No . . . doing too well at poker. When my luck turns sour, Ah'll head out. What brings you to Prescott?"

"Mining."

Holliday looked puzzled. "Only small mines here . . . mostly played out."

"We're interested in supplying the needs of miners," I interjected.

Holliday looked at me as if I had just sat down. After sizing me up, he said, "In that case, Virgil Earp has a sawmill for sale."

"Virgil Earp's here in Prescott? What about his brothers?" I was embarrassed by my enthusiasm, but a book that included the Earps and Holliday would sell like hotcakes.

"The rest of the Earps left, and Virg's only staying until he sells the mill. Then we'll follow his brothers to Tombstone."

Sharp scratched his chin. "In another locale, a lumber mill might fit our needs, but Prescott's too far from the new silver strikes."

"*Everything* in Prescott's too far from the new silver. What are you looking for?"

"A man," Sharp answered.

"Who?" Brow interjected. "I know everyone."

I answered, "Elisha Campbell."

Holliday and Brow immediately stiffened.

After an awkward silence, Holliday bowed slightly. "Ah'll be leaving you gentlemen now. Good day."

Brow pushed away from the table. "If you men are friends of Elisha Campbell, perhaps I should leave as well."

"We're not," Sharp said. "In fact, that man cost me a great deal."

"Are you looking to kill him?" Brow asked evenly.

"No," Sharp answered, a bit too forcefully.

"Then you may be the only man in Prescott that doesn't want him dead."

I glanced at Sharp but couldn't read his face as he evenly said, "Wantin' him dead an' killin' him are two different things. But, in truth, I don't want him dead . . . not yet, anyway."

"What business do you have with him then?"

Sharp looked as if he were getting angry. "Steve, this is yer affair."

I hesitated and then lied. "Mr. Campbell might have information about my family. I need to talk to him. Afterwards, I don't care if he's lined up in front of a firing squad that includes every man in town."

"A few women might join as well," Brow quipped.

"What the hell did he do?" I asked.

"He owes money to everyone, including me. He's even got a marker with Doc. The son of a bitch hides behind Governor Frémont—another damned debtor. Campbell romanced a couple of wives when their husbands were away. Took their pride and their husbands' money. He's got three lawsuits going, one against me. If you got anything, that sniveling tinhorn sues, borrows, or seduces his way to get it, all the while using the governor for protection. He's not without his charms, but he's just a common crook with an engaging smile."

"How can I find him?" I asked.

"Why should I tell you?"

"Because he may have something I'm willing to buy. If I do a deal with him, I'll let you know before he skips town."

Brow laughed uproariously, and I noticed a curious look from Holliday, seated at a poker table across the room.

"You're a man after my own heart." Brow laughed some more. "He's out of credit on Whiskey Row, so he usually does his drinking in the home of a political figure seeking favor with the governor. He stays at Cunningham's boardinghouse on Goodwin Street, so you might find him there."

Sharp jumped to his feet, wearing a fierce expression. Following his gaze, I saw a neatly dressed man in his fifties strolling into the Palace like he owned the place.

Brow exclaimed, "Oh, my God, that's Campbell there!"

Without hesitation, Sharp marched across the saloon and smashed Campbell across the face with a huge fist. Campbell stumbled backward and collapsed against a table, spilling the drinks of four men. Two of them charged Sharp, but he easily dodged them, using his boot to trip one while flooring the other with a roundhouse punch that must have broken his jaw. It had all happened instantly, and now the saloon was so quiet, I heard a chair creak from a customer's shifting weight. Moving carefully, I scanned the room, but nobody looked threatening.

Sharp moved forward until he loomed over Campbell. "Eli, don't let me see ya again, or next time, so help me God, I'll kill ya with my bare hands."

Without a glance or hesitation, Sharp left the deathly silent saloon.

Chapter 9

I rapped on Sharp's door. Getting no answer, I knocked again. "Jeff, it's Steve."

"Come in, it ain't locked."

I open the door to find Sharp sitting on his bed, rubbing his hand. His Winchester lay on the bed beside him. He looked angry, and his eyes challenged me. I had never seen Sharp like this before, and I wasn't about to risk his rage by reprimanding him for hitting a longtime enemy.

"How's the hand?"

"Sore. What happened after I left?"

"Not much. I offered Brow five dollars for the damage, but he wouldn't take it. Said he'd have paid ten to see that punch. So I gave the five dollars to that stranger you clobbered to pay for the drinks and to make up a bit for his sore jaw. He was pretty drunk and seemed to blame himself more than you. Still, he took the five dollars."

"What about that son of a bitch, Campbell?"

"Brow told the barkeep to throw him out, but Campbell scurried out on all fours first. As soon as the two of you left, the saloon went back to normal."

Sharp started to reach into his pant pocket and grimaced. "Damn!" He shook his hand, rubbed it, and then sucked on his fingers. "Steve, I'll pay you the five bucks when this hand works again."

71

"Forget it. I'd have paid ten dollars to see that punch too."

The anger faded, and he looked like an eight-year-old boy caught by a schoolmarm while doing something rotten to the little girl sitting in front of him. Sharp smiled wanly. "Steve, I'm sorry I ruined yer plans."

I was sorry too, but I realized I wasn't blameless. This venture had always been about finding a man Sharp hated. Now that the inevitable had happened, I couldn't heap all the blame on my friend. Besides, everything had happened so fast, Campbell probably didn't know we were together, so I would just have to work him alone. I hadn't been looking for a lot of help from Sharp for this phase anyway.

I put my hand on his shoulder and squeezed lightly. "Don't worry. We'll figure something out . . . but tomorrow. Tonight, I'm bone tired."

"Ya know, if Campbell's that broke, he probably already sold those shares. Edison Electric Light Company ain't exactly a secret."

"Not many believe the story. To most people, power comes from steam or rushing water, and it's used to move things like locomotives or textile looms. People can't imagine electricity creating light. No . . . I don't think he would find many buyers on the frontier. Besides, he's maneuvering Governor Frémont to get the investigations dropped. He'd gamble everything he's got except those shares. I'm sure he'd keep them for his triumphant return to New York."

I really was tired and wanted to sleep on a soft mattress for the first time in over a week. I said good night and walked toward the door. Sharp stood and walked a pace behind me. I thought he was escorting me out, but then he stepped into the hall and turned toward the stairs.

"Where are you headed?" I asked.

"Saloon." He must have seen something on my face because he quickly added, "I'm just goin' down to buy a bottle for my room."

"Do me a favor, don't make any more trouble."

Sharp laughed. "Trouble is the furthest thing from my mind."

Chapter 10

I woke before sunrise but felt well rested. After washing my face and brushing my teeth, I stuck my head out the window to see what the weather was like. A brisk breeze tousled my hair, but the sky was crystal clear with the deep iridescent blue of a pending sunrise. It was going to be a grand day.

After dressing, I grabbed *Roughing It* and ran down the outdoor staircase that led to an alley behind the Palace. My lifelong practice had been to read while I ate my morning meal. On the ride from Nevada, we ate breakfast in the saddle, so I was looking forward to getting back to old habits.

As I entered the Palace through a rear door, I saw that they had covered a few tables with gingham cloth, and a couple of early-rising patrons were eating food that smelled terrific. As soon as I chose a table, a buxom, matronly lady came over, wiping her hands on her apron.

"Good morning, gent. Coffee?"

"Yes, ma'am."

Before I asked what was on the menu, she was gone, but she returned in quick order with a hot coffeepot she held with the bottom of her apron. She expertly filled a blue enameled mug already sitting on the table. After pouring, she said without preamble, "Steak and eggs, chop and eggs, oatmeal, mush, flapjacks. What'll it be?"

"Flapjacks, chop, and eggs. All together."

Without a word, she whirled and, barely breaking stride, filled two more coffee cups on her way to the kitchen.

In less than ten minutes and four pages of my book, she returned with two plates, sliding them in front of me without the slightest clatter. Then she reached into her apron pocket and handed me a cloth napkin wrapped around my tableware.

"How's that look, gent?" she asked with a smile and both hands on her hips.

"Perfect," I answered.

"Well, you enjoy yourself." And she was off to another table, wiping her hands on her all-purpose apron.

I unwrapped the napkin to find a fork and a knife for the chop. The food looked and smelled delicious, and the service was friendly and efficient. Perhaps the Palace didn't have the elegance of the St. Charles Hotel in Carson City, but it was a huge improvement over Pickhandle Gulch.

After I was halfway through breakfast and another ten pages, Brow sauntered into the now half-filled saloon with the confidence of someone who liked what he saw. That is, until he saw me. His expression immediately turned troubled, and he approached with a hesitation that made me wary.

When he loomed over me, he said, "I'm sorry about your friend."

I was confused. "What? You mean Jeff Sharp?"

He appeared confused. "You don't know?"

"Know what?"

Brow sat down. "He was arrested last night for the murder of Elisha Campbell."

I sat stunned a moment before blurting, "From that single punch?"

"No, from a rifle shot to the back of the head. Close range."

I shook my head. "No. Jeff wouldn't do that. He'd never shoot anyone from behind."

"If a man hates enough, he can do anything."

"I've seen back-shooters threaten Jeff's life. He still fought fair. Only way he knows. There's been a mistake."

"I don't think so." He held my eyes. "Sharp's Winchester did the killing. It was found close to the body—two spent shots." He looked down, as if embarrassed. "His name was carved into the stock."

"Wait a minute. Where did this happen?"

"Base of Thumb Butte."

"How far?"

"Almost a mile from here."

"And Jeff was found that far away?"

"No. He was found in his room . . . in a drunken stupor."

"This is bullshit!" The more I learned, the more

76

it looked like someone had framed Sharp. "What time did this happen?" I asked.

"The killing? Somewhere around midnight."

I had left Sharp about eight o'clock . . . so I guessed it was possible. Still, it didn't make sense. When Sharp left his room for a bottle, he didn't seem angry anymore.

"Were you in the saloon about eight o'clock?" I asked.

"I'm always in the saloon at night."

"Did you see Jeff Sharp come in about that time?"

"Sure. Big event. At first he tried to order a bottle, but men kept buying him drinks, and he spent most of the night right over there." Brow pointed to the end of the bar. "Pretty drunk when he staggered out."

"What time was that?"

"Let's see, Julie had just started singing, so it must have been about eleven."

"See him again?"

"No."

"Did you see Campbell in the saloon again?"

"You ask a lot of questions, but no, I never saw Campbell again."

I took a sip of my tepid coffee. "How did you learn about this?"

"About one in the morning, a deputy came in to ask if I had a Jeff Sharp registered. Not long after, someone spread the word that a man had been

arrested for killing Campbell. A cheer went up."
When he saw the look on my face, he quickly
added, "I'm sorry. That was rude. It's just that
everybody hated Campbell, and nobody knows
your friend."

I lifted my coffee cup toward the waitress, and
she hurried over to fill the cup of a "gent"
talking with her boss. I used the distraction to
think. The timing seemed implausible to me. In
two hours, Jeff would have had to follow or lure
Campbell out to Thumb Butte, kill him, and get
back to his bed so he could pass out. And he had
to accomplish this while falling-down drunk. As
I thought it through, I realized he didn't have
even two hours, because within that time, the
body would have been discovered, the arrest
made, and word spread to the saloons. The
timing would be extremely tight for a sober
man, but impossible for Sharp if he was really
drunk.

I took a shallow sip of the hot coffee and looked
at Brow. "My friend didn't kill Campbell."

"I guess a court will decide that, but it doesn't
sound good if he was killed with your friend's
rifle." Brow looked uncomfortable. "He
threatened to kill Campbell right here in this
saloon. Everybody heard."

"With his bare hands, if memory serves. Jeff
would never back-shoot a squirrel." I shoved my
breakfast away. "He didn't do it."

Brow just shrugged.

"Where can I find him?"

"The jail is in the basement of the courthouse."

"Who's the sheriff?"

"Virgil Earp's the town constable. He's the one in charge."

Chapter 11

Because of the early hour, the courthouse was quiet, but I found a watchman to ask about seeing a prisoner. After some preliminaries, he took my gun and then unlocked a door that led to a dark stairwell. He repeatedly pulled a wire attached to a tinkling bell at the bottom of the staircase. Eventually, a door opened, and light leaked up to us from a lantern in the room below.

A large, scruffy-looking man peeked around the doorjamb. I hoped he wasn't Virgil Earp.

"Visitor!" the watchman yelled down. Then he turned an appraising look on me. "The night jailer is named George. He'll let you talk to the prisoner for five minutes . . . but . . . if you buy us both breakfast, you can talk as long as it takes us to eat it."

"Sounds reasonable," I said evenly. "I'll go to the Palace and bring back something. What do you and George want?"

He winked. "A silver dollar'll do. I've got someone to fetch food."

"And you'll keep the change, I suppose."

"Won't be no change. George and I are big eaters."

"Very well." I handed him a dollar coin.

"George, I'll be sending breakfast down soon."

The watchman made a sweeping wave with his arm to signal that I could descend the stairs.

As I approached the bottom of the stairwell, George backed away from the door and kept a hand on his pistol grip.

When I reached the last step, he said, "Take your coat off and hang it on that peg." He nodded toward four pegs on the wall. After I hung my coat, he ordered me to slowly turn in a circle, and then he told me to lift my pant legs above the top of my boots.

"The man upstairs took my gun," I said.

"Don't mean ya don't have another or a knife. Gotta be careful." He dropped his hand away from his pistol. "Who're ya here to see?"

"Jeff Sharp."

He nodded. "Last cell. Stand back against the wall, away from the bars. Do not pass anything to the prisoner. Do not accept anything from the prisoner. Do not approach the bars. I'll be watching."

"I understand."

As I walked down the hall, I was surprised to see every cell full—most held two men. When I got to the end, Jeff was lying on a wood army cot with his face against the stone wall. No one was on the other cot. A chamber pot, wood stool, and small writing desk comprised the remaining furnishings. With no windows, the only light came from a couple of lanterns hanging outside, along the corridor. The odor of vomit I had smelled coming down the hall came from this cell.

"Jeff?"

After a long moment, Sharp slowly rolled over and peered at me with bloodshot eyes. "Is it morning?"

I pulled out my pocket watch. "Almost seven."

"Damn." He gently swung his legs off the cot and rubbed his eyes with the heels of his hands. "Any chance of gettin' coffee in this fine establishment?"

"I'll check."

When I turned, I saw George leaning against the wall in the office area. He held up a hand to stop me from walking toward him. "I heard. He'll get coffee with his breakfast at eight o'clock. One mug." Then he smiled. "For his information, this ain't no fine establishment."

"But I can smell coffee," I said.

"Do yer talkin'. He'll get coffee in short order."

I looked at Sharp, and he seemed miserable but awake. "Jeff, what happened?"

"Not sure. But I know what didn't happen. I sure as hell didn't kill Campbell."

"I know that." I took half a step forward, then remembered my instructions and retreated to the wall. "You need to explain what happened so I can get you out of here. Let's start at the beginning: Why did you stay downstairs in the saloon? I thought you went down for a bottle to take back to your room."

"When I walked in, I was treated like a hero. Before I knew it, I had three full shot glasses in front of me. I'd blame others, but hell, I wanted to celebrate too." Sharp looked at his hand and gave it a shake before rubbing it again. "I'd dreamed about punchin' that cheatin' bastard for years."

"When did you leave?"

"Hell, I don't know. I was drinkin' for a couple hours. By the time I walked out, I was lucky to move under my own power." He alternated between rubbing his forehead and his hand. "I remember climbin' those damn back stairs. I had to take each step careful-like while holdin' tight to the handrail."

"What else do you remember?"

"Not much. I recall a bunch of men roustin' me out of bed. I was too drunk to resist, so I guess they just led me over here to this cell. Woke up pukin' a few hours ago, an' that jailer told me I was under arrest for the murder of Elisha Campbell—way out at this Thumb Butte, for God's sake."

"Did you go to Thumb Butte last night?"

"Hell, I don't even know what it is."

"That big outcropping we saw on the way into town. It's about a mile away."

"I couldn't have traveled a mile. I barely made it out of the saloon."

"Jeff, it doesn't look good. Your rifle was lying next to the body of a man you threatened to kill earlier in the evening. A bullet had been fired into the back of Elisha Campbell's head."

"Shit." Sharp looked worried, but I could see that his thinking was still muddled from over-drinking. He sat still for a time until he said, "I need three things. A damn good lawyer, an alibi, an' a cup of hot coffee. Can ya get 'em for me, Steve?"

I must have been mistaken about his mental state, because that list was anything but muddled. "I'll get you the best lawyer in the territory, but the other two might be more difficult."

"Bribe that son-of-a-bitch jailer. I need to get a clear head. Then talk to people that were in the saloon last night. Ought to be plenty to testify I was fallin'-down drunk. I never could have gotten out to some butte."

"Jeff, did you lock your door when you went down to buy that bottle?"

"Ya know I didn't. Ya was standin' right there. I meant to be right back."

"And your rifle?"

"Yep, in my unlocked room the whole time I was drinkin' myself under the table."

"I think someone wanted Campbell dead, and you provided a handy scapegoat."

"Handy an' stupid." Sharp leaned over the

chamber pot as if to puke again, but then jerked back up straight.

"I need a fourth thing: Can ya kindly pay someone to empty an' clean this damn chamber pot?"

"I'll take care of it."

He looked up at me with forlorn eyes. "What d'ya think?"

"I think we're in a strange town. If this goes to trial fast, we may not have enough time to discover the real story. We need help."

"Joseph?"

"Joseph."

Chapter 12

Another two dollars secured Sharp an endless cup of coffee and a clean commode, so I ran over to the Western Union office to send a message to Captain Joseph McAllen of the Pinkerton National Detective Agency.

My next stop was the second floor of the courthouse: the governor's office. A secretary behind a carved mahogany desk guarded the governor's closed office door. As I approached, he stood and raised a hand to stop my progress. He was a young man, probably early twenties, impeccably dressed in a three-piece suit that was obviously tailored in the East. I, of course, was dressed like a cleaned-up ranch hand.

"Good morning. I'd like to see Governor Frémont. My name is Steve Dancy."

"He hasn't arrived yet, and he's booked the next few days. I'm Jonathon Winslow, his personal assistant. May I ask the subject of your business?"

"Personal matter. I sent him a letter announcing my pending trip a few months ago. Could you please tell me where I can find him?"

"No."

"Excuse me?" I wanted to verbally tear into this civic minion, but that would have made him even more impertinent. "I'm a personal family friend of John Frémont, recently arrived from New York City. My family was a major donor to his presidential bid. I've run into a bit of trouble, and I need to speak to the governor as soon as possible. Where can I find him at this hour of the morning?"

"I'm under strict orders never to reveal the governor's whereabouts . . . *especially* if the subject is personal. I can make you an appointment for next week or possibly the week after." He leaned over a leather-bound appointment calendar. "Will fifteen minutes be sufficient?"

"You won't tell me where he lives, will you?"

"Of course not."

"Well, I suppose it's not a secret to townsfolk. Good day, sir."

He let me walk ten paces before adding in a quiet voice, "You won't find him at home."

I stopped and slowly turned to face him. "Then I'll speak with Jessie. She'll tell me how to find her husband."

The sneer faded. "Perhaps it's best if we don't disturb Mrs. Frémont this morning. If you tell me what your problem is, I'm sure I can handle it. I do all sorts of tasks for the governor."

"I'm sure." I pretended to contemplate his offer. "But I think this should be handled personally by the governor. You did understand that the Frémont and Dancy families are not only friendly but politically connected?"

"Do you want money?"

"What? No."

"Does the problem involve a woman?"

"No."

"Just a moment." He disappeared behind the closed door. After a moment, he reappeared and waved me into the office.

John C. Frémont sat alone at a long committee table, eating breakfast. He wore a beard and a full head of unruly gray hair. He had grown old, and he looked beaten. I was struck by this inglorious end to a glorious career.

I approached with an extended hand. "Governor, I'm Steve Dancy. I'm sure you don't remember, but you once bounced me on your knee."

Frémont wiped his hands on a napkin and shook—not a politician's handshake, but the gesture of an erstwhile hero resigned to mundane routine. It must be difficult to go from being nationally celebrated to holding an obscure posting on the frontier.

"Steven Dancy? From New York City? I'm sure you're correct, but I have no such recollection. How long ago was it?"

"In 1855, twenty-five years ago. You were the Republican nominee for president. My father and you were friends and political allies."

"A heady time. Lots of gentlemen to greet, lots of wives to dance around the floor, lots of babies to kiss . . . and lots of children to bounce on my knee. It's all just a blur, I'm afraid."

This wouldn't do. "Governor, may I remind you, the Dancys were among the largest and earliest donors to your campaign. My family introduced you to New York society, which garnered additional large contributions. You bounced me on your knee, not at some political event but in our parlor, which you visited often to discuss political strategy with my father."

"Please excuse me. I lost a good friend last night. My mood is dark and my mind addled."

He still hadn't acknowledged knowing us. Perhaps he was afraid I had come to collect a return favor—or money for some long-forgotten debt. I had originally hoped to use his influence to assist with my enterprises, but now I wanted his help to free Sharp.

"I presume you are referring to the death of Elisha Campbell," I said.

"I am. Did you know him?"

"No, but I traveled from Carson City to see if we could make a business arrangement together."

He raised an eyebrow at the mention of the Nevada capital. I was sure he was assessing my political influence. I may have been dressed in trail clothes, but I had told him my family was consequential, and he surely had noticed my educated speech.

"Were you able to make this business

arrangement with Mr. Campbell?" he asked, seeming a bit more cautious.

"Unfortunately, no. We arrived yesterday, and I didn't have the opportunity to seek an introduction. I had intended to come to you in the hopes you might provide that service."

Frémont physically relaxed after hearing that I had been merely seeking an introduction to one of his associates. I assumed that he felt comfortable handling such simple matters.

"Then this is your loss as well. Mr. Campbell was astute at business. In fact, he was helping me with a few issues."

I wondered how to ask him to help me free his friend's murderer. I guessed that I'd need to find out as much as possible before he learned that fact.

"Governor, I need a good lawyer. Can you make a recommendation?"

"Of course." He looked pleased. Politicians always want people beholden to them, and a recommendation was an easy way to curry favor. "George Blanchet is the best in the territory."

"What are his specialties?"

"Government relations, deeds, claims, and business transactions. If you want to do business in the territory, you want Blanchet on your side of the table."

"Does he have any experience with criminal cases?"

"Not really." Frémont laughed. "Do you intend to commit a crime?"

"No. My friend has been wrongly accused of a crime."

Frémont must have guessed, because he immediately stiffened. "What friend? What crime?"

No use equivocating any longer. "Jeff Sharp has been accused of murdering Elisha Campbell."

The governor leaped to his feet, almost spilling the remainder of his breakfast. "Elisha was a friend of mine!"

"Be that as it may, Jeff Sharp didn't kill him."

"I can't get involved with this. Please leave."

"Governor, I know it's been many years, but the Dancy family was critical to furthering your political career. I only want a fair hearing."

"The Dancys furthered my political career? Do you see where I am?" Frémont reached into his pocket and threw a few coins on the table. "There, that ought to repay everything I owe for this grand posting." He plopped into his chair and waved his fingers, dismissing me. "Please, go."

I started to leave the pathetic old man but stopped with one hand on the door. "Just one more question, and I'll leave. Did Campbell ever mention the Edison Electric Light Company?"

Frémont was back on his feet. "Get out before I call capitol troopers. Now!"

I took that as a yes.

Chapter 13

After leaving the governor, I went to see Bob Brow at the Palace. I needed a lawyer, and in my experience, saloon owners knew all about the townspeople. I hoped that he could direct me to a lawyer who didn't just trade favors with politicians. Saloon owners weren't early risers, but he had come in while I was eating breakfast, so he might still be around. But when I entered the Palace, Brow was no longer in sight. I was about to ask the barkeep for his whereabouts when I spotted Doc Holliday eating alone. It was mid-morning, and gamblers seldom stirred before noon. The thought struck me that everyone got up early in this town.

I ordered a cup of coffee from the bar and walked over to Holliday. "May I join you?"

"No." He gave me a curious look. He continued in his easy Southern drawl. "Ah'll excuse your rudeness because you're new to town, but Ah do not abide being interrupted at breakfast. Everybody else knows it. Now you do too."

I bowed slightly. "I apologize, Doctor. Is there a time I could see you?"

"About what?" There was curiosity in his voice.

"I need legal help for my friend."

"When you address someone as doctor, it means they're most probably not in the legal profession."

"At present, if I'm not mistaken, you're a gambler, and gamblers know people—or they don't stay in the profession long. I thought you might direct me to a lawyer with skill and character."

I worried that I had overstayed his patience, but Holliday laughed instead of snarling at me. "A lawyer with character. Next, you'll want me to find you a generous banker. Well hell, you might as well sit, sir." He waved me into a seat across from him. As I sat, he bellowed out to the room in general, "Don't none of you jackals get the idea you can bother me at breakfast. I'm likely to put a bullet in your fat yaps."

As I sipped some scalding coffee, Holliday gave me a sly wink before asking, "What are you looking for?"

"The best lawyer in the territory. One with experience defending criminals but also savvy in delaying trials. I have money."

"That's always handy."

I shrugged.

"Why do you want a delay?"

"I have a detective en route, but it will take him a while to get here."

"You believe your friend's innocent?"

"I know he is."

Holliday seemed to mull that over. "Lots of people are happy Campbell's dead . . . including your friend. What makes you think he's not the one who did it?"

Now I thought. Sowing a little worry around town about what we might know or what evidence we might possess could be advantageous. "I can't disclose that at the moment, but we need time. I need a lawyer who knows how to tie the proceedings in knots that'll take weeks to untangle."

"You want Mac Castle."

"What can you tell me about him?"

"A rarity—an honest lawyer. If he distrusts you, he'll send you on your way. But if he accepts you as a client, he's the best around. That boy's clever as a saloon gal sizing up the clientele. When he's in court, everybody comes to watch because he's entertaining, sarcastic, and irreverent." Holliday chuckled. "A man after my own heart. But somehow his cranky style appeals to juries as well as the grandstands."

Castle seemed like my man, but I had to ask, "What do you think of George Blanchet?"

Holliday jerked back like I had shown him a photograph of a circus freak. "If you steal a claim or commit fraud, Blanchet will gladly defend you. He's as shifty as they come, but Ah wouldn't hire him to defend your friend."

I nodded. "Just checking. Someone else recommended him."

"You trust this person's judgment?" He sounded incredulous.

"I wouldn't be interrupting your breakfast if I did."

He gave me an odd look. "You trust me?"

I tried a friendly smile. "I trust your judgment." I stood. "If you'll excuse me, I need to find Mr. Castle."

"Not hard. His office is next door. Good day, Mr. Dancy."

I left the Palace, pleased that Doc Holliday had remembered my name.

Chapter 14

I climbed to the second floor of the narrow building and saw a long hall with a series of mahogany doors painted with gold lettering. The third one read, "Mac Castle, Attorney at Law."

I knocked, and a male voice yelled at me to enter.

When I opened the door, a man in shirtsleeves sat in a leather chair reading what looked to be a legal brief.

I walked over. "Mr. Castle, my name is Steve Dancy."

Without attempting to get up, he asked, "What can I do for you?"

"I need a lawyer experienced in defending tough criminal cases. I was hoping for a few moments of your time to interview you."

"Usually the client is the supplicant." His amused expression told me I hadn't offended him.

"This case is so important to me that I must hire not only the best but also the most experienced in cases similar to mine."

"And what type of case would that be?"

"Murder."

"The Elisha Campbell murder?"

"Yes."

"You said, 'in cases similar to mine.' My

understanding is that another man has been arrested for that crime."

"My friend, Jeff Sharp. This morning, he asked me to find him an attorney. That's why I'm here."

"Take a seat." He pointed at a leather chair.

Mac Castle had an almost typical law office: cluttered rolltop desk, dark wainscoting, framed portraits, and bookshelves of law books arranged with exquisite neatness. That is where the similarity ended. Castle appeared to be in his thirties and wore an open-neck shirt, without coat or tie, and slippers. The opposing leather chairs, like those at my father's club, put the client and Castle on equal footing.

"Tell me about yourself and your friend."

"We rode into town yesterday afternoon and got rooms at the Palace. After a bath, we had drinks in the saloon. We were tired from a long ride and left early, but about eight o'clock, Jeff went back downstairs. I retired. He stayed in the saloon drinking until about eleven and then returned drunk to his room. While he was gone, he left his door unlocked with his rifle inside. Sometime before one o'clock, Campbell was discovered dead at the base of Thumb Butte, shot with Jeff's rifle. The rifle was found beside the body."

"You're omitting the most important fact."

I knew what he meant. "Earlier in the evening, my friend punched Campbell and threatened to kill him if he ever saw him again." I paused. "Have I told you anything you don't already know?"

"Not yet."

When he offered nothing more, I told him a little about Sharp's business interests and some of our history together—omitting the violent episodes. I then talked about Sharp's character and why he could never commit murder.

When I finished, he asked, "Would you like a cup of coffee?"

"I would."

He got up and left the office without another word. I sat for a moment but couldn't resist peeking at the papers Castle had been reading when I came into his office. I actually heard the intake of my own breath. Damn. The papers were a civil complaint against Elisha Campbell for misrepresentation in the sale of Edison Electric Illumination Company stock. They were being filed for Lew Davis, the barkeep at the Palace saloon.

I flipped through the pages like a raccoon rifling through a picnic basket. It seemed that when Davis submitted the certificate through his bank to New York, he was informed that the company was valued at only a few pennies per share. Attached to the complaint was a stock certificate that looked as real as any I had ever seen. Damn. Campbell knew the value of his

Edison shares, or he would never have thought to sell shares in a shell company with a similar name. I was interested in shares of the Edison Electric Light Company, not the Illumination Company.

When I heard a footfall in the hall outside, I dropped the papers back on the side table. I heard Castle tap the door with his shoe and jumped up to let him in. When he stepped through the door, his hands carried two steaming china mugs of coffee.

"Sorry it took so long. I ran down to the Palace to get these. I put cream in. If you want sugar, there's a cone on the table over there."

"This is fine," I said as I took one of the mugs from him.

After we settled back in the twin chairs, he said, "Now tell me about the history between Sharp and Campbell."

"What makes you think there's a history?"

"You told me Sharp is a fine, upstanding citizen. Fine, upstanding citizens do not hit random customers as they saunter into a saloon. Tell me how Sharp knew Campbell."

"I left that out on purpose."

"Because it could be construed as motive." It was a statement, not a question.

I shrugged. "Are you accepting Jeff Sharp as a client?"

"Does Mr. Sharp have two hundred dollars?"

"He does."

"In that case, I'll represent your friend if he decides to engage me." Castle then described his legal experience. His practice involved mostly fraud and property title cases resulting from the primitive legal institutions in the Arizona territory. He had defended numerous criminals for armed robbery, assault, and murder. He told me that he had lost all but two of these cases but got fair sentences for the remainder. Castle said he had a much better record on prosecuting civil fraud cases.

"Why did you win only two criminal cases?" I asked.

"Because generally, people who are arrested are guilty. If they go to trial, the attorney general has witnesses or hard evidence. In the case of your friend, he has both."

"There are no witnesses to the murder."

"There are reliable witnesses to assault and battery. The threats to kill the victim are quite damaging. A rifle with his name carved into the butt at the scene of the crime is hard evidence."

"But his door—"

He held up a hand to stop me. "Access to the weapon may have been available to others, but the rifle was owned by Sharp and last known in his possession. It puts the burden of proof on the defense, or at least the burden of building sufficient doubt. In addition, there were pine needles on the stairs leading to his room and stuck to the bottom of his boots."

I sat back. "I never heard that. What does it mean?"

"It means he may have been at Thumb Butte last night."

"There are pine needles all over."

"But none in the Palace saloon. Tell me, did Sharp have his clothes and boots cleaned while he took a bath?"

"We both did." I was starting to worry. "Do you believe Sharp's guilty?"

"I consider it unethical to say no to get a client, but the truth is . . . I don't know."

"But you know a lot about this case. How?"

"I ate breakfast with Constable Earp." He sipped his coffee. "But he probably doesn't know everything, so why don't you tell me something I don't know?"

I hesitated. "Perhaps we should wait until after you talk to Jeff. I'd feel more comfortable sharing information if a formal attorney-client relationship were in place."

"I won't even bother to talk to Mr. Sharp unless you're forthright with me. Now tell me everything."

I had already determined that Castle was a good attorney. He had me over a barrel. We needed him more than he needed another client. I decided to tell Castle almost everything. It would all become public knowledge soon anyway. I told him about Sharp and Campbell being partners in a New York City import business. I told him about Campbell's despicable betrayal. I told all about Sharp's mines and alluded to my own financial well-being. I told about the violent confrontations Sharp and I had in Nevada and Colorado. I didn't tell him about the Edison Electric Light Company.

When I finished, he picked up the two empty mugs and disappeared out the door. I didn't want another cup of coffee, but I didn't have a chance to say anything before he was gone. Besides, I suspected Castle used these errands to think.

After he returned, he asked, "Did you, at any time, have an association with Elisha Campbell?"

"No. Why do you ask?'

"Campbell was a swindler who made enemies wherever he went. You're both from New York City. You're a violent man who settles scores with a gun. You knew about Sharp's unlocked door, and you knew his name was carved in the stock of his Winchester." His face remained completely blank. "Mr. Dancy, you had the best opportunity to frame your friend. I want to know if you had motive."

"I never saw Elisha Campbell before he walked into the Palace last night."

"I'll accept that for now, but understand that if I take Mr. Sharp as a client, I will go anywhere the evidence leads me to get him acquitted."

I nodded. "Good, because I did not kill Campbell, nor did I frame my friend."

"I certainly hope that's the truth." He picked up the brief he had been reading when I came in and waved it in my direction. "What did you think of this?"

I started to protest but then smiled as I realized he had left me alone with the brief so I would read it. "You intend to get him off by putting the blame somewhere else."

"Delivering an actual murderer is more effective than trying to convince a jury that the evidence is too weak to convict."

"Why did you want me to read this brief?"

Castle sat back and interlaced his fingers as he pondered me. "I wanted to gauge whether you had been a victim of the same scam. I'm aware of two other victims who bought shares in this worthless company."

"I wasn't a fourth." I had to make a decision. Did I tell him we came here to buy stock from Campbell? This man was far too clever to remain ignorant of any aspect of this case. I had to trust him. I pointed to the brief. "When you worked on these cases, did you discover that Edison had a company with a different name?"

"Yes, the Edison Electric Light Company."

"Jeff and I have reason to believe that Campbell possesses stock in this real company."

The way Castle leaned forward told me this was

news—the first real news that interested him. "How do I know you didn't just hear about these certificates he's been selling all over the territory?"

"Our information came from New York, not Arizona. Campbell got the shares from a consortium led by Commodore Vanderbilt's son. It's certain he had them at one time but uncertain if he still has them. We came to Prescott to find out."

"How valuable would they be?"

"Not certain. But with further engineering, Edison's lighting system could change mining. That's our interest."

Castle looked puzzled. "I'm confused. Or I should say, I suspect you're lying somewhere. If Sharp wanted these shares, why would he open negotiations with a punch to the jaw?"

"I told you, Campbell had stolen Sharp's fortune and ruined his reputation. He thought he could put that aside until after we got hold of the shares, but when he saw him for the first time, he lost his temper." I decided I might as well tell Castle everything. "By the way, I already own those shares. Campbell ran away from New York before paying a credit line extended by Corny Vanderbilt." I reached into my inside coat pocket and pulled out my legal documents. "We weren't here to buy them; we came to collect my property."

I handed the documents to Castle. He read them quickly, then looked up with a quizzical expression. I explained that my attorneys in New York had recommended that I collect the certificates if possible to avoid someone contesting ownership.

"Yes, an innocent buyer, or holder in due course, could cause you untold difficulties, especially if they pursued their claim outside New York courts—someplace like the territory of Arizona perhaps."

He leaned forward to hand them back to me.

"No. I'd like you to retain them. If the occasion arises, I'd like you to represent my interests."

"Is a retainer of twenty dollars acceptable?"

"Yes."

"Very well. But as your attorney in this matter, I must advise you not to grab the certificate if you happen upon it." He held up my documents. "With these, I'll have no difficulty handling the matter in a way that will never be contested. Understood?"

"Yes." I withdrew my wallet and handed Castle twenty dollars.

After putting the money in his pocket, he interlaced his fingers again and remained silent for a long moment. Eventually, he stood up. "Have you eaten your noonday meal?"

"No."

"Try Mrs. Potter's on the other side of the

courthouse. Food's good and all the government people eat there. Try to eavesdrop on their conversations. My bet is they're talking about the murder."

"I'll try." He was obviously shooing me away. Before we separated company, I had to mention one more thing. "By the way, I have a detective on the way."

"What? Who?"

"I wired Captain McAllen of the Pinkertons. He was with us in Nevada and Colorado."

"I don't like this. Who will he work for?"

"Me . . . but I'll instruct him to share everything with you."

"I'll need to think about that."

"Think about it all you want, but McAllen is going to be neck deep in this. He's a friend of ours, and we trust him."

"I'll ask Mr. Sharp about him. In fact, I'm going over to the courthouse now."

"I'll come with you."

"Not if you want me to defend Sharp. I talk to him alone. You go over to Mrs. Potter's."

Castle was a smart lawyer. He wanted to verify what I had told him without my presence to influence Sharp. I bet he could spot a single lie in a one-hour conversation. I suddenly realized that I had revealed far more than I had intended. I had started the meeting by saying I was going to interview him, but in the end he had been measuring me, and I had not emerged from this initial encounter with his full confidence.

"May I write Jeff a note?" He looked hesitant, so I added, "You may read it."

"I'll give him your note. But I'll decide whether to give it to him at the beginning or end of our talk."

"Very well." Without asking permission, I went to Castle's rolltop desk and wrote a short message. It read, "Jeff, I strongly recommend you accept Mac Castle as your lawyer."

I folded the piece of paper in half and handed it to Castle. He read it, then gave me a hard look he had not yet used with me. It was cold and calculating.

"Mr. Dancy, make no mistake, if I accept this case, Mr. Sharp will be my sole client in this matter. To be clear, our arrangement involves an entirely different matter. If the evidence in this case leads to you, I will use it unmercifully to defend my client. Do not get in my way or use your damn Pinkerton to misdirect this investigation. Are we clear?"

"Yes. You may also tell Jeff I believe we've found the right lawyer."

Chapter 15

As soon as I opened the door to Mrs. Potter's Café, the enticing smell of good food reminded me that it had been a long time since breakfast. The décor was more refined than I expected in a town on the frontier. I saw crocheted white tablecloths, blue willow china, and red flocked wallpaper. An American flag adorned one wall, bracketed by photographs of presidents Rutherford Hayes and George Washington. I assumed the patriotic flair meant that the owner wanted statehood for Arizona.

The place was busy and all the tables occupied. I spotted an open seat next to the young man I had encountered outside the governor's office. I hesitated because his companions may have been closer to my age, but they were no less expensively dressed than he. I had not brought a suit from Carson City, and although I had put on fresh clothing that morning, I looked like a well-groomed trail hand. Despite my appearance, I approached their table.

"Excuse me. I was wondering if I might join you."

One of the men responded, "I'm sorry; we're doing some personal business. Seating should free up in just a few minutes."

I started to leave when another gentleman

stood. "Are you associated with the man that was arrested this morning?"

"I am."

"Then why don't you take this seat? We should get to know each other."

"Thank you." I extended my hand. "Steve Dancy."

"George Blanchet. I understand the governor recommended that I represent your friend. This is Jonathon Winslow, the governor's assistant, and Herb Locklear, a councilman in the territorial assembly. Please, take a seat."

"We've met," Winslow said with extreme disinterest.

I shook hands with everyone before I sat. Blanchet looked like the hail-fellow type who practiced law based on who he knew, not what he knew. The bearded Locklear, on the other hand, presented a solid appearance, both in physical stature and demeanor.

"Thank you," I said, looking around the café. "This appears to be a busy place this hour of the day."

"All the political busybodies eat here," Locklear said.

"If the food's good, then I'll make a habit of eating later in the day. After the crowds."

"Then adjust your habits my friend, because the food is as good as you'll find in Prescott," Locklear said, his voice loud enough for Mrs. Potter to hear wherever she was.

I turned to the young man. "Thank you for granting me access to the governor. We rekindled family ties."

"That's not what I hear," Winslow said. His tone was snobbish.

"From whom?"

"From the governor. He scolded me for letting you interrupt his breakfast. He has no recollection of your family. Besides, a supposed campaign contribution to his presidential run is ancient history."

I bit my lip and signaled for a waitress. I wasn't about to debate with an overblown underling. "Any recommendations?" I asked to change the subject.

Locklear answered. "If you've never experienced it, their Mexican tamales are fantastic. If you want to stick with standard fare, order the Stockman Special. It's a great piece of beef, with potato and peas. But whatever you order, leave room for cake. Mrs. Potter bakes like no one else in the territory."

I had never heard of tamales, nor experienced Mexican food. Not being adventurous with my diet, I ordered the Stockman Special.

"Tragedy about your friend," Blanchet said. "I'm sure he had good reason, but justice is swift and severe here in the territory. If he'll engage me, I'm sure I can use his drunkenness to lighten his sentence—perhaps to just prison time."

Blanchet took on an expression meant to convey compassion. "We all make mistakes."

"I appreciate that," I said. "I'll mention your offer and the governor's endorsement this afternoon."

"You've not seen him since you talked with the governor?" Blanchet asked.

"No."

All three men exchanged glances at my simple response.

"Are you from New York or just related to people in New York?" Winslow asked, in his haughty tone.

"I grew up in New York City. Yourself?"

"Boston. I graduated from Harvard last year. I'm out here to build a curriculum vitae." He snickered. "Also, I guess, to kill time until I'm twenty-five years old." He lifted an eyebrow at me. "My family's highly connected politically. In fact, we supported Frémont's appointment to this post. Much more recent than your contribution to his presidential run twenty-five years ago. Politicians have such short memories. That's why my family makes broad contributions to many politicians every year."

"It was my mistake to bring such a trivial matter to the governor's attention. You're right, it was ancient history." I didn't want to argue with Winslow, because he probably controlled the governor's schedule, and I might need access to

Frémont again. Better to butter up the narcissist. "In what district do you plan to run for Congress?"

"The eighth . . . Daniel Webster's old seat. A family friend is holding it for me until I come of age." He tilted his head at me. "Perceptive of you."

"Not really. You mentioned politics and said you were building a curriculum vitae while you waited for your twenty-fifth birthday, which is the constitutional age requirement for the House of Representatives."

"That I did. I must learn to be more careful around strangers."

"Is your future candidacy a secret?"

"No, not at all, but my father tells me to keep things to myself." He laughed. "He says I talk too much."

"From what I've seen, not a handicap in Congress."

"You've been to Washington?"

"I was just making conversation." Actually, I had been to Washington many times, but I thought Winslow's father had given him good advice. I turned slightly toward Blanchet and asked, "Did you work with Campbell?"

Blanchet stiffened. "Why do you ask?"

"I understand Campbell fraudulently sold stock in a worthless company."

Now Winslow and Locklear stiffened as well.

"And you thought I was involved?"

What open wound had I stuck a stick in? Blanchet sounded as indignant as a woman whose profession had been misidentified. I found it informative that he hadn't denied working for Campbell, and Locklear and Winslow's reaction gave me information as well.

"Excuse me, I didn't mean to give that impression." I tried to look embarrassed. "I just didn't want to recommend you to my friend if you had represented the man he supposedly killed. I framed the question clumsily. Please forgive me."

"I still don't understand. What would I have to do with stock sales?"

"I thought he might have duped you into believing they were shares in Edison's new company and unwittingly enlisted you into his scheme. I understand he has used reputable lawyers in the past to further his frauds."

"Where would you hear this?"

"Pinkerton National Detective Agency. I spent my morning trading telegraphs with them. They should have an agent here shortly to assist with the case."

Blanchet vehemently shook his head. "You're going about this the wrong way. Once I represent Mr. Sharp, I'll engage anyone necessary." He regained his composure and patted me on the shoulder. "You must leave this to professionals. It's easier than you think to prejudice a case."

I acted chagrined. "I suppose, but I had to do something. My friend had been arrested for a hanging crime."

"Understood. As soon as I finish my meal, I'll concentrate my considerable talents on helping your friend. Don't worry . . . and cancel that Pinkerton. I already have resources right here in town."

Castle had said he knew there were two other victims, but he never said they were his clients. I examined the other men at the table. I was almost certain they had hired Blanchet to recover money paid for shares in a shell business. My guess was that I had interrupted a meeting on the topic. With Campbell's death, Blanchet had probably told them that any further legal effort was futile, and invited me to sit at their table to change the subject. Ever since Doc Holliday had described Blanchet as a shyster, I suspected that he and Campbell might have gotten together as naturally as a flea finds a dog. I was trying to confirm my suspicion with my question about his working with Campbell. I thought it also might sow a few doubts in Locklear's mind. It had worked. Both Locklear and Winslow were looking at Blanchet with curiosity.

"Can you recover anything from Campbell's estate?" I directed my question to Blanchet.

"What estate? He had nothing," he answered before thinking.

114

Now I was sure these two had been swindled and engaged Blanchet. I decided I had pushed things as far as I wanted at this first meeting. To veer away from my previous questioning, I innocently asked, "Mr. Winslow, is there something I can send to the governor to make amends? Perhaps a gold pen or a cigar case?"

Chapter 16

After we finished our meal, Blanchet wanted to walk me over to the courthouse, but I told him I needed to send a telegram first. Actually, I wanted to see if Captain McAllen had responded to my earlier telegram. He hadn't, so I hurried over to the courthouse and descended into the basement. Blanchet was waiting with a different jailer, who told us the rules allowed only one visitor at a time, which was convenient for me because I could warn Sharp to act dumb about Mac Castle. I told Blanchet I should go first to convey the governor's recommendation, and he readily accepted my reasoning.

As I walked down the hall of cells, I noticed they were now empty. Evidently, all the men I had seen earlier had been arrested for drunkenness and released in the morning with a fine.

"Hello, Jeff."

Sharp looked more like himself. Probably two meals and rest had helped him overcome his hangover. Maybe the hot coffee he held in his hand helped as well.

He gave me a friendly nod. "Steve."

"I see you got your coffee."

"Yep, but my dear jailer reminded me that two dollars does not last beyond sunrise."

"I'll take care of it. What'd you think of Mac Castle?"

"I liked the man just fine. He's got a good handle on the case, an' he knows all about Campbell swindlin' his way around town. But his insinuations didn't sit well." Sharp came over to the bars. "Steve, he suspects ya might've killed Campbell."

"I know. He came at me straightaway."

"Before or after ya wrote that note?"

"Before. Jeff, you want a lawyer who thinks through all the possibilities, no matter where they lead. Fact is, his suspicions of me and willingness to bring them out in the open convinced me that he was the right person to save your weathered old neck. Did you hire him?"

"Yep. Sorta. Listen, everythin' except me an' my rifle is back in that room. Can ya collect my gear an' stow it someplace? There's a wallet in my saddlebags. Pay Castle two hundred bucks an' take care of these jailers for a week."

"Room key?"

"Jailer's got it. When they rousted me, Earp locked the room, so everythin' should be like I left it. When ya see Castle, give him my wallet for safekeepin'."

"Don't trust me, huh?"

Sharp laughed. "Not on a good day, an' this ain't one of those. No, he's gonna have expenses, an' ya got yer own dough. I don't want him

117

holdin' back on anything that might help. 'Sides, I think he's a trustworthy sort." After a sip of coffee, he added. "Castle's cautious. After I vouched for ya, he promised to keep ya abreast of everythin' . . . but I suspect he might hold back."

"We'll learn to trust each other. It'll just take time. He wasn't comfortable with McAllen either, but I assured him that McAllen would share all he learned with him."

"Ya know that's a lie. McAllen probably won't tell me everything. Man's tight-lipped as hell. But I think Castle's okay with him, leastwise fer the moment. Told him we was longtime friends."

"It'll be fine—McAllen knows how to handle a lawyer. Speaking of that, there's another lawyer at the end of the hall who wants to defend you. Governor Frémont recommended him, so I can't ignore him. Doc Holliday says he's a shyster. By the way, Holliday's the one who directed me to Castle. I didn't tell this lawyer you already had an attorney."

Sharp craned his neck to see if he could spot the man through the bars. "Ya might as well tell him now."

I hesitated. "Maybe you should hear him out. I think he was representing two people who might have been defrauded by Campbell. If you string him along, maybe you can learn something."

"Like what?"

"Like if he was in cahoots with Campbell."

"Ya think Campbell had a partner?" His tone was skeptical.

"I'm not sure. He might have fingered the marks or sewed up the legal transfer. Who knows? The man's name is George Blanchet. Doc said he specialized in representing claim jumpers and fraudsters." I shrugged. "Birds of a feather—"

"Flock together. I take yer point." Sharp shook his head. "Don't make sense, though. A good-for-nothing lawyer might befriend crooks, figurin' they'd end up in court sooner or later, but I don't think an officer of the court would actually partner up with a fraudster. Lawyers are afraid of bein' disbarred."

"Well, if you have better things to do."

Sharp laughed. "Ya got me there. I'll talk to him, but ya better alert Castle. Don't want to look like I'm playin' both sides against the middle."

"Wouldn't want that. They might throw you in jail."

Sharp smiled weakly this time. "How do ya suppose I ought to go 'bout gettin' somethin' outta our friend?"

"Keep asking questions about Campbell. He'll never tell you direct, but you might get a notion about their relationship."

Sharp rubbed his neck. "I'll start by tellin' him I want an attorney who knew what kind of man Campbell was. Might be able to discover somethin' from inside this cage, but I'd feel more comfortable if McAllen was workin' outside."

"I sent him a telegraph first thing, but when I checked a short while ago, he hadn't responded."

"Damn."

"It's only been a few hours."

"I'm just worried he's off trackin' outlaws in some wilderness."

I had already thought about that. "If I don't hear back by the end of the day, I'll send a general query to the Denver office. I'll get you someone."

"I want—"

"I know. I want McAllen too."

We looked at each other, and I saw fear in his eyes. I suspected I had the same fear in my eyes. I blinked it away.

"Why don't I send Blanchet down? Keep you busy. Tell him you already talked to Castle, but you want the best attorney possible. At the end, tell him you need time to decide which one to hire. If he gets pushy, snarl. I've seen you back off stronger men than him with nothing more than your mean temperament."

Sharp nodded assent, but he was not amused, nor had the hint of fear been cleansed from his eyes.

Chapter 17

After I climbed the stairs from the basement jail, I knocked, and an armed deputy on the other side opened the locked door into the courthouse proper. As I stepped into the entrance hall, a rushing Jonathon Winslow almost knocked me down.

"Excuse me," he said, without looking to see whom he had bumped.

"Mr. Winslow?"

"I don't have time right now." He kept walking away. "I'm late for a meeting."

"Could we set an appointment?" I yelled after him.

He finally stopped to look at me. "No. The governor doesn't want to see you again."

"Not the governor. You. Can I buy you breakfast tomorrow, perhaps?"

His expression turned sour. "Mr. Dancy, are you addled? The governor doesn't want to see you, which means I don't want to see you. You really are impertinent to keep pushing yourself on people who are busy with important matters. Now, if you'll excuse me, I must get to my meeting."

He disappeared down a corridor before I had an opportunity to excuse him. Was it possible that Winslow could make me dislike him more? I chuckled as I realized that wouldn't even be a challenge for him. I looked out of place in trail clothes with these self-important men running around in tailored suits, but in my experience, clothing was far less important in the West. Rich ranchers and miners frequently dressed in the same garb as their hands. It was their cleanliness that differentiated them. I was scrubbed, so I saw no reason for Winslow to treat me like some lower social order.

When I turned to leave, I saw a young girl playing jackstones on a small table along the lobby wall. I would have hurried by, except that she was exceptionally skillful. She'd bounce the small ball and pick up a jackstone before the ball hit the table, then do it again, picking up two jackstones, all the way to five, and then start all over without the slightest hesitation. Her rhythm was as smooth and unfaltering as a shuttle flying back and forth in a power loom.

I watched because I was fascinated with her skill, but I kept quiet so I wouldn't disturb her concentration.

Without missing a beat, she said over her shoulder, "Mister, my pa doesn't like strange men ogling me."

As I turned to leave, I heard her mutter, "How many men do I have to send on their way? Golly."

The voice was familiar. "Maggie?"

She missed. Jackstones flew everywhere, and

the ball bounced across the floor. Throwing me a haughty look, she exclaimed, "Look what you made me do! How dare you say such a thing to me?" She threw her arm in the direction of the door. "Leave, or my pa will be upset."

"I apologize. I mistook you for someone else." I kneeled to pick up a jackstone, and she knelt beside me.

"Go now, or you'll ruin everything." She had whispered, but it had been an order.

I stood and walked briskly out the door. I had found that it was best not to disobey a McAllen.

Maggie was the fourteen-year-old daughter of Joseph McAllen. Her mother had long ago divorced him and married a preacher. The new family had moved to Durango, Colorado, but McAllen and his daughter still saw each other on occasion. The previous fall, Sharp and I had rescued Maggie from a bad situation. At first, everyone believed Utes had abducted her, but we eventually discovered that it was an old enemy of the captain's who wanted to exact revenge by forcing him to help rob a silver shipment.

What was she doing here? There was a familiarity in her whispered order, so she had recognized me. I looked over the men on the street. McAllen had to be close by. He would never let his daughter venture into the territory without escorting her. I didn't see him on the street, so he had to be inside. I decided to wait

123

until the two of them came out. I realized I was on the Whiskey Row side of the town square, and any respectable family would exit on the opposite side, where Mrs. Potter had her café. I hurried around the outside of the building and arrived in time to see Maggie and two other people leaving the courthouse. Neither of the two were Captain McAllen . . . nor were they her family from Durango.

I immediately turned my back and knelt to straighten my cuff. As I fidgeted, I peeked around my leg and watched them walk to Gurley Street and turn right. As soon as they disappeared around the corner, I followed, walking as normally as possible given my anxiety. When I turned the corner, they were gone, but I knew immediately where they had gone—Prescott House was only half a block away.

I climbed the two steps into the hotel, and there they were, chatting amicably with a man I assumed was the proprietor. I ignored Maggie's annoyed glance and waited for them to go upstairs to their room.

As soon as they broke off their conversation, the innkeeper turned his attention to me. "Yes, sir. How can I help you?"

I kept my eyes only on him but spoke loudly enough for Maggie to hear as she started to climb the stairs. "Do you offer afternoon tea?"

"It's a bit early, but yes, we do."

I handed the man a coin. "I'll take a newspaper to read while I wait. When you start, would you be so kind as to bring me service for one?"

"Of course, sir."

He went behind a counter, and I had an idea. "Do you have old issues?"

"A few."

"Give me a current issue, and then when you're not busy, collect all the old issues you can find. I like reading old newspapers when I come into a new town. I found it's a fast way to get familiar with people and events." I nodded toward the coin in his hand. "You may keep the change."

I saw him rub the silver dollar with his thumb. He handed me a newspaper and made a little bow, before saying, "Of course, sir. Take any seat you'd like."

The lobby was small and lavishly decorated. There were so many chairs and divans that the room felt crowded with no one around. The walnut chairs and sideboards kept the powder blue and red from being too obnoxious. This was definitely a woman's room.

I picked a chair in the corner and sat down. Now the onus was on Maggie or the man and woman who always kept to either side of her. It didn't take long. In less than five minutes, a nattily dressed man came down and sat in the chair opposite me. The lobby was unoccupied, so I felt no need to be restrained.

"Mr. Schmidt, I'm pleased to see you again."

He shook my hand. "If memory serves, you are Steve Dancy."

"Correct. Are you investigating a fraud?"

"We were. It appears your friend killed our target. I just met with our client at the courthouse, and he informed me that our services are no longer required."

"Jonathon Winslow." The meeting he was rushing to must have been short.

"Our work is confidential."

"Where's the captain?"

"I don't know."

"Bullshit. He wouldn't let you use his daughter as part of your disguise if he wasn't close. We need him. Where is he?"

"I'd prefer that you not take that tone with me, especially in public."

Carl and Mary Schmidt were a husband-and-wife team that worked covertly for the Pinkertons to investigate swindles and frauds. As he had explained to me last October, they were normally hired by marks who felt foolish and wanted to get even with the person who took their money. Revenge was far more important than money to these people, and since fraud victims were generally wealthy, business was lucrative. Sharp and I had met the Schmidts because McAllen had asked us to leave Maggie in their protective care while we thwarted a silver robbery.

I took a deep breath and spoke calmly. "Is Captain McAllen in the area?"

"Yes. He's our supervisor on this assignment. But he stays away from us because his Pinkerton status is known. Mary goes riding with Maggie every day, and the captain meets up with them. She reports on our progress as the captain and his daughter ride along together. He stays away from us the rest of the time."

"Then I'd better go riding with them today."

Schmidt thought about that. "If the contract were really closed, I don't think you joining the women would be a problem. You see, Jonathon Winslow fired us, but he's not really the client."

He paused dramatically, wanting me to fill in the rest. So I did. "I presume the Pinkerton agency was engaged by his family in Boston. The swindle isn't public yet, but if it makes the papers, our future congressman would look like someone who lacks judgment or is still too young to hold a weighty position. A trial has a way of exposing a lot of things besides the crime. So you're thinking that a well-worded telegram to the parents can keep this engagement open, only now the assignment would be to keep young Jonathon's name out of any proceedings or newspaper articles. Have I got that about right?"

"Not about . . . exactly right."

"Let me explain something. Sharp didn't kill

Campbell. If you proceed along the path I just described, you'll interfere with our best defense, which is that Campbell was killed by someone he swindled. Your goals will clash with mine. Sharp's lawyer wants to use the stock scam to expose the real killer or at least sow doubt in a jury's mind. Winslow's name will likely surface because the other victims know that he also bought shares in the bogus company. So . . . extending the engagement could wreck my friend's chances of going free. One last point: Jeff Sharp is a longtime friend of Captain Joseph McAllen."

"I think it will be a pleasant afternoon for a ride."

"You're coming along."

"Of course. I take orders from my supervisor, not you."

With that settled, I asked, "Why's Maggie here?"

"It was the perfect excuse for her to see her father every day. She's in no more danger than she would be walking the streets of Durango, and she gives us perfect cover."

"Joseph's idea or hers?"

Schmidt smiled as he got up to leave. "What do you think?"

"Maggie's. She's a headstrong McAllen."

"I'm going upstairs to change. Are you riding like that?"

"I am." I marveled at how westernized I had become. In the East, I would never ride in street clothes. Of course, in the East, I wouldn't be walking the streets in denim and boots.

Chapter 18

Schmidt led our party of four out of town toward Thumb Butte. As we came around a bend, I spotted a man sitting ramrod straight on a horse to the side of the road. Despite his *jorongo* and sombrero, I knew it was Captain McAllen even before Maggie spurred ahead.

I guessed that McAllen was somewhere in his early forties, but he was not the type of man you asked personal questions. His no-nonsense demeanor was reinforced with terse conversation and a rigid sense of honor. Even from a distance, I could see that, despite his irregular wardrobe, he was clean-shaven and well-groomed. He also looked formidable, even when sitting perfectly still.

I reined up Liberty to let Maggie say hello to her father before making my own greetings. I noticed that Carl and Mary Schmidt did the same.

As we had ridden out of Prescott, Thumb Butte dominated the landscape. It was unusual and dramatic, but it didn't look like a thumb to me: more like a rock outcropping extending up from the top of a hill. As we got closer, the angle changed, and it looked like an ordinary forested hill. It was probably my one-eyed accountant cast of mind that kept me from seeing the butte as anything other than a butte.

The Schmidts hadn't said a word, so I asked if they remembered Jeff Sharp.

They looked at each other, and Carl responded. "Of course. Man in his fifties with little education, sturdy built, confident, no sidearm but carries a rifle, says whatever he thinks, and has big appetites. A rough sort."

I didn't like the description. "He has little formal education, but he knows more than most college graduates, and I'm not talking about what he's seen and experienced. The man reads everything."

"I'll take your word for that." The tone was dismissive.

I turned in my saddle to look straight at Carl Schmidt. "Do you have a problem with Sharp . . . or me?"

Schmidt looked as if he had been jerked out of a reverie. "I don't really know you or Mr. Sharp. We met only briefly outside Leadville."

"You're bullshitting me. You hunt con men, so you've got to be good at judging people right off."

Schmidt turned in his saddle to look me in the eye. "You're correct on every count. I am bullshitting you. I am an expert at judging people, I don't like Mr. Sharp, nor do I believe a self-educated man from the backwoods can achieve erudition or class. Mr. Sharp is the type of man who is fully capable of killing an enemy, and the evidence that he did so in this situation is substantial."

Schmidt looked taken aback when I started laughing.

"What's so amusing?"

"Harvard, Yale, or Princeton?"

He looked wary. "I graduated from Harvard. Why is that amusing?"

"Only a Harvard man could take a playacting job and still feel superior."

"Our work is important," Mary Schmidt protested from the other side of her husband.

"I wasn't addressing the job; I was addressing the haughty attitude."

"Who made you an expert on Harvard graduates?"

"Columbia University."

Carl Schmidt tipped his hat in mock homage. "I never would have guessed."

"I know. Perhaps you're not as good at judging people as you suppose. For example, you're right that Jeff Sharp is the kind of man that's capable of killing an enemy, but you missed the most important part of his character . . . he would never shoot a man in the back."

"He was falling-down drunk."

"Drunk or sober, Jeff would fight fair."

"I'll take your word for that." Again, the tone was dismissive.

I was about to argue further, but McAllen waved us over. It was just as well. I was growing to dislike Carl Schmidt. I also understood that he resented my interfering with his work. I presumed that was the reason he took pleasure in needling me.

As we drew near, McAllen stood in his stirrups, leaned across his saddle, and shook my hand.

"Good afternoon, Captain," I said. "Thank you for responding so fast to my telegram."

McAllen smiled with closed lips. "I suppose that means you sent me a telegram after Jeff got himself arrested."

"I did."

The smile faded. "We usually ride the trail around the base of Thumb Butte." He tugged his reins and wheeled his horse around. "Best to be off the road."

For about fifteen minutes, McAllen rode along a well-used trail, chatting with his daughter. As we approached a small glen, he pulled up and dismounted. We all followed suit.

We let the horses graze and gathered in a rough circle. It was so quiet, I heard a lizard or snake slither in the brush thirty feet away. The day was sunny but still crisp enough that I felt comfortable in a sheepskin coat over a wool shirt and long johns.

"I was surprised to learn you were in Prescott," I said.

"Been here almost two months. Routine until now. What the hell are you and Jeff doin' here?"

"We're looking for mining investments."

"In Prescott? Mines around here would be tiny for an operator like Jeff."

I noticed that last sentence caught Carl Schmidt's attention. Harvard men were always impressed by money.

"I insisted we stop to see Frémont. At one time, he was a family friend, but . . ." I shrugged, "he seems to have forgotten." I wanted to get away from McAllen's line of questioning, so I asked, "What do you know about the murder and Jeff's arrest?"

"Everythin'."

"Everything?"

"At least everythin' there is to know at the moment. Jeff and you arrived in town about this time yesterday. Jeff hit Campbell in the jaw and threatened to kill him in front of witnesses. Later that evenin', he got drunk at the Palace. You were nowhere in sight. He left before midnight. Campbell was killed with a single shot in the back of the head from Jeff's Winchester, which was dropped next to the body. Two shots had been fired from the rifle. All of this was discovered by the constable and me. Pine needles were found on the stairs at the Palace and stuck to Jeff's boot heel." McAllen swung his arm around to point out the pine trees that circled the glen. "This afternoon, Jeff hired Mac Castle to defend him." McAllen looked thoughtful and then added,

"Last, and most damnin', Campbell destroyed Jeff's business and reputation in New York City." He paused again. "That about it?"

"Wait a minute. How do you know the last part?"

"Constable Earp asked Jeff why he slugged Campbell. Jeff foolishly told him."

"Virgil Earp talks to you about this case?"

"I live in his home, not far from where we stand."

I was surprised to hear that McAllen lived a short distance from the murder. "Did you hear a shot last night?"

McAllen hesitated, trying to figure out how much to tell me. "Yes. The Earp home is a quarter mile from the murder. I was with Earp when he went to investigate the noise. After inspectin' the site, I suspected Campbell wasn't murdered there. Too little blood around the body, and it looks like someone covered up tracks by brushin' the dirt— tracks that might have been caused by draggin' a body."

"Doesn't it seem odd that a man barely capable of exiting a saloon could drag a body all the way out here?"

"Lots of things ain't right about this case."

Maggie wore a broad grin. "Does that mean we stay? Can you move into town?"

"I thought you liked all the secret doings," McAllen said noncommittally.

"At first, but now they're boring, Pa. If you board at Prescott House, I can help you solve this mystery."

"What makes you think it's a mystery?" Mary Schmidt asked.

"Mr. Sharp didn't kill Mr. Campbell, so it's a mystery." She said this so matter-of-factly that I smiled.

"Maggie, dear, sometimes things don't work out the way we want." Mary Schmidt gave her a condescending look. "If you want to be a detective someday, you need to follow the evidence, not your heart."

Maggie struck a defiant pose with hands on both hips. "My statement does not come from my heart. Lots of men in this town had a grudge against Mr. Campbell. Any one of them could have taken advantage of Mr. Sharp's drunkenness. You forget, I know Mr. Sharp, and that rifle was like his arm. He'd no more drop it in the woods than I would leave a shop without my purse. Someone else left it to make him look guilty."

I was impressed. She was right. I had never questioned the incongruity of the Winchester being left with the body. Carrying that rifle was such an ingrained habit that even drunk, Sharp would never leave it behind.

"Mag, if I moved into town, I wouldn't have any more private talks with Constable Earp,"

McAllen said. "But with this turn of events, I can see you more—come into town."

"Captain, if I may," Mary Schmidt said. "If you show the town that Maggie's your daughter, they'll know we're Pinkertons. It may be a bit early to make that decision."

"You're right, Mary. Let's keep things the same for a few days." He put his hand on his daughter's shoulder. "Mag, I'm sorry, but you need to play the dutiful daughter to the Schmidts a bit longer."

"But Pa, I can help. No one pays me any never-mind. I can go anywhere, overhear conversations, watch people."

McAllen lifted his hand away from his daughter. "Mag, you do exactly as the Schmidts say, or you'll find yourself on a coach home. Do you understand?"

"I do."

I watched her face. It was firm and resolute. I had seen that expression on her father. My guess was that her *I do* conceded only understanding, not obedience.

Carl Schmidt spoke for the first time. "Captain, I came with Mary because questions are being raised about this entire engagement."

"Who's raisin' questions?"

Carl Schmidt nodded in my direction. That got me a stern glance from McAllen.

"Jonathon Winslow is the one questioning this engagement," I said in defense. "I believe he fired your team. Mr. Schmidt wants to wire Boston and beg Winslow's father to keep working on a case that no longer exists."

Carl Schmidt became indignant. "*Begging* is a highly inaccurate term. And we weren't fired. We were engaged by Jonathon's father. Only he can terminate our agreement. I'm sure he'll want us to remain on the case to protect the family name."

Harvard men generally weren't smarter or better educated, but they were successful because they helped each other, and if the situation warranted, they would protect each other from impolite assaults from lesser beings. In truth, the same was somewhat true of Columbia, but moving up the rungs of society by using family connections was one of the reasons I had left the city for the frontier. Out here, a man made it on his own—or he didn't make it.

McAllen's next words surprised me. "Carl, send Mr. Winslow a telegram to inform him that it is likely that their son's business dealin's with Campbell will come out at trial. If he authorizes another retainer, we'll try to keep the worst of it out of the newspapers."

"Yes, sir."

Without a further word, Carl Schmidt walked over to his horse, mounted up, and rode away.

"Captain, I won't pull back on Jeff's defense to protect that doltish assistant to the governor.

Continuing this engagement puts Jeff in jeopardy."

"No it doesn't. We can do both. More important, protectin' Winslow allows me to stay in Prescott so I can help Jeff."

"I can hire you and your team."

McAllen gave me one of his stares that brooked no further discussion. "Steve, I would consider it an insult for you to offer me money. Jeff's my friend, and someone made it look like he committed murder. We'll work together to get to the bottom of this, but I can do my job at the same time."

Carl Schmidt seemed to know the right thing to say when McAllen gave an order, so I followed his example. "Yes, sir."

McAllen's eyes flamed briefly, but he let my impertinence go. "Have you found any evidence that helps Jeff?"

"No, but it didn't take long to find several people who might want Campbell dead."

"Who's on your list?"

"Lew Davis, Jonathon Winslow, and Herb Locklear were all victims of Campbell's scam. Blanchet and even the governor may also have been victims, but I think it more likely that Blanchet was a partner."

Mary Schmidt spoke up, "The governor, his assistant, the leader of the Republicans in the Council, a highly connected lawyer, and the day manager of the Palace. That's a list of most of the important people in Prescott. We can't shove aside the obvious suspect, Jeff Sharp."

"Jeff didn't kill Campbell," I responded a bit too sharply.

"Take it easy, Steve. Pinkertons are trained to never discard a suspect until hard evidence proves them innocent. Mary is right to keep him on her list." He turned his eyes from me to Mary Schmidt. "Did you suspect any other victims of this fraud?"

Her eyes twinkled with humor, and I guessed she could play coy better than a barroom hussy. "I presume you mean beyond Carl and me. Actually, we hadn't closed the deal yet, or we would have put Campbell in jail." She dropped her coy act. "Captain, in answer to your question, we haven't run across anyone else in town. There was a rancher down south, but we haven't seen him in Prescott. That doesn't mean there aren't others who have hidden their involvement due to embarrassment."

"What about Bob Brow?" I asked.

"Why would you suspect him?" She looked puzzled.

"Brow told me he was being sued by Campbell. He also mentioned that there were several women that he romanced out of money . . . and other valuables."

She hesitated, then shook her head no. "Brow's unlikely, but I want to learn about these women."

"Why are you dismissing Brow?" I asked.

"He can spot a cheat from twenty paces, and Castle would've handled any legal issues for Brow. I think he's doubtful."

"Is there any chance Mac Castle should be on the list?" McAllen asked. "It wouldn't be good if Jeff's lawyer was the murderer."

That hadn't occurred to me, and I looked at Mary Schmidt to hear her answer. "Not a chance. Castle would never buy stock without telegramming New York." Again, the twinkling eyes. "That man has checked every term and condition in the Bible."

I chuckled to make light of my next comment. "I might as well mention that Castle has me on his list. Campbell and I were both New Yorkers. He says I knew that Jeff's door was unlocked and that his name was carved in the stock of his Winchester. He also accused me of being a man who solves problems with a gun."

"I think I'll like Mr. Castle," McAllen said, with his closed-mouth smile. "I'll put you on my list as well."

His expression turned serious again. "Mary, talk to Winslow. See where he was last night. Ask him if he told anyone you were Pinkertons. If not, caution him to keep it quiet. Check Locklear's whereabouts too, but be discreet. Steve, go see Jeff and let him know I'm here. See if he remembers anything more."

"I need to see Castle as well."

"Fine, but meet me at Earp's for dinner at seven."

I looked McAllen up and down. "Should I dress as a Mexican bandit?"

No smile. "Steve, come however you damn please." He snuggled the sombrero on his head. "A jorongo is warm and allows access to my gun. Great for ridin'. And a sombrero shades the harsh Arizona sun. Now, if we're done, may I spend some time with my daughter?"

McAllen and Maggie swung easily into their saddles and were gone. I guessed that last sentence wasn't really a question.

Chapter 19

I was in a hurry to get back, so I left it to Mary Schmidt to escort Maggie back to town. I had learned from Carl Schmidt that Campbell had a room at a boardinghouse on Goodwin Street. I wanted to search for the genuine stock certificate before anyone else rummaged through the room. I scolded myself for being concerned about personal affairs when Sharp was in trouble—but not for long. After all, this was a short detour, and Sharp would be my partner in this enterprise. As I rode, I tried to figure out how I would get access to Campbell's room.

By the time I tied up Liberty outside the light-green clapboard house, I still hadn't come up with a good answer. As I trudged up the three steps, I decided to claim I was a distant relative and come for his effects. The woman who answered my knock was younger than I expected. She was trim, neatly dressed in a polka-dot blouse and a pale yellow skirt. Her brown hair pulled back in a tight bun showed off an attractive face unadorned with makeup.

"Yes?"

"Hello. I'm Steve Dancy, here to collect a few things from your deceased boarder, Elisha Campbell."

"No. You may not take a few things. Take it all

or nothing. I need to rent that room. Anything in that room tomorrow morning will be donated to my church."

"Yes, ma'am."

She gave me an appraising look. "My name is Mrs. Cunningham. Follow me."

She led me upstairs without requiring further explanation. At the landing, she said, "You'll need help. My son's available for two bits an hour, plus tip."

Was this a request for a small sweetener? I couldn't imagine that I'd need help emptying a single room. Then she opened the door. I had never seen such clutter. Stuff was strewn everywhere, even across the bed. It would be difficult to find enough space to even lie on the bed.

"Did someone make this mess searching the room?" I asked.

She gave me a quizzical look. "Did you know Mr. Campbell?"

"Only through correspondence," I lied.

She held her arm out, palm up. "Well, this is how he lived. Can you get all this stuff out of here?"

"Yes, ma'am."

"Today?"

"With the help of your son. Would it be okay if I put some of this stuff in boxes for your church?"

"Of course. My son's name is John. I'll send

him right up. He'll know where to stack the boxes out back." She gave me another stern look. "I need this room rented immediately."

"I understand."

She started out of the room but stopped. "What's your relationship to Mr. Campbell?"

"I'm also from New York, and we have common friends. I promised to ship his personal effects."

She looked disappointed. "Should have guessed. Mr. Campbell was three weeks behind in his rent. I was hoping you were family and would make good on his chalk."

"No, ma'am. But if I run across anything of value that's not personal, I'll set it aside. Perhaps you can sell it to settle the account."

"Good luck." She flicked her head at the room. "I looked through this mess and found only stuff that even my church will probably throw away."

"Did you find any legal papers? I'm been requested to look for a will."

She pointed to the corner. "There's a satchel over there. If Mr. Campbell has any assets, he owes me twenty-one dollars. City statutes say I get paid first." She gave me yet another stern look to make sure I understood. "I'll send John right up. Pay him four bits in advance."

I nodded, and she disappeared into the hall. I suppressed irritation that she was asking me to pay her son—in advance—for work he would have had to do for free if I hadn't shown up. I reminded myself that for a few coins, I would get to rummage through Campbell's room. This was a stroke of luck.

I investigated the satchel first, but it contained only receipts, telegrams, letters, a pocketknife, and ink. I was about to set the satchel aside when I noticed a narrow inside pocket that contained two black tubes. I recognized the tubes. One was a Cross stylographic pen and the other, a Cross propel-repel mechanical pencil. I recognized them because I owned two sets of these writing instruments. I had bought the A. T. Cross sets thinking they would help me write a great novel. That reminded me that my book would be published in a few months. For some reason, that thought made me more excited than the potential of a license for Edison's inventions. I rolled the pen in my hand. It felt good and familiar, but I had other things to do. I shoved both instruments into my pocket.

Not finding what I was looking for in the satchel, I threw everything off the bed and lifted the mattress. Nothing. Next, I peeked behind the headboard. Again nothing.

"What are you looking for?"

The boy looked to be about fifteen, maybe older. It surprised me, because his mother looked to be well under thirty.

"John?"

"Yep. What are you looking for?"

"A will."

"What's that?"

"A written statement that tells people what to do with a person's belongings after they die."

"If Mr. Campbell has any valuable belongings, my ma gets paid first. She says it doesn't matter what any piece of paper says."

Evidently Mrs. Cunningham had given her son clear instructions before she sent him upstairs.

"Understood," I answered. "Do you know where to get boxes?"

"Yep. At any one of the forty saloons along Whiskey Row, but they charge a nickel for each wood box. You got money?"

John was definitely Mrs. Cunningham's son. I reached into my pocket and handed him a silver dollar. He flipped it in the air with his thumb and deftly caught it. As he slipped it into his pocket, he said, "Four bits for me and ten boxes. Right?"

"Right."

"It'll take five trips, so I better get at it." He disappeared before he finished the sentence.

While he was gone, I searched the room. There was no stock certificate, either for the genuine Edison company or the fake. Mrs. Cunningham had been right: except for a few items of expensive, but threadbare, clothing, the room was filled with worthless odds and ends. It looked as if Campbell had been too lazy to throw anything

147

away, or perhaps he took comfort in being surrounded by stuff he had accumulated.

By the time John had completed his five trips, I had separated the true trash from the things a church might sell at a bazaar. As we worked together to clear the room, two questions nagged me: Where were the stock certificates, and what had Campbell done with his ill-gotten gains?

After the last box had been carried downstairs, I realized that this room was large and had good furnishings. A dollar a day for room and board seemed a bargain, and there was enough space for Jeff's things until he got released. Maybe I would talk to Mrs. Cunningham.

I trotted down the staircase just as John came bursting back into the house.

"Mr. Dancy, I guess it's time for that tip."

"What makes you think you earned a tip?"

"Because I was fast, I carried all the boxes, and I didn't bore you with idle chatter."

I had to smile. "Well said." I handed over another four bits.

"John, since you've been paid handsomely, start carrying those boxes over to the church." Mrs. Cunningham had entered the hall from behind us.

"Ma?"

"No back talk. When you've got a job in front of you, it's better to do it today than tomorrow. You can get four of them over there before washing up for supper."

148

"Yes, ma'am." He looked dejected, but I saw him rubbing the two coins together as he went out the door.

"Supper smells good," I said.

"Mr. Dancy, I appreciate your help, but I'm not in a position to offer free meals."

"Is that room let?"

"No, would you be interested?"

"I am at a dollar a day."

"Then it's yours." She held out a hand. "I require one week in advance."

I handed her a ten-dollar silver certificate. She started for a sideboard, but I stopped her progress by saying, "I should be here at least ten days, so no need for change."

"Thank you. I'll give you a day's notice when the next week is due."

"What time is supper?"

"Excuse me, one dollar buys the room. It costs another dollar for board."

"You told me Mr. Campbell owed you twenty-one dollars for three weeks. I assumed that was for room *and* board."

"Mr. Campbell mooched his meals elsewhere." She looked highly disappointed. "Do you want your money back?"

My room at the Palace didn't include meals, so two dollars a day was still fair—unless Mrs. Cunningham was a lousy cook. But bargaining was in my nature. "Keep the ten for one week's room and board. If we're happy with each other by the end of the week, I'll pay two dollars a day."

She looked indignant, and I thought she was going to show me the door, but then she looked down at the ten dollars in her hand. "All right, Mr. Dancy, but if you pull this again, I'll send you packing. Are we clear?"

"Yes, ma'am." I reached into my pocket and pulled out the black tubes and handed them to her. "These are the only things of value I found in Mr. Campbell's belongings. They're an A. T. Cross pen and pencil. Not one of their gold models but recently invented and very fine instruments. My guess is that someone in the courthouse would pay five or six dollars for them . . . perhaps more if they're a novelty in Arizona."

Her reaction surprised me. She looked like she might cry. "Mr. Dancy, I apologize. I was so mad at myself for letting Mr. Campbell get the better of me that I was rude to you." She held the pens up in her fist. "This means more than you know. It's not the money; it's my pride. I run a good house, but there's very little room for error, so I get angry when I make a mistake."

"Mr. Campbell took much greater advantage of others . . . some prominent citizens." With that comment, a thought struck me. "Ma'am, before we settle this fully, I should inform you that I'm friends with the man accused of killing Mr. Campbell."

She lifted her chin. "I . . . Did he do it?"

"No, ma'am. But someone in this town did, and some important people might get pretty mad as I try to uncover the real murderer. You could come under some pressure because I board here."

"Mr. Dancy, as long as you pay in advance and don't disturb my other boarders, you are welcome in my house."

"Thank you, ma'am."

As I left my new lodgings to go visit Sharp, I wondered about her second condition.

Chapter 20

When I stepped out of Mrs. Cunningham's house, it was dusk. Where had this day gone? Had it been only one day? It had started with a calm breakfast, a visit to Sharp in jail, my interview with Castle, lunch with Blanchet and his cronies, another visit with Sharp, the discovery of Maggie, and the ride to meet her father, and had ended with my search of Campbell's room. I suddenly felt exhausted.

Damn. I had forgotten I was supposed to be at Earp's for supper, and I still had things to do. I ran around the side of the house to find John. After a quick negotiation, he accepted one dollar to move our belongings from the Palace to my new room. I told him to stack Sharp's stuff neatly in a corner. Then I rode the half block to the Palace. Luckily, newly arrived in town, we had bought our rooms for only one night.

I found Brow at the bar, watching over the gaming tables. He gave me a friendly nod as I approached, but kept his eyes on a couple gamblers at the faro table.

"Mr. Brow, I want to thank you for the hospitality, but I've taken a room at Mrs. Cunningham's."

He threw me a glance, then said offhandedly, "I heard a room recently became available in her

152

house." Evidently satisfied with the play at the faro table, he turned toward me. "I hope you'll still honor us with your business in the saloon."

"Of course." I signaled to the barman for a beer. "Mrs. Cunningham's son will be over shortly to move our stuff out. Any charge for the delay?"

"Naw. Any news about your friend?"

"Only that Castle has agreed to defend him. Did Earp question the customers that were here last night?"

"He did."

"Did he learn anything?"

"The constable doesn't share his work with me."

My beer arrived and I took a healthy swallow. It tasted good after an hour of cleaning up Campbell's mess. "Mr. Brow, you mentioned that Campbell was suing you. What for?"

"I'd tell you it was none of your business, but everybody already knows. Campbell stayed in one of my rooms at first. He got behind, so I sent Lew to take his trunk as collateral. He was suing to get it back."

I tried to keep the excitement out of my voice. "Do you still have it?"

"Campbell never paid his bill. What do you think?"

"Can I buy it?"

"For his tally, plus five dollars. That's a good price. It's a Saratoga trunk."

"What's in it?"

"How the hell would I know? I never broke the lock."

I would have paid more. A locked steamer trunk might hold the stock certificate and maybe even some evidence about who had committed the murder. After I gave Brow the money, he promised to have it delivered to Mrs. Cunningham's.

I finished my beer and ran up to Sharp's room. I wanted to retrieve his wallet. No sense putting temptation in front of John. In no time at all, I was back in the saloon, buying beer in a tin pail for Sharp.

When I got to the jail, the night man was already on duty. Before I was allowed to walk down the aisle to Sharp's cell, the jailer swirled his pistol barrel around in the beer to make sure I wasn't hiding something beneath the brew. Instead of being insulted, I admired Earp's selection and training of men.

Sharp heard my steps and was at the jailhouse bars as I approached. "Good evening, Jeff. I brought you beer."

"That's neighborly, but can ya get me out?"

"Not yet, but I have good news. McAllen's already in town."

"In Prescott? Here?"

I nodded too enthusiastically to retain any poise. "He was supervising the Schmidts on a case. Guess which one."

"Well, I'll be damned. Gotta be Campbell."

"He's been here setting up the Schmidts as ideal victims. Maggie's here too." I handed the pail through an opening in the bars meant to pass food trays to prisoners.

After a healthy swallow, Sharp said, "Thanks. That's the best news I've had since they dragged me to jail. Tell Joseph to look hard at Blanchet. That man's as crooked as a dog's hind leg."

"What'd you learn from your talk?"

"Nothin' specific. He just kept talkin' on an' on 'bout how connected he was. That ain't the way good lawyers talk. That sleazy bastard really wanted to defend me. He just kept at me. Took it hard when I finally told him to go pound tar. I wasn't gonna string him on." Sharp gulped down more beer. After he wiped his mouth with the back of his hand, he added, "Steve, he talked 'bout Campbell like he admired him . . . and knew him a good while. Be just like that pettifogger to murder Campbell, then weasel his way into bein' my attorney. My butt'd be hangin' out in the wind."

"Could they have been partners, and maybe Campbell tried a double cross?"

"Who knows? Just tell Joseph to look hard at that son of a bitch."

"I'll tell him tonight. Jeff, I need to hurry. We're having dinner together, and McAllen gets testy when a person's late for an appointment."

"All right, but do me a favor an' take care of that jailer before ya go. I'd like to have decent meals, coffee when I call for it, an' my chamber pot changed twice a day. An' next time, bring a book an' newspaper. Might as well read what they got to say 'bout me."

"Damn, I should've thought about that already. Sorry, Jeff. I'll bring back issues of the newspaper as well. Maybe you can learn something. Writing material?"

"Nope." He nodded behind him with his head. "Castle already brought me writin' paper an' one of them newfangled pencils that push the lead on out whenever ya want." Sharp laughed. "Castle said that for some damn reason they won't allow me a knife so I can sharpen a wood pencil."

"Did he ask you to write down what you remember?"

"Yep, but it ain't much. He stopped by 'bout an hour ago to pick it up. Smart fella, asked good questions after he read it."

"Jeff, I've got to go, but I'll see you in the morning."

"Bring Joseph."

"If I can. He sets his own agenda."

I turned to leave, when Sharp added, "Tell Joseph that there's somethin' else that ties Campbell an' Blanchet together. They're both good buddies with yer friend John Frémont."

With that jab, I hurried out of the basement jail.

I was late for my supper appointment, but the real reason I took the stairs two at a time was that Sharp's last comment reminded me that I had coerced him into coming to Arizona. As a result, my friend was in trouble, and my guilt went well beyond a twinge. I had to get him out of there. Not only because it was partly my fault, but because I knew he would do the same for me.

Chapter 21

Virgil Earp lived in a log house within sight of his lumber mill. I thought of it as a house rather than a cabin because it appeared to have four rooms, and the roof was shingled. It looked similar to what locals called the Old Governor's Mansion. I assumed the name was a joke until I learned that when the eight-room log house served as the governor's home, it was the biggest and best house in the territory.

Before I dismounted, McAllen stepped onto the porch. He lifted a whiskey glass in salute, leading me to expect a cordial greeting. Instead, I got a McAllen greeting.

"You're late."

"Business."

"We have business here." Without a further word, he turned around and reentered the house.

I tied up Liberty, removed my saddle, and cleaned my boots with a brush that was lying on the porch. Earp's house surprised me. It looked homey, with a large oval hooked rug, family photographs on the wall, comfortable furniture, and a table set with matching china that belied the rustic exterior.

McAllen nodded toward a woman standing next to a substantial man. "Steve, I'd like to introduce Allie, Virgil's wife, and this is Virgil Earp."

Allie curtsied, so I returned a half bow before stepping forward to shake hands with Earp. "It's a pleasure to meet you both. Thank you for having me at your table."

"You're welcome," Allie said. "I've been holding supper. If you sit right down, I'll serve. Please hang your gun on that peg by the door."

When I had first arrived in the West, I didn't wear a gun, but a couple of incidents convinced me that it was dangerous for a man to go unarmed. Even so, I was glad to unhook and hang up my holster, because I needed to be careful about my sitting posture with a pistol on my hip. Nothing startles a hostess like a gun clattering to the floor.

"Can I offer you a whiskey?" Earp asked, as his wife went to a stove in the back of the large room. His voice was so deep, it almost sounded like a growl.

"That would be much appreciated," I answered.

Virgil Earp was dressed in a dark suit that made me feel like I should have changed clothes for supper. His tall stature was accented by sandy blond hair, and his droopy mustache dominated a stern face that had yet to smile.

By the time we had our drinks and sat down, Allie brought over a platter with a roasted chicken surrounded by potatoes and carrots. The sight and smell made me very hungry.

"My compliments. That looks and smells great."

Another curtsy. "Thank you, sir. I hope it tastes even better than you expect."

"That would be a challenge, because your presentation has raised my expectations to a considerable level." I looked at my host. "Mr. Earp, you're a lucky man to have such a capable and attractive wife."

A broad smile and a third curtsy told me I had atoned for my late arrival. A nod from Earp confirmed my repaired status.

Supper conversation revolved around territorial politics and the lumber business. Evidently, Earp had little respect for Governor Frémont and doubted that the territory would soon become a state. The lumber trade had slowed to a crawl because miners and the greedy had deserted Prescott to rush after silver in Tombstone. After the meal, we went outside for whiskey and a smoke.

McAllen looked impatient as I packed, tamped, and lit my pipe. When I finished, he asked, "What did Jeff have to say?"

"He doesn't trust Blanchet and wants you to take a hard look at him. He suspects he might have been in cahoots with Campbell." I didn't feel a need to inform Earp that Sharp had also requested that I bribe the jailer.

Earp expertly rolled a cigarette. After an initial puff, he said, "Blanchet's a weasel and a coward. I don't see him being violent." He looked at me. "Winslow's the one with the most to lose. He

160

guards his reputation with more care than his money.

"I'm not sure a small fraud in some distant backcountry would harm a congressional race in Boston."

"Jonathon's prideful," Earp said. "As that young pup likes to remind people, the Winslows came over on the *Mayflower*. He thinks that means his family owns this country. And believe me, his ambitions go beyond a congressional seat. I'll bet his parents wouldn't let some ne'er-do-well ruin their boy's career."

McAllen had relit a half-burned cigar. "Steve, we need to keep an eye on that Winslow kid. That's why I told Carl to wire his father to extend our engagement."

I didn't like Winslow but believed he was an unlikely suspect. "If you think he or his parents had this done, why'd they hire a Pinkerton team that might get in the way?"

"I'm not privy to the ways of the rich," Earp said.

"I am. There's a possibility the boy did it, but his parents would never hire someone they didn't know for something this sensitive."

Earp gave me an appraising look. "Joseph tells me you've killed on occasion."

"I never met any Winslow before today . . . and I didn't kill Campbell and then frame my friend."

"Glad to hear it." He took a draw on his

cigarette before adding, "But you should know, Castle has you on his *possible* list."

"He told me." I tried to be nonchalant. "Constable, does this mean you believe Jeff is innocent?"

"Mr. Sharp is my number-one suspect, but Joseph convinced me that we need to investigate to be certain. I'm only saying that if I had to pick someone else, it would be that sniveling Winslow . . . or his family."

"Locklear?"

"Herb? He's plenty pissed he got took, but killing's too messy for him. He'd write it off as a bad bet and try to keep it quiet."

"Looks like he hired Blanchet."

"Naw. Probably asked for free advice. That would be more like our dear councilman."

Something occurred to me. "Castle said a couple of women got fleeced. Any possibility of an irate husband?"

Earp stepped off the porch and crushed his cigarette under his heel.

McAllen made an aside to me. "Lots of sawdust around. Be careful with matches and dumpin' out your bowl."

I nodded understanding.

After Earp stepped back on the porch, he leaned against the rail before saying, "Three women, to my knowledge. Amy Hill was one. Her husband owns the hardware store. Mrs. Potter. She's a widow. And Mrs. Cunningham. Her husband ran off to Tombstone."

The last one caught me by surprise. "I just took a room at Mrs. Cunningham's. She only mentioned that Campbell owed her back rent."

Both Earp and McAllen glared at me.

"You took Campbell's room?" McAllen asked, nonplussed.

"I did."

For some reason, Earp laughed. "You know, men have killed to get close to a pretty woman."

"She's married."

"Story has it that her husband was killed in a street fight in Tombstone."

"Story?"

"It was reported in the *Tombstone Epitaph*, but Mrs. Cunningham says it was a mistake. Claims to have received mail from her husband. Few believe her though."

I thought about it. "That eliminates her unless she has a man friend. She's not nearly strong enough to get Campbell all the way out here. Even with a wagon."

"Mrs. Potter, as well," Earp said. "Elisha Campbell courted both, so I don't think another man is around."

"No jealous suitors?"

"Possible, I guess," was all Earp offered.

After a moment of silence, I asked, "Captain, what do you think?"

Instead of answering, McAllen stepped off the porch to crush out his cigar. After he resumed his position against the railing, he said, "In my experience, this isn't woman's work. Back shootin' usually means a cowardly man, so I'm going to look closely at Winslow and Locklear. Problem is findin' new evidence. We've already got the weapon, and I've gone over the site. Nothin'." McAllen looked at me. "Steve, see what you can discover about Blanchet."

"I will, but you don't sound confident."

"I'm not."

"Then we're going to have to work harder. There are five of us, counting the Schmidts. We ought to be able to discover something."

"Six of us," McAllen said in a quiet voice.

"Six?"

"Maggie insists on helpin'."

"Maggie? You're not going to allow her to get involved in this, are you?"

"Not much choice. Appears she picked up a single-mindedness from somewhere. Better to make her part of the team than to pretend she'll stay out."

"What'll she do?"

"Whatever you say."

"Me?"

"Yep. She insists. Won't work with the Schmidts."

"Because they'll keep her on small stuff."

"Probably. Anyway, she wants to help you."
McAllen finished his whiskey in one gulp.
"Steve, keep her safe."

"Yes, sir." This time I said it with respect.

Chapter 22

When I stepped out of Earp's cozy home, I was startled by the darkness. Clouds blanketed the sky, shielding even the minimal light from a new moon and the stars. Earp left the door open, so I had enough light to saddle Liberty and cinch the flank strap properly.

"Stay on the road; it'll take you right into town," Earp said.

"Trust Liberty," McAllen added. "A horse sees better than you in the dark. Just don't take him from a lit barn into the night and expect him to see right away. Horse's eyes take a long time to adjust."

McAllen had been teaching me the ways of the West for nearly a year. I guess he wasn't done.

I mounted up and said, "When will I see you?"

"I'll be movin' into the Palace tomorrow. Be about town from now on, but tell Maggie to ignore me for a day or two."

"I'll pick her up after breakfast. Do we have a story?"

"Make one up. Ride careful." With that, McAllen went back into the house. Earp followed, and after he closed the door, I found myself sitting astride Liberty in the pitch dark.

I nosed the horse around, and he seemed sure-footed as he walked along at a leisurely pace. Town was only about a mile, so even at a slow tempo, I expected a short trip.

In a few minutes, I could see the edges of the trail, but I held a loose rein so Liberty could find his own way. If not for the chill, it would have been a pleasant ride. After about fifteen minutes, I grew anxious without cause. I was about to shake it off when I heard a yell.

"Stand and deliver!"

I pulled up. "Deliver where? I can't see a damn thing."

"Just drop yer valuables to the ground and keep ridin'."

I thought about going for my gun. If I couldn't see, then how could the robber know what I was reaching for? While I was making up my mind, I heard a gunshot. I immediately recognized it as rifle fire. I found myself on the ground. Damn. Had I been shot? I ran a hand over my face and felt nothing wet or out of place. I saw another muzzle blast and rolled off the road. Where the hell was Liberty? Had the robber killed my horse? Suddenly anger welled up, and I went for my Colt. After I pulled my coat up, I discovered that my holster was empty.

Things were still for a moment, so I hugged the ground and squinted to make out any unusual shapes on the road. I saw something that could be my pistol and crawled as flat as possible until I could reach out my arm to the object. It was my Colt, thank God.

As I rolled away again, I saw Liberty. He was behind me, not ahead. The road bandit must have fired a warning shot to hurry me up, and Liberty had bolted, throwing me to the ground. Now my horse was over twenty feet away . . . with my Winchester in a scabbard strapped to his side.

I looked across the road but saw nothing. I had only five shots, so I had to wait for another muzzle flash, or I'd waste bullets *and* give away my position.

What was the robber doing now? Why was it so quiet? I vowed not to be the first to make a noise.

At last, I heard, "Throw yer purse out, but I wanna hear yer gun fly 'cross the road first. I got all night, cowboy."

I could tell his voice was directed away from me. My bet was that he had his back against a tree and was yelling in the opposite direction. Not a bad plan. I swung my legs in an arc behind me and found a tree close by. As I moved to hide behind it, another shot rang out, and my hat was no longer on my head. Damn, that was close. I had been too busy moving low to see the flash, so I still didn't have a fix on his position.

Now safe, I yelled my own warning. "You don't have all night! Virgil Earp will be here shortly."

"Bullshit. Let's hear yer gun, or I'll put this-here next bullet in yer head."

"You're dumber than a half piece of soap. Earp lives less than a quarter mile up this road. He heard your shots."

I waited. Then I heard him scurry away in the brush. I started to throw a couple shots after him but held back because I didn't want to be responsible for any more killing. Instead, I sat behind my tree and listened. Finally, I heard a horse off in the distance. The road agent was running away.

I felt safe enough to collect Liberty. When I got to him, he was skittish as hell but settled right down with a neck rub and a few mumbled assurances. I realized that this was the first gunfire Liberty had encountered. Horses had to be trained to remain calm around loud reports. It also occurred to me that I hadn't practiced with my guns since last fall. I needed to remedy both of those omissions.

In a few moments, I heard, "Who goes there?"

"It's Steve, Virgil. It's all clear now."

Earp approached carefully, with a shotgun at his waist. I looked for McAllen but heard his footfall before I saw him. He was walking to the extreme side of the road with his rifle at the ready.

"What happened here?" Earp asked.

"Highwayman, but he ran away."

Both men came up to my position and looked around. I'm not sure what they thought they could see. Maybe more than I thought, because

McAllen picked up my hat and handed it to me. I started to put it on my head, when I felt something. It was a hole through the crown.

"Damn, that son of a bitch almost killed me." I showed the hat to McAllen.

"Doesn't make sense," Earp said. "Everybody knows I live just down the road. Tell me exactly how this happened."

After I told my short story, both men shook their heads in disbelief.

"Either that was a stranger, or someone was out to kill you," Earp said.

"I don't think he wanted to kill me. He could have shot me as I rode up. Why give me warning?"

"Don't know, but better come stay the night at my place. You can ride back in the light tomorrow."

I thought about the Saratoga trunk waiting for me in my room. I was anxious to see what was inside.

"I'll be fine. It's a short ride from here and he won't try again." I mounted up. "I'll see you tomorrow."

"Suit yourself, but something ain't right. We've had some highwaymen to the south but never up here."

I rode away slowly. I was concerned, but in less than five minutes, I could see a glow in the sky that must have come from lanterns along

170

Whiskey Row. In another ten, I was riding into the livery.

After grooming and feeding Liberty, I rushed over to Mrs. Cunningham's, carrying my rifle. I never left my rifle at a livery. I nodded politely to a couple of men in the parlor of the house and scampered up the stairs. The trunk was at the foot of my bed. I hung my sheepskin coat on a peg by the door and looked around the room. John had followed my instructions and transferred our things from the Palace.

Although some men wore a knife at all times, I wore mine only in the wilderness. I wasn't good with a knife in a fight, so wearing one around town made no sense. Besides, the one time a man had charged me with a knife, I shot him. At the moment, however, not wearing my knife meant I had to hunt around the room to see where John had stored it. I found it in a top bureau drawer.

The steamer truck was well built, and I tried many times before I was able to force the lock with my knife. I opened the lid with a little trepidation. At first, I saw only clothing. As I threw them aside, I noticed they were summer garments. At the bottom, I found what I was looking for. Or at least I hoped so. There were papers, writing utensils, stamps, and gold foil seals. On closer inspection, I discovered that the papers were preprinted stock certificates for the Edison Electric Illumination Company. These were the phony certificates. Campbell used the stamps and seals to make them look official. I rifled through everything but couldn't find the genuine article. Then I used my knife to slit the lining to check for a hidden certificate. No luck.

I sat on the floor, disappointed. Nothing had gone right since we rode into Prescott. The man I had come to see was dead, my friend was accused of murder, and the stock certificate for the Edison Electric Light Company was nowhere to be found. My priority had to be Sharp, but I still wanted to complete the business that had brought us here. I thought I couldn't be more dejected, and then I saw light leaking through a hole in my coat. I got up from the floor and examined it. The hole was new, with a companion hole on the backside. I put the coat on and stuck my finger through the holes, which were to the side. Damn, a bullet had just barely missed me. I had been lucky twice.

Then a realization struck me. This shot had to be the bandit's first attempt, the gunfire that had spooked Liberty and thrown me to the ground. The implication was undeniable. There had been no warning shot. That man had been sitting in ambush to kill me.

Chapter 23

The knock was loud and authoritative. As I rolled out of bed, I noticed that the light seeping around the drawn curtains was bright. How late had I slept?

As I stumbled toward the door in my nightshirt, I yelled, "Damn it, just a minute!"

When I flung open the door, I couldn't have been more surprised.

"Mr. Dancy, we have work. Do you intend to sleep the morning away?"

I quickly closed the door to a crack and stuck my head in the opening. "Maggie, what are you doing here?"

"Waking you, evidently."

"To what purpose?"

"To find Mr. Campbell's killer. Don't you care about your friend?"

"Of course. I was up late with your father and Constable Earp. We were discussing the case."

"Discussions are what men do when they sip bourbon. Mysteries are solved by investigations."

"And you know this from your extensive experience with the Pinkertons."

"I do."

I had meant the comment sarcastically. She

either didn't notice or refused to be intimidated. Maggie was proving herself a McAllen with her every utterance. Then it occurred to me that that was exactly what she was doing. Because her mother had moved away after she remarried, Maggie saw her father only once or twice a year. She idolized him. She probably saw him as a knight of the frontier, saving the good folks from outlaws and brutes. When I first met McAllen, I considered him an employee, but we eventually became friends. Perhaps he was a paladin. He certainly had rescued me from a desperate situation more than once. Then another thought occurred to me: For nearly two months, Maggie had watched Mrs. Schmidt perform the duties of a Pinkerton agent. No wonder she thought it was appropriate for a woman to engage in this line of work.

"Is Mrs. Cunningham still serving breakfast?"

"She was about to put it away, but I convinced her to hold it until I woke you."

"Tell her I'll be down shortly." I closed the door with a firm snap.

I shaved, scrubbed, dressed, and ran down the stairs. The dining room was empty except for Maggie and Mrs. Cunningham. The two sat close together, their heads bent in even closer. As I entered, they straightened abruptly as if I had caught them conspiring. Perhaps I had.

Mrs. Cunningham immediately stood. "Take a

seat, Mr. Dancy. You can eat a biscuit until I bring you the rest of your meal."

"Have you eaten, Maggie?"

"Hours ago."

What was I in for? I had checked my watch as I dressed, and it was half past eight o'clock. Not sunrise, but I had certainly not "slept the morning away."

I plopped into a chair and grabbed a biscuit. Maggie slid a crystal dish of preserves in my direction. Both were superb. If this was any indication, Mrs. Cunningham knew how to cook.

In a few minutes, Mrs. Cunningham returned and distributed several bowls in front of me. One held steaming porridge, another two boiled eggs. It was the third bowl that caught my attention. "An orange?"

"You mean, where did I find fruit way out here in the wilderness?" She looked pleased with herself. "Yuma. That's a navel orange from Brazil. They grow quite well along the Mexican border."

I grabbed the orange and peeled it, dropping the skin into the bowl. It was cold and juicy and sweet. I had seldom tasted anything so good. I hadn't eaten an orange since New York City, and it was an unanticipated pleasure. Mrs. Cunningham smiled in satisfaction before retreating to her kitchen.

After I finished my meal, I looked up to see

Maggie watching me with interest. I wiped my mouth with a napkin, took a sip of coffee, and looked back at her with what I hoped was an expression of disinterest.

"I propose we start with Mr. Winslow," she said without preamble.

"Why?"

"I don't like him."

"This is what you learned from your extensive experience with the Pinkertons?"

She was only flustered for a moment before saying, "He thinks he's going to be president someday. Protecting his precious reputation is motive."

"I'm sorry to inform you, but your father is still in charge of this investigation. He instructed me to find out what I could about George Blanchet. Since he also said we were to work together, that means you'll accompany me today as we find out what we can about the esteemed counselor of Prescott, Arizona."

"What about Mr. Winslow?"

"Your father said he would personally look into Mr. Winslow. Now, I intend to follow your father's instructions. If you want to participate in this case with me, you need to assure me that you will do the same."

"How do you propose we start?"

"Did I miss your assurance?"

"Mr. Dancy, Captain McAllen is not only the

supervisor of this investigation, he is my father. Need I say more?"

"You do." I sipped the last remnants of my coffee while I continued to put on an appearance of indifference.

Finally, I got a glowering response. "You seem to be a very annoying man, Mr. Dancy. Very well, if you insist. I give you my assurance that I will abide by my father's instructions."

"Which includes doing what I tell you. No sleuthing on your own. Captain Joseph McAllen's orders. Do you understand?"

For a moment, I thought she was going to argue, but then she gave me what appeared to be a genuine smile and said, "I understand."

I was about to demand something beyond an understanding but decided it would be wasted effort. I would just need to keep her close at hand. Maybe if she felt engaged, she would be more obedient. It was worth a try.

"Tell me what you know about Mr. Blanchet," I asked.

"He's not a very good lawyer, but he knows the governor and all the moneyed interests in the territory. Let me rephrase that. Mr. Blanchet is a staunch Republican, and he serves the men behind Republican interests in the state."

This was news to me. President Hayes was a Republican, and he had appointed Frémont, the first Republican presidential candidate. I had assumed that Republican interests dominated the territory. "Are there Democratic interests in the territory?"

Maggie gave me a look that made me feel stupid. "The southern part of the territory is Democratic. That's why Tucson and Tombstone keep trying to get the capital moved, but Hayes will never let that happen. Tombstone mines produce ore valued at up to six thousand dollars per ton. If the capital gets moved south, with that kind of money coming out of the ground, this will be a Democratic state one day."

I was impressed. "Very astute for a fourteen-year-old."

"Fifteen. I've had a birthday since you saw me last." She gave me another disdainful look. "They come around regular . . . once a year."

I ignored her sarcasm. "What else do you know about Blanchet?"

"He and Campbell ate breakfast together nearly every day."

I felt my posture straighten. "How do you know that?"

"They ate at Mrs. Potter's Café. Same as us."

"You didn't eat at Prescott House?"

"God, no. Worst food in town."

"Don't use profanity."

"I apologize. A bad habit I picked up from the Schmidts."

"Break it. Anything else?"

She actually stuck her finger under her chin and struck a thoughtful pose. "No. Why would my father be interested in Mr. Blanchet?"

"Not sure, but he'll be more interested in him once he knows he regularly ate breakfast with Campbell."

"He already knows. I told him weeks ago."

Of course. They probably shared a lot on those afternoon rides. Then it occurred to me that McAllen was using his daughter. She was a fixture about town and a child. Most likely, nobody gave her any notice. Because of her keen sense of observation, McAllen probably learned as much from her as from the Schmidts. Possibly more. I doubted the Schmidts would speculate, because they struck me as a couple who abhorred being in error.

"Any suggestions on how we proceed from here?" I asked.

"Let's follow him."

There was excitement in her voice, and I pretended to consider her idea. Finally, I said, "In business, the person who knows the most about someone is usually a competitor. Let's see Mac Castle, Jeff's lawyer. Perhaps he can give us some history on our Mr. Blanchet. Besides, I need to give him money for his services."

"Let's visit Mr. Sharp first. I'd like to say hello." She jumped out of her chair, holding up two biscuits. "I owe these to Mr. Sharp for the rock candy and jerky he gave me on the trail after rescuing me."

Maggie had been abducted the previous year, and Sharp and I had helped rescue her. When she was free, Sharp had given her rock candy and then jerky to rebuild her strength.

"If you remember, I was the one that brought you your horse. How will you repay me?"

"You may ride with Pa and me this afternoon." She stuffed the biscuits in her skirt pocket and looked anxiously at me.

"Do you need to use the privy first?" I asked.

"Mr. Dancy, I've been lollygagging around here for hours waiting for you to wake up. Then I sat and watched you linger over breakfast. My God . . . I mean, my gosh, you savored that orange like it was the finest chocolate. Now we've arrived at a course of action, and you remain seated. May we, at long last, proceed?"

"Of course. I just need to go upstairs to get my hat and gun."

As I sprinted up the stairs, I couldn't help but smile. This could be fun.

Chapter 24

The day was crisp, but at least the walk to the courthouse would be short. As we hunched our shoulders against the morning chill, Maggie said something that stopped me in my tracks. "One more thing about Mr. Blanchet: he wants to take me to his bed."

"What?"

"Mr. Dancy, I'm fifteen and attractive. I didn't mention it earlier because I didn't think it relevant. Many older men make advances."

"What kind of advances?"

"Men in general, or Mr. Blanchet?"

"Mr. Blanchet."

"He buys me a peppermint stick whenever he runs into me at Hill's Hardware or the Goldwater store."

I smiled. "Perhaps he just thinks you're a cute child."

Her expression made clear she thought I was stupid. "He tries to hide it, but I catch him watching me suck on the peppermint stick."

That took me aback. "You probably misunderstand."

"Mr. Dancy . . . I spend a great deal of time on my aunt's ranch. I know all about breeding."

"All?"

She blushed. "Perhaps not all, but I can tell

when a male is interested. Every woman can."

I stopped myself from making a comment about her not yet being a woman. Fifteen-year-old girls might take that as a challenge. As I contemplated whether this revelation had any meaning, I heard someone angrily yell out Maggie's name.

My hand was on my Colt as I turned to see the Schmidts marching toward us.

"Where the hell have you been?" Mary Schmidt demanded. "We've been looking all over for you."

"Not all over, or you would have found me at Mrs. Cunningham's." Maggie remained unusually calm in the face of adult wrath.

"Your father made us responsible for you." Mary took a step toward Maggie. "Never leave without telling us where you're going."

Maggie held her ground and even seemed to lean in toward Mary. "You told me to never interrupt when you were together in your room."

Maggie had said this with an innocent tone, but for a moment, I thought Mary was going to slap her. Mary took a long, slow breath, before saying, "A note on our door would have been helpful."

"I'll be working with Mr. Dancy now." She hooked her arm through mine. "I'm his responsibility."

Her intimacy was unwelcome as far as I was concerned. She was playing some kind of game with her guardians, and I didn't want to be a part of it. I pulled my hand out of my pocket and let my arm dangle, but instead of taking the hint, Maggie took hold of my arm above the elbow. What was this girl doing?

"Our instructions come from your father, and Captain McAllen said you're still our charge . . . at least for the next few days. You may accompany Mr. Dancy, but only during the day. Until he says so, you are to disclose to no one that you're not my daughter."

Mary turned her angry glare at me. "What's your story?'

"My story?"

Her angry expression turned to exasperation. "Are you courting my daughter or just corrupting her?"

"Neither."

"Well, if you walk down the street arm in arm, that's what people will say."

"I take your point." I wasn't good at this but went ahead anyway. "I'm your brother. I came to Prescott to see you and my niece. Maggie follows me around because I'm her favorite uncle."

"That should work. Don't elaborate. The less detail, the less likely you'll get tripped up. Keep us informed of your whereabouts."

I nodded, so she turned to Maggie.

"Young lady . . . you will be polite to your parents at *all* times. Understood?"

Maggie released my arm, smiled coyly, and

dipped in an approximation of a curtsy. "Then how will I keep up the pretense of being your darling daughter?"

If possible, Mary's expression grew even angrier. "Just do as I say." She whirled, grabbing her husband by the elbow. They marched off together in the opposite direction.

As we watched their backsides, I mumbled, "Carl never said a word."

"Mary's the boss, both on the job and in the home. Carl's a weasel."

"Why don't you like the Schmidts?"

"I've heard them talk when they think I'm not listening. If they didn't work for Pinkerton, they'd be crooks. Those two are self-seeking scoundrels."

I thought about it. As I again looked at them walking away, I could swear Mary Schmidt sensed my stare and started to sway her derrière in a sensual rhythm. "Perhaps that means they have the requisite talents to catch other scoundrels."

"Oh, they're good all right. Pa says there are none better. It's what got them this assignment. The Winslows are very rich and very important." With that, she thrust her jaw out, and her mouth became a thin, straight line across her face. "I wish they could make that arrogant, overindulged dandy do something that would land him in jail."

"What? Who are you talking about?"

"Master Jonathon Winslow, the second most powerful man in the territory. At least by his reckoning." She threw me a glance, then spoke in a snickering voice. "Can you imagine a measly assistant getting so puffed up?"

"Did he make a pass at you as well?"

"He did, and he's not put off as easily as Mr. Blanchet. My guess is they have a bet between them on who can despoil me first."

Did girls her age really think this way? None that I had ever encountered *talked* this way. I looked down at Maggie standing beside me. This one was scary. "Blanchet, Winslow, and the Schmidts—is there anyone you like?"

Now her smile looked genuine and not a bit coy. She again hooked her arm in mine before saying, "Yes, Mr. Dancy, I like you."

With no one looking at us now, I threw her arm away. "Miss McAllen, I don't know what your game is, but young ladies do not hold the arm of their favorite uncle in that fashion."

Her expression showed no displeasure at my outburst. "Mr. Dancy, may I speak bluntly?"

"I thought you had been exceedingly blunt already." I gave her a thoughtful look. "I'm not sure I want to hear what you consider blunt."

Maggie continued to smile. "Don't worry; I have no designs on you. I'm tired of playing jackstones to appear childlike. Now I have you. When the reprobates in this town see me on the arm of a notorious gunman, they'll leave me alone."

I tried a firm voice. "First nobody knows I'm a so-called gunman . . . and uncles that seduce their nieces are frowned upon, even on the frontier."

"I didn't know about being your niece until a moment ago." She appeared to think. "I like it. A notorious and protective uncle works even better. May I spread the word about you killing so many outlaws?"

"You may not. I want to stay friendly with this town. But I'm happy to hear that you were playacting with me."

"Are you surprised?" She shook her head. "I'll never understand the conceit of men. You're far too old for me." She gave me an appraising look. "But not for Mrs. Cunningham."

"What?"

"She likes you."

"She doesn't know me."

"She wants to know you. I spent the morning answering her questions."

That got my attention. "You didn't tell her about my gunplay?"

Her chagrined expression answered my question.

"Now the whole town will know."

"She's not a gossip."

"But she *is* married."

"No. Her husband was killed in Tombstone. She

tells men he's still alive for the same reason I play jackstones and sidle up to you. Women are sought-after game on the frontier. They need a poisoned bite or protective coloration to make them invisible."

"Do all fifteen-year-olds think the way you do?"

"Of course not. How do you think so many of them end up pregnant and married? Usually in that order, I might add."

"But not you."

"Not me. I'm a McAllen."

Chapter 25

"Maggie! Wow, ya've grown!"

Sharp looked to be in a good mood, considering the circumstances. He leaned his cheek against the bars, and Maggie gave him a passing kiss that probably never touched his two-day growth of beard.

"Back away from the cell!" the jailer yelled in a loud and shrill voice. He was nervous because I had bribed him to let us both go down to the cell.

Maggie dutifully retreated, but she didn't look the slightest bit remorseful that she had broken the rules. When she had backed up against the wall, she said, "I've had my fifteenth birthday, and I've solved my first crime."

This was news to me. "What crime?"

"Nothing big. I overheard a Goldwater clerk complain that a man had snuck out of the store with a lady's garment. I knew immediately that he was no gentleman, so I walked along the boardwalk peeking into the saloons. Soon I saw a grisly scoundrel trying to buy the favors of a saloon dancer with a new dress. I informed Constable Earp, and Goldwater's rewarded me with a new hair ribbon."

"What did Mrs. Schmidt reward you with?" I asked.

She waved offhandedly. "No matter. I don't

know why I brought it up." She held out the biscuits. "I brought you some biscuits, Mr. Sharp. Mrs. Cunningham made them fresh this morning, and she's a wonderful cook."

"Well, thank ya, Maggie. That's very thoughtful." Jeff turned one of his wicked grins at me. "An' Steve, what did ya bring this poor maligned prisoner?"

"Maggie, to brighten your otherwise dull day."

"And a great gift she is. How ya doin', darlin'?"

She curtsied. "Very well, thank you. I'm working with Mr. Dancy to get you out of here."

We had both rescued Maggie from an abductor, but Sharp was definitely Maggie's favorite. I felt rebuffed but consoled myself that Sharp was always the favorite of the ladies.

"Don't get yerself in trouble, young lady," Sharp warned.

"I won't. I have the greatest gunman in the territory looking out for me, and the greatest detective in the world for a father. The real murderer should be quaking in his boots."

"Well, on that score, I have a bit of news. Lew Davis, the day manager over at the Palace, brought me a bucket of beer yesterday afternoon, an' he said somethin' that's been naggin' at me."

Instead of answering, I lifted an eyebrow.

"He said he was sorry for my troubles—like he knew I didn't do it. An' why the hell should he be sorry? I barely met the man."

"Maybe he's feeling guilty. Making amends," Maggie said, with too much excitement.

"Did he say anything else?" I asked.

"Nope. Nothin' of interest about the murder anyway."

"Jeff, is this your gut speaking? Because it sure seems weak."

"Maybe. Somethin' just didn't feel right.

I thought it over. "Well, he was swindled by Campbell, and he works days, so he was free to wander about late at night." I pushed myself away from the wall. "We'll look into it."

"Yes, we will," echoed Maggie.

Jeff's revelation disturbed me, but I chose to ignore it for the moment. Instead I concentrated on how to discover more about Lew Davis. First, I would talk to Bob Brow. He seemed outside our circle of suspects and, as owner of the Palace, he was Davis's boss. Could Doc Holliday add anything? I decided to approach him as well. He could give me a read on Brow and Davis. Besides, the more I talked to Doc, the more likely I could convince him to be a character in my next book.

"Jeff, do you need anything?" I asked.

"Clean clothes, soap, sponge, a miner's pan, toothbrush, bakin' soda, an' hairbrush."

"Planning on going out on the town?"

"Grand idea. Bring along a key to this-here lock, if ya can manage it."

"I'll do my best."

He turned his attention to Maggie. "I'd like to see yer pa as well."

"I'll tell him, but he's busy getting you free."

"How? By kissing the derrière of Constable Earp?" Sharp seemed angry for some reason. "Tell him to bring whatever forces he can to this town. He knows I'll pay."

"Yes, sir, I'll tell him, but you've already got Mr. Dancy and me. We'll solve this before any more Pinks can get here."

"Jeff, we also have the Schmidts. More people might get in the way."

"I know. I'm just pissed at everythin'. This is my second day in this dungeon. I'm gettin' bored, a bit scared, an' very ripe smellin'. So if it's all the same to you, I'd like ya to get me outta here . . . an' do it in a way so my feet stay solid on the ground."

"Then we'd better get busy. I'll send the things over later in the day."

As we were leaving, I stopped by the gruff-looking jailer. "Thanks for caring for my friend," I said, as we shook. The two silver dollars I had secreted in my palm were no longer there when I withdrew my hand.

At the door, I turned back toward the jailer. "By the way, are you getting my friend a ration of beer on occasion?"

"Yes, sir. As ya requested. Coffee throughout

the day, beer in the afternoon." He flipped a silver dollar in the air and caught it with a deft move. "I'll take care of yer friend, as long as ya remain friendly."

"Much obliged." I climbed the stairs back to daylight.

Chapter 26

"Who's this?" Castle asked.

"Maggie, my niece. Mary Schmidt is my sister. Perhaps you know her. She's been staying at the Prescott House for the last couple of months."

"I know who she is."

Did that mean he knew she was a Pinkerton? I decided to let it go, and I could see he was going to do likewise. My flimsy story would never sound reasonable to someone who already knew about the Edison Electric Light Company.

I waved Maggie into one of the opposing leather chairs. "Maggie's also a friend of Jeff Sharp. We all spent some time together last fall in Colorado."

"I think she should step out into the hall. I want to ask you some sensitive questions."

Maggie used both hands to flare her skirt as she gracefully settled into the chair that faced the attorney. After she had folded her hands in her lap, she said, "That won't be necessary. I can probably answer those 'sensitive' questions."

Castle looked like he was going to protest but must have decided to let it go, turning to me. "Are you wanted in any state of the union?"

I pulled over a wooden captain's chair and sat down. "No, I'm not wanted anywhere. Why do you ask?"

"You have been involved in killings."

"Self-defense. There were never any charges."

"How fortunate for you." Castle didn't look sympathetic.

"Not really. What was fortunate for me was that none of those outlaws were successful. We discussed this previously. Why bring it up again?"

"I took tea at Mrs. Cunningham's house this morning. By her accounts, you can be a much more brutal man than I had supposed."

I gave Maggie a reproachful look. Evidently, Mrs. Cunningham was not above gossip.

"Not by her account, by mine," Maggie interjected. "I fear I enlarged stories about my uncle while we waited for him to waken." She looked down shyly. "I guess I was trying to impress her. I hope you'll forgive a young girl's vanity."

I wasn't sure what Maggie wanted to be when she matured, but my guess was that she could find employment as a thespian.

Castle looked dubious. "I would brush this aside except I understand you were involved in gunplay just this past night."

"When someone takes a potshot at you, it's seldom referred to as gunplay. I might add that I was returning from supper at the home of Constable Earp."

"Someone shot at you last night?" Maggie asked with concern.

"Just a highwayman. I'm not sure he even shot at me . . . probably aimed over my head."

"Nonetheless, you will remain on my suspect list," Castle said.

"Fine. Now, can we get down to business?"

Maggie said in an authoritative voice, "As you will remain on my suspect list, Mr. Castle."

"*Your* suspect list?" He whipped around to me. "Who is this girl?"

Before I could think of a response, Maggie said, "I'm the daughter of Carl and Mary Schmidt. Mr. Campbell was trying to purloin money from my parents." She kept her hands folded in her lap and remained exquisitely still. "You're well-to-do. Did Mr. Campbell steal from you?"

"He did not."

"Can we get to business?" I interjected. "We just came from visiting Mr. Sharp. He says he hasn't spoken to you since your initial interview."

"Nothing to talk about yet." Castle addressed me but kept wary eyes on Maggie. She remained still while leveling a steady gaze at him. Obviously, she had unnerved him after only a few short sentences. Then I recalled that she had done the same to me on the walk over to the courthouse.

"You've discovered nothing?"

Castle reluctantly switched his eyes to me. "I discovered that Mr. Campbell was broke and desperate to raise enough money to return to New

York. Evidently, the authorities in New York dropped their investigations. He was working a swindle on"—he looked at Maggie—"your parents. Unsuccessful to my knowledge."

"Anything else?"

"Not much. Oh, Blanchet will prosecute the case."

"What the hell? He asked to defend Sharp."

Castle shrugged. "Two sides of the same coin. Due to his relationship with the governor, he gets hired to prosecute cases all the time."

"What can you tell me about George Blanchet?" I asked.

"He's an adequate prosecutor. Usually takes on easy cases, which is not a good omen." He added offhandedly, "He'll disqualify any juror that has publically criticized the governor or President Hayes."

"How long has he lived in Prescott?"

Castle rubbed his chin. "Maybe five, six years."

"Where did he come from?"

"I don't know. Why?"

"We suspect he may have partnered up with Mr. Campbell," Maggie interjected. "Besides, he's a nasty man."

Castle chuckled. "What would you know about nasty men, young lady?"

I didn't want to give Maggie an opportunity to answer, so I quickly asked, "Has Blanchet had any illegal dealings since he arrived?"

"Nothing illegal that I'm aware of, but he's not what I would call overly ethical."

"And you have no idea where he may have come from."

"I said I didn't know, not that I had no ideas." He looked a bit too pleased with himself. "One time, Blanchet acted very odd when an Omaha visitor came to town. He stayed in his lodging house and seldom ventured out until the man headed down to Tombstone. As soon as the stranger was gone, Blanchet returned to his normal routines."

That was the best news I had heard in a while. McAllen could check with the Pinkerton Omaha office. If necessary, I'd pay for a full investigation.

Castle went over a number of legal technicalities, all of which meant that the trial could start within two weeks, and Sharp's chances didn't look good. He opined that there was nothing more unsettling than an undisclosed murderer in the midst of law-abiding citizens. Everybody knew Campbell, and those who had not been subject to his avarice liked his charming ways and good humor. There might be an occasional shooting on Whiskey Row, but townsfolk could avoid those haunts if they were frightened. One of their own shot from behind was different from a saloon brawl. The territorial authorities wanted a clean, fast conviction to show that Prescott was once again safe under their leadership.

"What about Mrs. Cunningham?" Maggie asked.

"Mrs. Cunningham? What are you asking, child?"

"I'm asking if you consider Mrs. Cunningham a suspect. Campbell owed her money, and she's quite angry."

"My understanding," I offered, "is that he tried to swindle her as well, which could account for the strength of her anger."

"He had more than a desire for her cash," Maggie said with certainty. "He may have seduced her."

Castle bolted out of his chair. "That's a bold-faced lie!"

"Which?" Maggie asked innocently. "That he tried, or that he succeeded?"

"Young ladies should not talk that way." He paced the room and shook his head. "How old are you?"

"Beside the point," she said dismissively. "We have a murder mystery. Everyone must be considered. Was Mrs. Cunningham jilted by her lover?"

"No!"

Castle marched around the room in a huff. Then he stood between us with his back to Maggie. "Mr. Dancy, I shall talk to Mr. Sharp about our continued consultations. If he insists they continue, I will not countenance this girl's presence."

"Mr. Castle, I—"

Maggie interrupted me. "No, it is I who must apologize, Mr. Castle." She stood and did a graceful curtsy. "My mother encouraged me to speak my mind, but my father tells me that I am old enough to control my tongue. I'm certain that your assessment of Mrs. Cunningham is correct. It was a desperate allegation on my part. I just wanted to help Mr. Sharp, who was extremely kind to me in a difficult situation last winter. Please forgive me. I'll be silent in future meetings."

"Why would you want to attend our consultations?"

I could tell from Castle's calmer voice that he had been mollified to some extent.

Maggie laid her hand on my shoulder. "My uncle rode all the way from Carson City to visit me. He needs to return in less than a week for business reasons, and I can't allow this incident to separate us for even a few hours. I'm being sent east for schooling and probably won't see him again for years."

A long silence ensued. Finally, Castle said, "Very well. Mrs. Cunningham is a dear friend and a woman of the highest standards. I'm aware that this whole affair has been unnerving for you both.

I'll do my utmost to defend Mr. Sharp, but I refuse to sully the reputation of every citizen in town to raise a maelstrom of doubt around this case."

"Of course, sir," Maggie said in a contrite voice. "You will have no further interference from me."

"Very well." Castle returned his attention to me. "Did Mr. Sharp have any requests?"

"Only one . . . acquittal. This afternoon, if you can arrange it."

Castle laughed, and I knew we were back in his good graces.

"Actually, he did have a request." I pulled out his wallet and counted out two hundred dollars. I held the two hundred dollars in one hand and the wallet in the other. "He asked me to pay your fee, and he wants you to hold his wallet for safekeeping. You can use the money remaining if you need additional funds, but please let him know in advance."

"How much remains in the wallet?"

"Four hundred and thirty dollars."

"He's a trusting sort."

"Jeff doesn't having a trusting bone in his body, but he believes lawyers fear disbarment."

Castle emptied both of my hands. "Mr. Sharp is smarter than he appears on the surface."

"He is, and he's giving you that cash so you don't skimp."

"I already knew that. Good day, Mr. Dancy." He just nodded at Maggie.

After leaving his office, we remained silent until we had walked down the steps of his building. I was about to reprimand Maggie, when she said, "Let's go to Goldwater's general store. You can buy everything Mr. Sharp asked for and pick up a box of chocolates for Mrs. Cunningham. We have enough time before we return to her house for the noonday meal."

"Excuse me?"

"Mr. Dancy, did it escape your notice that Mr. Castle is courting Mrs. Cunningham? This makes him a suspect, by the way. Now we know one of the women on our list has a suitor. I hope he's innocent, because it would have been unwise of you to hire the murderer as defense counsel. We'll put that aside for the moment. The important thing is for you to make your intentions known, or you'll be left in the barn."

I stopped walking. "Maggie, what are talking about?"

She exhaled in exasperation. "Mr. Castle went to Mrs. Cunningham's for tea . . . and he delayed his visit until after she had completed her morning duties. This is the action of a courting man. Then his outrage at my completely reasonable inquiry confirmed my supposition."

I started laughing. "I think Mr. Castle and Mrs.

Cunningham will make a fine couple. I wish them a grand future."

"Luck will have nothing to do with it, I assure you."

Her tone of voice made me look down at the no-longer-a-child walking beside me.

Chapter 27

Against my better judgment, I allowed Maggie to lead me to the Goldwater store on Cortez Street. I decided to buy chocolates, not because I intended to court Mrs. Cunningham, but because I felt guilty for shorting her on the lodging. At least, that is what I told myself.

I couldn't help comparing the store to ours in Leadville. Goldwater's, a two-story brick structure with a colonnade porch all around, was the more imposing. Our building was a one-story clapboard affair in desperate need of a coat of paint. The top floor of Goldwater's was a Masonic lodge, so the merchandise space was about the same as ours. There were no other similarities. We catered to prospectors, miners, and Indians, whereas Goldwater's customers—politicians—used different tools to extract money from the frontier. They needed fine clothing, fine watches, fine writing materials, fine liquor, and fine tobacco. The politicos also needed to please their wives, so Goldwater's carried the latest fashions, home furnishings, and jewelry. Goldwater's motto was "The Best Always." We had no motto. I'm sure all of those fancy things could be bought in Leadville, but not at our store. Our dry goods were heavy and durable, and we sold guns, ammunition, knives, and dynamite. If a prospector wanted a pickax, Spanish pack saddle, blankets, or food that wouldn't spoil, they came to us.

"Can I help you?"

The thin shopkeeper was impeccably dressed and groomed. He sported a bushy mustache that completely hid his mouth. My guess was that he was about my age.

"I'm looking around at the moment," I said. "I'm a shopkeeper as well."

"Are you looking for employment?"

"No." I saw a flash of relief on his face. "I'm just visiting. My store is in Leadville, but nothing as grand as this."

"Thank you. I'm the owner." He extended his hand. "Morris Goldwater."

I shook. "Steve Dancy. This is my niece, Maggie."

Maggie started to curtsy, but Goldwater extended his hand, so she shook it with two firm up-and-down motions.

"I've seen you in the store many times," Goldwater said to Maggie.

"Yes, she's been here a few months with my sister and her husband. I rode down from Carson City to visit with them."

"I hope you enjoy our town. Let me know if I can help with anything. Merchandise or town matters. I'm the mayor too."

"Actually, you can help. I brought only trail

clothes with me. I never expected the sophistication of your fair city." I tugged at my wool shirt. "How long to fit a suit?"

He looked me up and down. "You're tall and sturdy built, so a fitting would be a bit of a challenge. Say, about a week. Quicker if you pay an extra fee."

"I'm in town for only a few weeks, so I'll pay the extra fee to get use of it while I'm here. How much for two-day delivery?"

"Two days? That would be extraordinarily fast." He grabbed his chin with his thumb and forefinger. "What quality suit were you looking for?"

As a shopkeeper, I knew this was a polite way of asking if the sale would be large enough for a special effort.

"The finest wool, with an eastern cut. Dark brown, preferably. I'll also need three shirts, three silk ties, hose, garter, shoes."

I could see him tally the purchase in his head.

"That would approach two hundred dollars."

"If your tailor is expert, and you can get it all in two days, I would find that acceptable."

"Excuse me," Maggie said. "We have an appointment." She looked at Goldwater. "A box of chocolates, please."

From the moment Goldwater had said he was mayor, I wanted to build a sense of confidence between us. He could be a valuable source of information about the denizens of Prescott. Besides, I felt out of place dressed in trail clothes in this territorial capital. A good suit was something I could always use.

I ignored Maggie. "How long would a fitting take?"

He craned his neck to look in the back of the store. "Our tailor doesn't seem to be busy. Less than a half hour for measurements."

"Let's get on with it then." Responding to a dirty look from Maggie, I added, "Maggie, you select the chocolates and bring the box back to me. Mr. Goldwater, could you have a clerk collect a bath sponge, soap, and a prospector's pan?"

"Of course."

A few minutes later, when the tailor was measuring my waist, Maggie showed up with a red heart-shaped box of chocolates.

"Very amusing," I said. "Now go back and get a plain box."

"These are less expensive. Left over from Valentine's Day, I suppose."

"I'll pay the extra for fresh."

"You don't know those are fresher. Valentine's Day was just a month ago. Those ordinary boxes could have been around for a year."

"Maggie, no." I tried for a firm voice. Why was she acting this way? A relationship with Mrs. Cunningham held complications I didn't want to contemplate. I needed to get my friend out of jail and had no interest in a time-consuming courtship, especially with a woman tied to a town I would leave as soon as I freed Sharp and found the certificate. Mrs. Cunningham seemed too desperate for a male protector since her husband died, and I resented her using Maggie to further her ambitions.

In short order, the tailor finished his measurements and assured me that he would put my order in before all of his other customers. I had picked a lightweight wool fabric in a lighter shade of brown than I really wanted. I had several winter suits back in Carson City, and the weather would soon be warming. In the meantime, I had extra-heavy long johns I had bought in Leadville, where it was considerably colder than Prescott.

When I reached the front of the store, Maggie, holding a square box of chocolates, was talking to Goldwater. When I approached, she looked defiant.

"How much do I owe today?" I asked.

"Half the cost of the suit, a dollar for the chocolates, and six bits for the toilet items. I understand the chocolates are for Mrs. Cunningham."

I looked down and shook a finger at Maggie. "For someone of your ambitions, you have a loose tongue."

Finally, she looked chagrined. "You may be

right, Uncle. I was just telling Mr. Goldwater why I exchanged the heart-shaped box. Mrs. Cunningham came up by accident."

"Just to be clear, Mr. Goldwater, I am not courting Mrs. Cunningham. As you know, she's a married woman. These are a kindness for a favor she did for me. A *thank you* should not be diminished by buying something inappropriate, even if it's a great bargain."

"I understand." Goldwater moved behind the counter and pulled a cash box from beneath. "I presume you'll pick the other items when the suit is finished?"

"Yes."

"Then fifty dollars will keep it simple."

"Uncle, what about the other things Mr. Sharp requested?"

She was enjoying the playacting a bit too much. "I'll find the rest of the items in his belongings. They're in my room."

I handed over a fifty-dollar certificate, and he wrote me a receipt.

"May I buy you a meal?" I asked. "I'd like to discuss shop keeping and local politics."

"I was about to go over to Mrs. Potter's Café. Or were you thinking of a later date?"

"No. That's perfect. Shall we go?"

"Let me tell my senior clerk, and I'll be right with you." He stopped in his tracks. "Mr. Dancy, if you want to use my political influence to free your trail partner, I'd rather buy my own lunch."

Obviously, word got around this town quickly.

"I'll let Mr. Castle apply whatever influence is necessary and appropriate. I assure you, I have no request associated with Mr. Sharp."

He gave me an appraising look and said, "Okay."

As Goldwater went to inform his clerk, Maggie said, "We should be returning to Mrs. Cunningham's. The meal is free."

"Hardly," I answered. "You've placed far too high a price on eating at Mrs. Cunningham's. Why are you so insistent on playing Cupid?"

"She's a beautiful woman who finds you attractive. Are you involved with another woman?"

"No," I answered too quickly.

"Then I don't see the harm. If she's willing to entertain, why turn her down?"

"Young girls don't talk that way. At least proper young girls don't. Maybe I should talk to your father."

"That won't be necessary. The subject is completely out of my head. Let's solve this murder mystery and get Mr. Sharp back on the streets."

Did she mean it? No, she was too headstrong, but I had found the secret of quieting her tongue. I suspected I would again need to threaten to go to her father. A thought occurred to me. Young girls wanted nothing more than to be taken as seriously as adults. That could cause them to act out the behavior of adults. I vowed to keep a sharp eye on Maggie and Mrs. Cunningham's son.

Chapter 28

Mrs. Potter's was busy, but we were led to a table ahead of other waiting guests. I supposed being mayor had privileges. The three of us took our seats, and I placed my purchases under my chair.

Goldwater opened by asking about my experience as a shopkeeper. I told him about my gun shop in New York City and then said that I had bought the Leadville store to take advantage of the silver boom. He had no need to know that Sharp and I had bought the store as part of our plan to recapture Maggie from her abductors. As we discussed the ins and outs of shop keeping, I could see Goldwater warming up to me. Maggie looked frustrated with the meandering conversation, but I knew these preliminaries were necessary for him to be forthright when I asked questions about people that I assumed were his customers.

After we ordered applesauce cake for dessert, I said, "Jeff Sharp did not murder Campbell."

"How do you know?" He didn't seem surprised by my statement. My guess was that he had been waiting for me to broach the subject.

"I've been in several dangerous situations with him, and he always acts with honor and courage. I know his character, and he's not a murderer."

Maggie jumped into the conversation. "I know Mr. Sharp as well, and he would never shoot a man in the back or leave his rifle behind. I owe my life to Mr. Sharp."

Goldwater laughed. "Your life? That's certainly a bit of exaggeration, young lady."

"It *is* not! I was—"

"Maggie is indebted to Mr. Sharp, but the particulars are of little interest right now." I saw no need to color Goldwater's impression of Sharp by bragging about his violent escapades.

"It's still of interest to me." She started to add something, but I could see her think better of it. Instead, she sat quiet and pouted.

After a silence, Goldwater said, "Constable Earp is a fine officer. He doesn't arrest men without good cause."

"I'm aware of Mr. Earp's credentials. He had no choice in the face of the evidence. I'll be the first to admit it looks damning, but my friend was framed."

"Suppose for the moment he was framed; who do you think did it?"

"Campbell was a crook. He swindled several in town. Any one of them could have killed him for revenge."

Goldwater rubbed his neck. "That was months ago. Why didn't they do something sooner?"

"Perhaps they saw Sharp hit and threaten Campbell. Or they could have just heard about it. That gave them an opportunity to blame someone else."

Goldwater didn't look comfortable but said, "I presume you have questions?"

"Did you know Elisha Campbell?"

"Yes. Spendthrift. Went through money fast: alcohol, gambling, women, and buying gifts for his supposed friends."

"Purchased in your store?" I asked.

"At first. I think he was broke at the end. I'm not sure, because he just quit coming into the store. I never extended him credit. Matter of principle. He had stolen from my friends.

"Do you know George Blanchet?"

"Of course."

"What can you tell me about him?"

"He trades on his connections with Frémont. To my knowledge, he was never swindled by Campbell. Why do you ask about him?"

"He's prosecuting the case."

"Sorry to hear that."

"Why sorry?"

"Blanchet likes to brag that he's never lost a case. If he's accepted the prosecutor role, it's because he thinks it will be easy to win."

I thought he might have another motive. If he were guilty of the murder, or even just had a loose partnership with Campbell, then as prosecutor, he could control the course of the trial. "Do you know anything about his background before he came to Prescott?"

Goldwater seemed startled by the question.

"You know, Blanchet's a braggart, but now that you mention it, I can't recall him saying anything about his past. Strange. Almost everyone talks about their upbringing and earlier life, but he's never mentioned a word, to my knowledge."

"You sound like you don't like the man."

Goldwater didn't hesitate. "I don't. Someone blackballed him when he tried to join the Masons. Everyone thinks it was me, but it wasn't. I wanted to, but he had a case pending against me at the time—a big one, and I didn't want him angry. It was foolish of me, because he still won through perjury. He's sued me so many times that I now think of it as part of running my business." He looked around to see who was in the restaurant. "A few customers order things, especially wives, and then complain that the product is shoddy or something when it comes time to pay. If I try to collect per our agreement, the obstinate go to Blanchet." He shook his head in resignation and then smiled. "You wouldn't be in the market for a ruby pendant . . . works better than a box of chocolates."

"No need. Do you think Campbell and Blanchet could have been partners?"

Another long thought. "Possibly, but I don't believe Blanchet would ever kill a man. My guess is that cowardice would hold his trigger finger more than his morals."

Maggie sat up straight. "Back shooting usually means a cowardly man."

I recognized her father's words.

"That's quite a thing for a young lady to say," Goldwater said.

"I assume you also know Herb Locklear." I wanted to change the subject.

Goldwater bridled at the question. "He's a member of my Masonic lodge, a fine, outstanding figure. I know he was swindled, but he wants to keep it quiet. Listen, our territorial legislature is made up of two branches. The assembly is the lower house and the council, the upper house. Locklear leads the Republicans in the council. If you suspect him, you're barking up the wrong tree."

"No, I don't, especially after your comments, but his victimhood is not as quiet as he would like. What about Lew Davis?"

"Taken by Campbell as well. Lew can be hard. Killed a man in self-defense once . . . or so I hear. But he does well by Brow. Keeps order during the day and doesn't steal." He turned thoughtful. "If someone else killed Elisha Campbell, my money would be on Lew. He has a temper, and he heard your friend threaten Campbell."

It was news that Davis had once killed a man. This was another piece of information for McAllen to investigate.

"Were you aware that Mrs. Cunningham was angry with Campbell?" I asked.

"Everyone knew. Surely, you don't suspect a woman?"

"Why did you bring her up?" Maggie demanded. "This is a man's work. Perhaps a man taken with Mrs. Cunningham, but she would not be a party to it."

"Your mother always says women can do whatever a man can do."

"Well, my mother says a lot of things. I ignore most."

"We've all noticed. Now, may I ask Mr. Goldwater another question?"

Maggie returned to her pouting. During the exchange, Goldwater had been glancing between us as if watching a tennis match. I vowed to get to the bottom of this as soon as I could get Maggie alone. I said to Goldwater, "Campbell owed her money. It still chafes. Is she a vengeful woman?"

"No. She won't let go of a slight, but all she does is grouse."

"How about Jonathan Winslow?"

"My best customer. Full of himself but harmless. He was swindled as well, but he's too ambitious to risk murder. The rich have other ways of taking care of these matters."

"Like how?"

"During a fitting, he told me he had hired

216

Pinkertons to build a criminal case against Campbell."

"Are there Pinkertons in town?" I asked, as innocently as possible.

"Is that a serious question?"

"What do you mean?"

He looked at Maggie. "Winslow told me your parents were employed by Pinkerton. They were here to catch Campbell red-handed and put him in prison."

Should I deny it? I decided against it because I needed to know something. "Have you mentioned this to anyone?"

"Of course not. This is a small town. News like that would spread faster than a summer forest fire."

"Please remain silent. My sister and her husband work secretly. They're still engaged on the Campbell affair."

He looked confused. "For what purpose?"

"I can't say, but please don't hamper them by disclosing their true purpose."

Without hesitation, Goldwater said, "You have my word."

"Thank you." Even knowing him for less than two hours, I knew I could rely on his word.

Chapter 29

After our meal, I escorted Maggie to the Prescott House so she could change clothes. I asked her to stow the chocolates and toiletries in her room until we returned from our afternoon horseback ride. This time, McAllen met us at the livery on Gurley Street, and he had our three horses saddled and waiting. Maggie kissed him on the cheek and then threw me a nasty look. Evidently, she wanted her father to know I had displeased her.

"Steve, I hope you had a productive mornin'," McAllen said, by way of greeting.

"Jeff's still in jail, so not as productive as I would have liked."

I told him about our morning and what we had learned. I omitted telling him that Maggie believed Blanchet and Winslow were trying to lure her into bed. I also chose not to relay Maggie's opinion about the Schmidts or that she was playing Cupid. The only hard pieces of news I had were that Davis had killed a man and that Blanchet was very closemouthed about his life prior to Prescott. I informed him that Blanchet would prosecute the case, which would probably start within a couple weeks, adding that the New York investigation against Campbell had been dropped.

After I finished, Maggie said, "We wasted a great deal of time jabbering about shop keeping with Mr. Goldwater."

"Why?" The question was directed at me.

"Goldwater is the mayor; I wanted to build common ground with him."

"Sounds reasonable. Maggie, why are you in a snit?"

The direct question caught her unawares. "No reason."

"She wants me to court my landlady, and she's displeased that I won't cooperate."

"Is this true?" McAllen uncharacteristically showed surprise.

"Not really. She expressed an interest, and I merely told Mr. Dancy. What he does is of no concern to me."

"Let's mount up. I want to get out to Thumb Butte."

After we were on our way, McAllen said, "Maggie, never interfere with a person's religion or choice of mate."

"Yes, sir."

"I don't want to hear any more on the subject. We have a tough task ahead of us. Steve, why didn't you mention Jeff's suspicions about Davis?"

Now McAllen's question caught me off guard. "Because his suspicion is based on Davis bringing him beer. Jeff thinks he feels guilty, but

I gave money to the jailer to provide Jeff with coffee and beer."

"Many prisoners have people outside that do what's necessary to get them provisions. But in the past, Davis has always sent over a boy with the beer."

I felt chagrined. I should have noted something so obvious on my own. "So you think it odd as well?"

"I trust Jeff's instincts."

"You saw him this morning?"

"I did. I knew most of what you told me, except that Blanchet is secretive about his past. Davis killed a man in Tucson, but he was acquitted. Self-defense. I'll send a telegram to our Omaha office when we finish our task this afternoon."

"What task?' I asked.

"We're goin' to walk the ground from the murder to town. Bit late, but maybe we can find somethin'."

"What are we looking for?" Maggie asked, excited.

"Anything Mother Nature didn't put there. If you find somethin', shout out, but don't touch it."

"This will be fun," Maggie said.

I didn't think so. The trail was heavily traveled, and we were going to find all kinds of discarded items. We'd be lucky to get back to town before suppertime.

"I'll take the trail and the three horses,"

McAllen said. "Maggie, you walk twenty feet on the right side. Steve, you take the left. Don't walk straight. Crisscross back and forth so you cover all the area between your assigned lane and the trail."

"Joseph, it was dark that night. The murderer would have stayed on the trail."

Without glancing in my direction, McAllen said, "Steve, you ever heard of tossin' somethin' aside?"

Damn. I always seemed to say dumb things around McAllen. Despite our history, I still wanted to impress him. I reminded myself to follow his example, keeping quiet unless I had something meaningful to say.

To get by the moment, I asked, "Did you learn anything this morning?"

"Winslow has a decent alibi. He claims he was with Elizabeth Mitchell, the highest priced whore in Prescott. Whores lie for money, but witnesses saw him eatin' supper with her at the Hassayampa Grill. She demands a high-priced meal as well as compensation for her services. 'Spose that makes it feel more like courtship." He paused and then added, "His parents reengaged us. Our job is to keep his name out of the trial, if possible. Out of the newspapers for sure."

I was surprised that he talked about whores so freely in front of his daughter, but in McAllen's line of work, whores were commonplace, so he probably thought nothing of it.

"Does that mean we drop Winslow as a possibility?" I was not happy with my favorite suspect hiring the chief investigator.

"Hell, no. I like him for the murder. His kind of people think they can get away with anythin'."

I was glad to hear that McAllen still considered Winslow a suspect, but by "his kind of people," McAllen meant the rich. Since I fell into that category, the comment irked me. I concentrated on the good news. McAllen had turned me away from looking into Winslow, not because he was protecting a client, but because he personally wanted to investigate him. As I thought about it, keeping me away from Winslow was probably a good idea. I was beginning to dislike the man so much that I might try a Sharp's style greeting one day, and look where hitting a man had put him.

Chapter 30

After two hours of trampling along the side of the trail, we had made very little progress. Just as I had suspected, the trail was strewn with people's discards. Every time Maggie or I yelled out that we had found something, McAllen had to come over to investigate, and we were never allowed to proceed further until he was done. The experience gave me an appreciation for what people discarded. Along with whiskey, patent medicine, and soda bottles, we found tobacco butts, tins, pouches, and juice. It seemed that when men went riding, they liked to drink and use tobacco. The only item we found from a female rider was a sweat-stained lace hankie. We found something else that I thought was interesting. Someone who frequented this trail liked to read a newspaper as he rode. After I found the third newspaper with a relatively current date, McAllen told me I could ignore any others I ran across.

I was beginning to wonder if we could finish our search in a single afternoon, when I heard Maggie yell with more enthusiasm than previously. Because McAllen was leading the three horses down the trail, one of us would usually walk over and hold the reins while he checked the other's find. This time, Maggie seemed so excited that I looped the reins around a bush and crashed through the chaparral to see what she had discovered. When I reached the two of them, McAllen was staring at the ground, while Maggie stared at her father with an expression of pride. I approached carefully and saw a jumble of leather straps.

"What is it?" I asked.

"A halter," McAllen said. He looked back to the trail, and I could see him mentally measuring the distance. Then he looked up at a tree above us. "Someone flung it from the trail, but it hit this tree and didn't go as far as intended." He picked it up and stretched it open with his hands. "This halter is too big for a ridin' horse." He turned it in different directions. "It's for a Shire, one of the big horses used to haul logs or lumber."

He took the halter out from under the shade of the tree and examined it inch by inch in the sunlight. He stopped, rubbed a part with his thumb, and even brought it to his nose.

He held it out for me to examine. "Steve, does that look like dried blood to you?"

I saw a dark blotch on dark leather. "Could be, but I'm not sure."

"Can I see it?" Maggie asked. I handed it over, and she almost immediately handed it back. "That's blood."

"How can you be sure?" I asked.

"When I geld sheep at my aunt's ranch, I wear

a leather apron. That's what dried blood looks like on dark leather."

"Steve, hold up your arms."

I did as McAllen ordered, and he slipped the halter over my head and down to my chest. When he nodded, I dropped my arms, and McAllen raised the harness to show how it had been adjusted to fit a man.

"The murderer used this halter and a rope to drag the body out to where we found it. Then he flung it out here so nobody would see him with it."

"Suppose you're right, how does that help us?"

"Not sure." McAllen wandered slowly back to the trail, so we followed him.

"About two hundred yards further up this trail is an abandoned livery," he said. "When the lumber business was boomin', that's where they kept the wagons, draft horses, and all the gear. It was a separate company back then. Now, the few remainin' Shires are kept in a barn next to the Earp house." McAllen pointed down the trail. "Campbell met his murderer late at night at that old livery." McAllen handed the halter to his daughter like it was a prize. "Let's go take a look."

He mounted up and we followed suit. The livery was only about a hundred yards beyond a slight bend in the trail. We all dismounted and loosely tied the horses to low tree limbs.

The place was dilapidated, with a collapsed corral, broken windows, and gaping holes where people had ripped off siding boards. McAllen threw open the big doors of the barn to chase away the dark inside. All three of us entered to find mostly nothing. The building had been ransacked of anything valuable a long time ago. I walked immediately to the back of the barn where I had spotted pieces of tattered tack hanging off wood rods.

"Joseph, this is the same type of tack. Thick and large. All the good pieces look to have been scavenged."

Without joining me, McAllen said, "That rifle shot passed right through Campbell's head. Let's look for blood and a bullet hole."

"Captain, two shots were fired from Sharp's rifle. Are you thinking Campbell was killed here, and then the second shot into the air was meant to draw Earp out to where you found the body?"

"That's exactly what I'm thinkin'. You might make a Pinkerton yet."

I took satisfaction in McAllen's compliment, but I could see from Maggie's face that he had made more trouble for me with his daughter.

After a twenty-minute search, we had found nothing. McAllen stood in the center of the barn and looked around.

"Steve, step outside, close the door, and then reenter. Let's playact Campbell enterin' the barn."

When I swung the door open, McAllen was nowhere to be seen. I walked into the barn and then heard McAllen say *bang* from behind me. When I looked back at him, he was pointing his finger at my head.

"As the door swung open, the killer hid behind this big barn door. The bullet should be on a diagonal, in the back wall."

All three of us approached the wall and examined the weathered wood. It was dark, this far back in the barn, but sure enough, McAllen soon said, "Here it is."

He used his knife tip to dig out a shallow-buried bullet and then held it between his thumb and forefinger. "Looks like this could be a .44-40," McAllen said.

"Does this help us solve the murder?" I asked.

McAllen flipped the bullet to Maggie, who looked startled but still managed to catch it. I guessed Maggie was the repository for our evidence.

McAllen walked to the barn door and looked out for a long moment before responding to my question. "Steve, if we can put together the sequence of events, then we might figure out why the events went the way they did. From that, we can probably guess the murderer."

"But we also need evidence."

"One step at a time." His voice was distant.

"Okay, first step?"

McAllen stepped outside the barn and rolled a cigarette. I followed and packed my pipe with a fresh load of tobacco. Maggie joined us and pulled something wrapped in wax paper out of her coat pocket. As she pulled the paper back to expose the end of a peppermint stick, the thought struck me that Thomas Edison had invented waxed paper. Before I could let that thought take me back to the missing stock certificate, McAllen started talking.

"I think we know the final steps. The murderer waited in the barn until Campbell closed the door and then shot him in the head before he even turned around. Then he used the halter to drag the body away from here. Once he got him to the base of Thumb Butte, he fired a shot into the air so the constable would find the body. The killer wanted the body found while Sharp was still drunk, and the memory of his threat fresh. On the ride back into town, he flung the halter off into the bushes."

McAllen paused, so I said, "And we know the first steps. Someone saw or heard about Jeff's encounter with Campbell at the Palace, then snuck up to his room to steal his rifle."

"Don't forget that after the murder, he went back into Mr. Sharp's room and stuck pine needles to the bottom of his boots," Maggie added. "That took nerve."

I swung around to look at Maggie. "Unless you

know he's passed out drunk. Could there have been more than one?"

"Of course," she said. "While someone met Campbell out here, someone else bought Mr. Sharp enough whiskey to get him stumbling-down drunk. The whiskey drinking kept him away from his room so they could steal his rifle, and allowed them to return later to plant the pine needles. We're looking for a pair of murderers."

McAllen flicked his cigarette away. "Good thinkin', Maggie."

She beamed, so I hoped we were evened up in the compliment category.

"Winslow and Locklear?" I asked.

"Don't jump to conclusions. One step at a time."

"Then what's the next step?" I asked.

"It doesn't seem obvious to you?" McAllen asked.

"No."

"Nor to me," Maggie added.

"We're standin' next to the key to this case," McAllen said. "The murderer moved the body away from here. The only reason to take that kind of risk is because the murderer believed that if the body was found here, it could lead back to him." McAllen walked over and untied his horse. Just before swinging into the saddle, he said, "My bet is that Campbell met regularly with the murderer . . . and they met right here."

Chapter 31

When we arrived at the livery on Gurley Street, it was already approaching dusk. "What are we going to do?" I asked.

McAllen dismounted and led his horse by the reins into the barn. This barn was in good repair, and a couple of livery boys rushed over to assist us. After we had unsaddled the horses, groomed, and fed them, we all three wandered out to the street. It didn't surprise me that McAllen hadn't answered. I was used to his ignoring me. It meant he thought my question was too silly to deserve an answer, or he was figuring out the answer, or he just didn't feel like talking. The latter was not a rare event.

"I'm taking my daughter to supper," McAllen said. "Alone." Out of the corner of my eye, I felt, more than saw, Maggie smile. "Steve, how about a beer while Maggie changes clothes?"

"I could use a cold beer and chatty company," I answered.

McAllen gave me a puzzled look but turned and walked toward Prescott House. We ordered beers at the hotel's tiny stand-up bar and drank them in the feminine parlor. Before we exchanged a word, Maggie came bounding down the stairs in a yellow floral dress that made her look grown up. She handed me the box of chocolates and toiletries. I had forgotten I had left the things in her room. Maggie then stood on her tiptoes and gave her father a kiss on the cheek. I was no longer a part of this party, so I gulped the rest of my beer and got up to leave.

"Sir?"

I looked over at the innkeeper, who plopped about four inches of newspapers on the counter. "You forgot these."

I seemed to be forgetting a lot lately. I had promised Sharp toiletries and reading material. Good thing someone reminded me. After dinner, I would take them to his cell. Maybe I could even get away with bringing him a bottle.

As I picked the newspapers off the counter, McAllen said, "We'll meet at eight in the morning at Jeff's cell."

I tipped my hat to Maggie and her father, and, without a word, started walking to Mrs. Cunningham's. I was glad the day was over and looked forward to a good supper and an early evening. Maybe Mrs. Cunningham had another orange.

As I stepped across her threshold, Mrs. Cunningham yelled from the dining room, "Mr. Dancy, so glad you could join us. You have just enough time to rush up to your room and wash up." She was distributing large bowls on the table and didn't sound particularly glad.

After I washed and changed into a fresh shirt, I

picked up the box of chocolates. Maybe they would improve her mood. The dining room was crowded, all seats but one taken. I glanced around, but everyone was a stranger to me, so I introduced myself and shook hands all around. When I finally sat down, Mrs. Cunningham looked impatient.

"If the greetings are over, Reverend Miles will say grace."

"Of course. Sorry for the delay."

As the minister said an overly long prayer, I pondered why Mrs. Cunningham was acting so annoyed. Perhaps she thought I had rejected her, but this was the first time I had seen her since Maggie told me she was interested in me.

After an excellent meal, the other guests left the house, probably for an establishment on Whiskey Row. I assumed the reverend was heading someplace else. When we were alone, I handed Mrs. Cunningham the box of chocolates.

"These are for you."

"What in the world for?" She held them away from her, as if they would bite.

"Just a small token." Her hard expression didn't soften, so I added, "I guess I felt guilty for bargaining hard for the first week's rent."

"I would have preferred the four dollars—that's a fair price for room and board." She said this with an edge that told me she did not welcome a box of chocolates.

What was Maggie trying to get me into? I was experienced enough with women to recognize when a woman was interested. Mrs. Cunningham was not. She was a money-grubber, and she was too irritated with me for bartering down the first week's rent to find me attractive. I also doubted that she had confided to a fifteen-year-old girl that she was attracted to me. Maggie had another game afoot.

I reached into my pocket and held out four silver dollars. "I meant to give these to you first. I apologize. I told you I would pay the full load if we were happy with each other. You're a great cook, and you serve excellent meals."

She looked at me askance for only the briefest moment before grabbing the coins. "Remember, rent is due the first day of the week." With that she whirled and marched off to the kitchen.

I stood rooted to the spot but soon followed her. When I entered, she didn't even turn around before saying, "Guests are not allowed in the kitchen."

"Then come out so I can talk to you."

"I have chores."

"It won't take long. I need a few answers. It's important."

"If you're looking for a woman, you can find one along Whiskey Row. A few cost no more than a box of chocolates."

"That was not my intent, and I'm insulted that you imply as much."

233

That caught her off guard. She was playing the role of the offended one. By claiming I took offense at her comments, I had stripped her of her defenses. She turned away from the sink and put a fist on her hip. "Ask quickly. I haven't got all night."

"What did you and Maggie discuss this morning?"

"Mostly she argued with me because I do not allow women to go upstairs. She was very anxious to wake you up."

"But you eventually let her."

"I did not. She was talking to my son in the parlor when I called him to carry in wood. When he finally complied, she snuck up on her own. She's a very headstrong girl."

I laughed, which puzzled Mrs. Cunningham. "That's for sure. I think she gets it from her father."

"You know her father?"

I had almost blundered. We needed to keep up the pretense that she was my niece. "Of course, he's my brother-in-law. Maggie's my niece."

"Oh . . . I misunderstood her eagerness to visit your room."

"You did. If you remember, we came down immediately and left right after breakfast."

"Together." She lifted her chin as a form of punctuation.

"Yes. I'm here to visit my sister and her. The Schmidts are staying at Prescott House. But this explains everything. Maggie was the one that insisted on the candy. She said it was an apology for an offense. I assumed she meant shorting the rent, but now I see that she was referring to her violating house rules and sneaking upstairs. Anyway, we both apologize, and we won't be any further trouble."

"Very well." She turned back to the sink and made busy washing dishes.

"Have I done anything else to anger you?"

She half-turned back toward me. "No, I don't mean to be rude. It's very difficult to run a boardinghouse of this size all by myself. John is easily distracted. I just get tired."

"Then I'll get out of your hair so you can finish your chores." I stopped just before leaving the kitchen. "By the way, did John and Maggie talk long?"

"Nearly an hour. I had to yell three times before he would leave the parlor and restock the wood bin." She actually laughed pleasantly. "I guess that set me off this morning. Been in a sour mood all day. I apologize."

"No need—you made up for it with exceptional meals. I'll see you in the morning."

Just before I walked out of the kitchen, Mrs. Cunningham said, "Mr. Dancy, I hesitate to tell you this, but John is smitten with your niece. I think it would be a good idea to keep those two young people away from each other."

"Yes, ma'am."

I left. I was dead tired. As I climbed the stairs, I realized that I was also apprehensive. I had seen the way Mrs. Cunningham clucked around her son like a mother hen. Perhaps Maggie wanted me to get her out of the way. I had a good idea why, but I was not going to be the one to tell her father.

It took me several minutes of rummaging through Sharp's things to find the rest of the items he had requested. I shouldn't have forgotten his request. He'd probably been fuming at me all day. I stuffed everything in a burlap sack, including the newspapers and my copy of *Roughing It*. Along the way to the jail, I stopped at the Palace and bought a bottle of Jameson Irish whiskey.

At the courthouse, the watchman took my gun and carefully examined the contents of the burlap bag. Then he held out his hand for the bottle. Instead, I handed him one silver dollar, then two. Two was the magic number that got him to unlock the staircase door. Next, he did something that made me less than happy. He yelled, "George, visitor. He got a bottle and paid only half the toll."

I had two dollars out before I reached the bottom of the staircase.

After again examining the bag, George said, "Here are the rules. Ya stay against the wall. He reaches out as far as he can through the food hole for these things and to fill his cup. Ya keep that bottle away from him. I'll be watchin', like always." He handed me an enameled tin cup. "No glass. Ya got any glasses in yer pocket?"

"No, sir."

"Then go on down. Ya know where he is." He grabbed my elbow. "Hold it. There's one more rule. That bottle ain't goin' back upstairs. Wanna guess where it goes?"

"To you."

"That's right. Make sure ya don't drink more than half."

After I walked down the aisle, I found Sharp standing at the bars. It was early in the evening, so all the other cells but one were empty.

"Hi, Jeff."

"Took yer damn sweet time."

"Been busy trying to get you out of here."

"I want to be mad, but I'm too glad to see ya."

"Before I tell you about our day, let's get this stuff inside the cell."

I handed over the items I had bought or scavenged from his belongings, one at a time, with both of our arms fully outstretched. The last thing I pulled out of the bag was the bottle of Jameson. I turned it so he could read the label.

"Ah, Steve, ya do know how to say yer sorry."

Chapter 32

I arrived back at the dungeon-like cell a few minutes prior to eight the next morning to find McAllen and Maggie already there.

"Good morning," I said cheerfully.

"Not as good as I had hoped," McAllen answered. "Jeff doesn't know who bought him drinks that night."

I looked quizzically at Sharp.

"Lew Davis bought my first drink, an' then Holliday bought me one. Then Davis told me my drinks were free all night. Someone who didn't want his name out there would make good on my chalk at the end of the night."

"Damn." I turned to McAllen. "Davis or Holliday surprise you?"

"Hell, Holliday'd buy Sharp a drink just for providing entertainment, and it would be natural for Davis to buy him a drink."

I turned back to Sharp. "No idea who footed the bill for the rest of the evening?"

"Nope."

I paced around a bit before expressing my thoughts out loud. "This might kill our two-man theory. If the murderer set up a drink purchase, he could leave the saloon to steal the rifle and kill Campbell. Damn, two men working together would've been easier to find."

I turned back to Sharp. "Did you see Blanchet, Locklear, or Winslow in the Palace that night?"

"How the hell would I remember?"

For some reason, McAllen found my question amusing. Then he reached into his pocket and handed Sharp some photographs. "Recognize any of these men?"

Of course, Sharp had only met Blanchet, and McAllen had already figured that out. I noticed there were more than three.

"Where did you get those?" I asked, as Sharp examined them.

"Borrowed from the *Arizona Daily Miner*. Newspapers always have photographs of prominent citizens."

Sharp handed them back through the bars. "Naw, don't think I saw any of those people."

I reached out and took them. There were photographs of Blanchet, Locklear, and Winslow, and another of Mrs. Potter standing outside her café. There were also group photographs of men. I handed them back to McAllen. "What are the group photos?"

"Masons, territorial legislature, governor's staff." He directed the next question at Sharp. "You looked at those group photographs?"

"Yep. Kinda small of each person, but nobody jumped out."

"Now what?" I asked.

"We try to find out who's been meeting at that

old livery, but first let's start with Lew Davis at the Palace. He knows who bought those drinks."

As the three of us walked across the town square, Maggie asked, "Did Mrs. Cunningham like the chocolates?"

"As a matter of fact, she did not. But we had a long talk about you."

Her brow furrowed, but she didn't say anything.

"She was upset that you violated her house rules."

"What rules?" McAllen asked, suddenly interested.

"No single females upstairs."

McAllen frowned. "What were you doing upstairs?"

"Waking Mr. Dancy. He was sleeping the day away."

McAllen glanced between us and said, "Maybe you ought to find another place to stay. This Mrs. Cunningham sounds finicky."

"No, no," Maggie exclaimed. "She had made her rule clear, but when she wasn't looking, I snuck up anyway. She has a right to be irritated with me."

"Joseph, she's a hardworking woman, trying to run a decent house. Besides, Maggie is smitten with Mrs. Cunningham's son. If I move, she won't have an excuse to see him."

"I am not!" Maggie yelled a bit too loud.

McAllen glanced between us, and for the first

time since I had known him, he looked confused. "What's this about?"

"Maggie is becoming a young woman," I said innocently.

"Mr. Dancy, that is not true."

"I'm sorry. I misunderstood. Perhaps you would like to wait out here and play jackstones."

Considering the look she gave me, it was a good thing Maggie was unarmed. She had tried to manipulate me. Perhaps now she would think twice before dragging me into her little intrigues. McAllen appeared more confused and then uncomfortable. I had to give my friend an exit, so I said, "Relax, Joseph." I laughed to show I was kidding. "I told you Maggie was trying to play matchmaker between me and Mrs. Cunningham. I was just trying to show her what it felt like."

Now McAllen appeared angry. "She already told me she would desist. You didn't need to give her another lesson."

"Of course not. I apologize. To you and Maggie." I stopped and put a hand on Maggie's shoulder. "That was mean. I'm sorry. Can we call a truce between us?" I took my hand off her shoulder and extended it. She gave me a dubious look, then grabbed my hand and gave it two firm pumps.

As we prepared to enter the Palace saloon, four men suddenly shifted position and put themselves between us and the door. They looked hard and smelled like they hadn't had a bath in months. They all carried Winchesters. One held his rifle with one hand, pointed at the sky, and the others used both hands to hold their rifles across their chests. All of the rifles were cocked, and each man had a finger on the trigger.

"We don't wanna kill no girl. Tell her to move aside," said the scruffiest of the bunch, the one holding his rifle straight up.

"I will not," Maggie responded immediately. "If I move away, my pa will kill you, and I don't want to be responsible for your deaths."

Maggie's bold threat—so sudden and unexpected—gave me time to assess the situation. These men meant to kill us, but they weren't professional gunmen, or they would have pointed their weapons at us. Instead, they thought a cocked rifle gave them all the advantage they needed. Wrong. At least it was going to be wrong for two of the four. A man quick with a gun can draw and shoot before another man's brain can register the action. McAllen and I were quick enough to each kill one before they brought their weapons around. Getting the second gunman was a bigger challenge. It depended on how well they were concentrating on the situation. That meant I needed to kill the savviest first.

I heard McAllen say, "Steve, kill the two on your side."

McAllen didn't bluff, so I drew and put a bullet center-chest in the one who looked the most alert. As I shifted my aim to the second man, I saw his eyes go wide, but his rifle hadn't moved. Everything had slowed down. It seemed like seconds had passed. I shot my second man before his eyes finished going wide. A rifle report told me he had reflexively pulled the trigger, but the gun was pointed up. I moved my Colt in the direction of the other two. No one was left standing in front of us. I glanced toward McAllen and saw gun smoke and his Smith & Wesson swinging in the direction of my two targets. Maggie was half off her feet behind McAllen, who had grabbed her with his left hand and swung her by the scruff of her coat. Time was still slow, and it seemed forever before she hit the boardwalk and rolled off into the street.

McAllen and I kept our guns at the ready as we reached forward and grabbed each rifle. We let the hammers down on the three unfired rifles before throwing them aside. We removed their pistols and then verified whether they were dead or dying. Satisfied, we turned to check the street in both directions. A few men stared at us stunned, but the shooting had happened so fast that people hadn't yet spilled into the street.

"Holster your weapon," McAllen ordered.

I did as he said, realizing we didn't want to

appear to be a threat to drunk men charging out of saloons.

Next, McAllen said, "Keep an eye on the boardwalk."

Nothing happened at first. Then men started running out to see what had happened. A few came with guns drawn, but they had waited until the smoke had cleared. Although none of them were a danger to us, I kept my eye on them. I felt, rather than saw, McAllen pick his daughter up off the dirt street.

I heard her ask, "What happened?"

Then I heard McAllen say, "Don't look."

I knew that was the wrong thing to tell a McAllen even before I heard her exclaim, "Oh, my God!"

From behind us, Virgil Earp yelled, "Everyone put your guns away! It's all over!"

I relaxed a degree with holstered guns and the constable's presence. When I returned my attention to the bodies, Earp was checking their condition. He stood, saying, "Four bullets, four dead. Never seen that before."

"Do you know them?" McAllen asked.

"Piddling ruffians from Wickenburg. Disreputable miners pay them to jump claims. To my knowledge, they've never gone up against someone who knew how to fight. Still, hell of a feat." He looked at us both. "You'll need to go over to the courthouse. The judge will decide if you spend tonight with your friend in the basement. Go on over there now. I'll meet you in a few minutes."

"What about Maggie?" I asked.

"We'll take our daughter." It was the Schmidts, who had appeared from the other side of the courthouse.

Mary Schmidt huddled and cooed over Maggie as they led her away. I heard Maggie say, "I warned them." But instead of bravado, her voice revealed that she had been severely shaken by the experience. Carl Schmidt shook McAllen's hand and patted him on the shoulder before chasing after his wife and Maggie.

There were now at least fifty men surrounding us, looking curious rather than threatening. Doc Holliday stood a bit taller than the others on the boardwalk. When our eyes met, he gave me a slight nod. I wasn't sure I liked it. I wanted to write about men like Holliday, not join their ranks.

McAllen and I walked over to the courthouse without speaking. He started up the stairs to the second floor, so I followed. Then he took a seat on a bench outside an office. The gold lettering on the hardwood door read "Judge Matthew Carter."

"Do you know Judge Carter?" I asked.

"Met with him a few times. Reasonable man. Earp should be able to find witnesses, so I suspect he'll let us go about our business until the coroner's inquest."

"Hope so. Difficult to help Jeff if we're cell mates."

"Been thinking on that. The Schmidts aren't investigators. If Carter throws us in the hoosegow, I'll send a telegram asking for people from the Denver office."

"Why would I throw you in the hoosegow?"

The man who inquired was dressed in a nicely tailored charcoal suit, a pressed snow-white shirt, and a red cravat.

"There has been a shooting across the street," McAllen said.

"I know. I saw it. Men who threaten a gunfight in front of a young girl deserve to be killed. You'll be free to go after you answer one question."

"What's that?" McAllen asked.

"Captain, what is this charade all about? Why have you been pretending that girl is not your daughter?"

Chapter 33

The judge had overheard Maggie refer to one of us as her pa and saw that she resembled McAllen. The captain told the judge the entire story, with several references to his position as a Pinkerton team leader. I kept quiet. I had little experience in front of a magistrate, and I knew McAllen would appreciate my silence.

A little later, Constable Earp returned to say that he had found four witnesses to verify what the judge had seen with his own eyes. Carter released us but said we had to stay in town, which McAllen clarified to include the Earp home out by the sawmill.

After we left the judge's office and were in the corridor, I pulled out my Colt to reload. When I stepped back into sunlight, I wanted a fully loaded pistol in case those four had not been alone. I noticed the captain doing the same. Suddenly a door opened, and Winslow and Locklear came out with their heads bent together. When they looked up and saw us with guns drawn, they were both startled, but Winslow looked terrified. Without a by-your-leave, he dodged back into the office. Locklear didn't budge until we reholstered; then he visibly relaxed.

"I heard about the shooting. I'm glad you gents aren't hurt," Locklear said.

"So are we," I said.

"Mr. Councilman, did you recognize those gunmen?" McAllen asked.

"No, sir. 'Course, I only saw them dead, but they didn't look familiar."

"Why did Mr. Winslow run away?" McAllen asked.

"Mr. Winslow is not from Arizona. He can't quit talking about what happened in the street right outside the capitol. Then we almost bump into you two . . . with your guns drawn, for heaven's sake." He glanced at the closed door. "You frightened him. Gave me a start as well, I might add."

Captain McAllen bent at the waist. "We do apologize. Please tell Mr. Winslow we meant no harm."

McAllen took me by the elbow and led me toward the staircase. After we were outside, I asked, "Is there anything to be learned from that encounter?" I asked.

"Yes. Winslow's a coward and Locklear is a straight shooter."

We stood in the warm sun a few minutes, and McAllen told me that, although he trusted the judge to keep a confidence, there was little reason to continue the charade with Maggie. His top suspect, Jonathon Winslow, already knew, and Goldwater knew as well. There was nothing to be gained by the subterfuge. Besides, he said he agreed with Benjamin Franklin, who always said that three men could keep a secret if two were dead.

By the time we got back to the Palace, someone had already removed the bodies and scrubbed down the boardwalk. Bloody corpses outside a saloon were bad for business. Evidently, a shooting was not. The Palace was practically shoulder to shoulder as all the men in town came around to hear about what had happened. Davis was frantically serving the men lined up along the bar, when a sudden quiet came over the large room. Every eye was on McAllen and me.

As soon as Davis spotted us, he drew two beers. With one in each hand, he walked them over and slid them in front of us. "On the house," he said.

"Thank you," McAllen said. "That's exactly what we want to talk to you about . . . free drinks. Who—"

"I'm sure Mr. Brow would be fine with as many as you like."

"Not what I meant," McAllen said. "Can we talk private?"

"Now?" Davis waved an arm. "I'm busy."

"We can wait a bit," McAllen said. "Got any help comin'?"

"Two barmen from nights should be here soon. We can talk after they arrive."

McAllen lifted his mug and saluted the crowd

of men who were still watching us. "Gentlemen, drink hearty."

With that, everyone resumed talking, laughing, and tapping glasses in toast. Davis raced down the length of the bar, serving beer and whiskey as fast as he could pour. I normally drank coffee in the morning, but now I appreciated being offered something cold. The gunfight had made all of my senses keen, so my beer smelled and tasted better than ever before.

After we each had savored a few swallows, McAllen said, "Now, what's this about Maggie?"

"I'm not sure I understand." I hadn't expected that Maggie would be foremost on McAllen's mind after what we had just been through.

"Yes, you do. What was that about her being infatuated with Mrs. Cunningham's son?"

"I told you . . . I was just showing her what it felt like to have someone butt into her business."

"Bullshit. Steve, I'm not the greatest father to Maggie, but part of my job is readin' what's on people's minds. I saw the way Maggie reacted. She was rattled, and she doesn't rattle easy. So what's goin' on?"

I took another swallow of beer, but somehow it wasn't as refreshing as before. "Exactly what I said. She's infatuated with John Cunningham. She tried to get me to court his mother so she could have time alone with him."

"Damn." Now it was McAllen's turn to delay by

taking a drink. "I knew this day would come . . . but so soon." Then he gave me a harder look than he did the gunmen outside. "You keep her away from this John, you hear me?"

"I'll do what I can, but I think we'd both better work on it." After another quick swallow, I added, "Mrs. Cunningham agrees with you, by the way."

"What the hell's she got against my daughter?"

Not the reaction I expected. "Nothing. She just thinks they're both too young."

"How old is he?"

"Not sure. Sixteen, seventeen."

"Damn it, Maggie's only fourteen."

"Fifteen. She had a birthday. They come around regular, I hear."

"Damn it, I know when she has a birthday." He waved Davis over for another round. "I remember birthdays; I just can't count."

He was taking this much more seriously than I had expected. McAllen was the most solid man I had ever met. In danger, he was deadly calm; in work, coldly calculating; and in moments of relaxation, generally humorless. McAllen was a man of control, and I realized I was less concerned with what was right for Maggie than I was in sheltering my friend from a situation he couldn't control.

Davis brought over two beers, and McAllen growled, "When are those two barmen gonna get here? I got another problem to take care of."

"Maybe you ought to go look after your other problem and come back later." Davis spoke evenly. Angry customers on the other side of the bar didn't intimidate him. "It's your fault I'm so busy."

"Fault? That's an odd word to use for someone defendin' himself."

"Poor choice of words. Mr. Brow and I are grateful for the business and pleased that both of you survived this dastardly assault."

"Damn it, don't smooth-talk me." McAllen, a man who never showed emotion, looked heated. "We'll wait. What I got to ask won't take but a minute."

Davis looked at the door. "Okay. They both just came in, so let me get them started, and I'll be right with you."

After Davis left to get his barmen working, I asked McAllen, "How do we find out who met at that old barn?"

"The liveryman can tell us who regularly took out a horse at night."

"Joseph, it's less than a twenty-minute walk."

"Thought about that. The murderer had a horse the night he killed Campbell—needed it to drag the body away from the old barn. Perhaps he always used a horse."

"Could've been privately boarded."

"Someone on a ranch or workin' a mine maybe.

But all of our suspects live in town, so they probably boarded or rented their horses at one of the liveries. We need to check it out, anyway."

"What about the four dead outside?"

"First, we talk to Davis and the liverymen. Then I'll check with the judge and get permission to ride down to Wickenburg. Maggie's goin' with me."

"Wickenburg's a full day's ride, and nobody's been out of town." I didn't like McAllen being away for two or three days, especially since I suspected he just wanted to get Maggie out of Prescott.

"You and the Schmidts work Prescott. I'll give you a list before I leave. If those hired men got loose lipped, it was in Wickenburg, not here. We gotta find out who met at that barn or who hired those killers. Those are our two clues."

Davis walked over as he took off his apron, which he threw into a box behind the bar. "There's a small room in back. Grab your beers and we can talk in there."

The Palace saloon was L-shaped. We followed Davis around the end of the bar to a door. He opened it to display a small room that could accommodate about ten men in captain chairs around a rectangular table. Davis held the door open and allowed us to go in first.

"What's this room used for?" McAllen asked.

"All sorts of private meetings, including

political committees that prefer to do their work where there's a ready supply of whiskey and food. Some big deals have been struck in this room."

"No need to sit," McAllen said. "All I want to know is who paid for Jeff Sharp's drinks two nights ago."

"That would be me, Doc Holliday, and Mr. Brow."

"Mr. Brow? He bought after the first two rounds?"

"Yep. When he saw men gather round to hear about Campbell being knocked off his feet, he told me to make Mr. Sharp free for the night. Your friend was drawing in business. Just like you boys are today."

"Why did you buy Sharp that first drink?" I asked.

"Are you serious? He did what I had wanted to do for months. I was so happy to see that son of a bitch on the floor, I would've bought him more drinks if Mr. Brow hadn't stepped in."

"Why didn't you ever hit him?" McAllen asked.

Davis rubbed his chin. "I might have if I had met him away from the Palace. Mr. Brow would fire me if I just up and hit a customer in here. That man stole money from me, but I wasn't gonna allow him to take my job as well."

"Did you want him dead?" McAllen asked.

"Did I want him dead?" He rubbed his chin

again. "I sure wasn't sorry to hear that he *was* dead, but I don't recall wanting him dead before he was. What I wanted was my money, and next best would be to flatten him out." Davis smiled. "I know what you're asking, so here's a direct answer: I didn't kill Elisha Campbell."

Chapter 34

There were two liveries in Prescott, and neither could recall anyone taking a horse out on the night of the murder. The Gurley Street livery had a night watchman, but the Granite Street livery did not. McAllen doubted that anyone would risk the accusation of being a horse thief, so if the murderer took a horse from the Granite Street livery, it was probably his own. For a two-dollar tip, the liveryman agreed to get us a list of all the owners by the next morning.

Disappointed with our lack of progress, we went over to Mrs. Potter's to meet the Schmidts and Maggie for lunch. The café was crowded, but the Schmidts had already secured a table.

Carl Schmidt stood as we approached. "Good afternoon, Mr. McAllen, Mr. Dancy. We're happy to see you come out of that shooting unscathed. We were also relieved to hear the judge didn't order you held."

"Thank you, Carl, but it'll be Captain McAllen from now on. Also, from this point forward, Maggie is my daughter."

She instantly beamed.

"I'll be taking a room at the Palace, but she'll continue to stay in her room at Prescott House," McAllen added.

"Pa!"

"It would be unseemly for you to stay in my room. Remember, we've been foolin' people. They may not immediately accept the truth. Besides, it's only for sleepin'. The rest of the time, I want you with me." He looked directly at Mary Schmidt. "Soon, the two of us will be taking a short trip to Wickenburg."

"Wickenburg?" Carl Schmidt looked unnerved. "Captain, the investigation is here, and we don't have much time. I spoke with Mr. Blanchet this morning, and he's planning to start the trial next week, possibly Monday."

"Those killers came from Wickenburg. I want to find out who hired them."

Carl looked at his wife for support, but she was intently watching McAllen.

"None of the suspects have left town," Carl scratched under his arm and looked nervous. "Captain, we'd know if any of them had been gone for several days."

"They could have sent a go-between, probably for the reason you just gave. It would be suspicious if they up and left town for an extended period."

"Then let me go to Wickenburg," Carl said. "You're much more valuable here. Besides, I have a knack. People open up to me."

McAllen looked at Maggie. I knew he wanted to get her away from John Cunningham. My guess was that when he thought about it, a couple of days wouldn't make much of a difference.

"Maggie?" he asked.

"I want to stay here . . . with you."

"Wickenburg's a rough town, more of a minin' camp and way station." McAllen seemed to be considering the idea. "Do you think you can handle it?" he asked Carl Schmidt.

"I've met the town marshal. He's a competent man. If I need help, I can rely on him."

McAllen weighed the subject a while longer, before saying, "I'd want you back here in three days, before the trial starts. It's a full-day's coach ride, so you'll have only one day to investigate."

"If there's something to be found, I'll find it in a day."

McAllen looked at me. I nodded agreement.

"Okay. Carl, take tomorrow morning's stage. This afternoon, I want you to talk to the troublemakers and good-for-nothings around town. Try to discover if any of their friends left for Wickenburg or disappeared for a couple days. If you can get a name, then when you get to Wickenburg, see if they met with those four gunmen. After you return, we'll work on findin' out who hired the go-between. Understood?"

"Yes, sir. What about Mary?"

"First, let me catch you both up on what we've discovered." Between ordering and the delivery of our meal, McAllen explained to the Schmidts everything we had done since the prior afternoon. At the end, he said, "Mary, I want you to ride around town and look for private stables. If you see any, find out whose horses are boarded there. It may not be just the homeowner's. People with barns take in other animals to make extra cash."

"That sounds like a pleasant afternoon," she said. "Horseback riding and snooping. Two things I love."

"We have another problem," Carl said. "Blanchet isn't going to bring up the stock swindles, so Winslow is protected through the prosecution phase. But Castle says he intends to make the swindles a key defense issue and refuses to keep Jonathon Winslow's name out of the proceedings. Worse, the editor over at the *Arizona Daily Miner* insists that he's going to publish the entire trial transcript."

Evidently, Carl was unaware that Winslow was McAllen's primary suspect, and that the captain had sought the Pinkerton reengagement so he could stay close to Winslow. Then I stopped thinking along this line. Captain McAllen was the most reputable man I had ever met. If his agency had been engaged to protect Winslow's reputation, he would fulfill the contract—unless he developed proof that Winslow was the guilty party.

"What do you suggest, Carl?"

"Sharp is your friend. Ask him to convince Castle he should leave our client out of this unless hard evidence is discovered."

McAllen looked uncertain. I could guess what

was going through his mind. Did he have greater allegiance to his employer or his friend? In the end, he just said, "I'll think about it."

It was an awkward moment, but Maggie helped us get past it by asking her father, "What are we going to do?"

"Right after lunch, Carl's gonna introduce us to the editor of the *Arizona Daily Miner*."

"He won't change his mind about printing the transcript," Carl said.

"I don't intend to try. At least, not today. I'm gonna give him an exclusive story about the four of us. The three Pinkertons and my daughter."

"Why, for God's sake?" Carl asked.

"I want people to know that Maggie is my daughter, and a personal ad doesn't seem like the correct way to do it. Second, we have a criminal to catch, and laying the Pinkerton National Detective Agency on the table might make the culprit nervous and cause him to make a mistake. Third, it's a damn good story, and the editor will be beholden to me."

"You can't tell him that the Winslow family hired us."

"No. A Mr. Steven Dancy of New York City hired us to chase Campbell."

I had to smile. "Me?"

"You were defrauded in New York and hired us to track down this scoundrel. Keeps the Winslows out and accounts for all of us being here."

"You'll tell Castle, I hope. He already believes that I'm a violent, wronged man, out for revenge."

"Of course." The closed-mouth smile told me he'd enjoy seeing me twist in the wind a bit.

I signaled the waitress over because I wasn't leaving without a piece of Mrs. Potter's lemon cake. After she left, I said, "Everyone has an assignment but me."

"I want you to see Castle. Tell him everything. I not only want him informed, I want to know what he sees in all of this. Any ideas or reservations. Then find out how he intends to defend Sharp."

"No difficulties with most of that, but I believe Castle keeps his courtroom strategy close to the vest."

"Then ask him what we can do to help. Hell, we're the best detective agency in the world. If he relies solely on legal maneuvers, Sharp may end up stretching a rope."

I nodded agreement but worried that Castle was more comfortable using legal maneuvers than catching bad men.

"Do you want to meet up this evening?" Carl asked.

McAllen gave Carl Schmidt a flat look. "Six o'clock at the Palace. Now, if you'll excuse us, I need to talk to Steve alone. Carl, I'll meet you outside, and we can walk over to the newspaper office. Mary, you might as well go change into your riding clothes."

The Schmidts stood and looked uncomfortable at being excluded from our conversation, but they left the café without protest.

I waited. I waited a long time because McAllen just sat there looking off into the distance. Suddenly, he grabbed his fork and took a bite of my cake. Maggie had ordered a piece of cake as well, but she had already finished hers.

"Pretty good." McAllen waved at a waitress until he got her attention, then pointed at my cake, and then himself. She nodded to let him know she understood the pantomime. McAllen remained silent until he was served and had taken two bites. Then he shoved the plate over to Maggie, who dug into the rest of the slice with relish.

"Instead of making progress, we're going backward," he said.

"What do you mean?"

"He means we haven't eliminated any of our suspects," Maggie said. "In fact, we haven't even elevated one or two as prime suspects."

McAllen looked proud of his daughter's pronouncements. "Correct, and now we have two more."

"Two more?" Maggie and I spoke almost together.

"The Schmidts."

"Did I miss something?" I asked.

"You did," Maggie said, excited. "Carl doesn't go anywhere or do anything without Mary. And he was too quick to volunteer to run down to Wickenburg. Especially since he isn't an investigator. He's half of a decoy team that lures in crooks." She glanced at her father for confirmation. "He was scared what Pa would find there."

Unbelievably, McAllen looked prouder. "Maggie has it exactly right. I've known those two for years. That was odd behavior for both of them. So odd that I don't trust them to find the go-between. Later this afternoon, Maggie and I will see Virgil Earp. He'll know the ne'er-do-wells in town."

"What could be the motive?" I asked.

"Money," Maggie shot back immediately. "Those two love money. But it would have to be a lot of money for them to go this far. Enough money for a lifetime of leisure."

"Yep," McAllen said. "Those two have the highest expenses of any agents in the entire nation. I'm constantly trading telegrams with the Washington office to justify their expenses."

The idea of big money was unsettling, because it might mean that they had taken possession of the stock certificate. I decided to go in another direction. "How was it odd behavior for Mary?" I asked.

"Mary is the senior partner, both officially and by nature. She outranks Carl, and she jealously guards her position. She never raised an eyebrow when he volunteered to run off to a mining camp for three days."

"Wait. If they hired those men, that means they tried to have you killed."

McAllen gave me another of his rare closed-mouth smiles. "That irritated me a bit, but I got riled when I remembered they also meant to kill you."

I smiled back because I knew he was joking. "Thank you for the concern, but it may have been only you. I just happened to be standing next to you. At times, you can be a dangerous man to hang around."

McAllen turned serious. "No. The Schmidts are careful . . . planners. If they had wanted only me, they would have waited until I was alone." He gave me a long, flat look before asking, "Steve, why would Campbell's murderer want you dead?"

Chapter 35

The mood at the table was tense. McAllen stared at me, and his daughter mimicked his behavior. I stared back, because many things were going through my mind, and I didn't like the conclusions I was drawing. The Schmidts were trying to expose a fraud by Campbell. Campbell had been notified that the New York City investigation had been dropped. He wanted to go home, but he was broke. He would have gone for the Schmidts' bait. Did they somehow stumble upon the fact that he possessed a real stock certificate? The Schmidts had to be savvy about investments as part of their work, and they would have instantly known the value of shares in the company that owned Edison's inventions.

But the Schmidts were Pinkertons. They liked the chase. They may have lived well on client money, but they weren't looking for a life of leisure. They enjoyed the game far too much. Just like me, they had left the East for the adventure and novelty of the frontier. And if they had stolen the stock, why would they want McAllen or me dead? That made no sense. If a few months from now they showed up in New York City with the certificate, what could either of us do about it with no evidence of wrongdoing? Unless we found something damning, there was no way they could be extradited back to the territory. Could there be another reason they would fear McAllen going to Wickenburg? Something completely unrelated?

In the last few days, they had had many opportunities to kill me. Why wait and risk going after both McAllen and me at the same time? Then I felt a chill. I remembered the supposed highwayman on the night of my return from Virgil Earp's.

I had never told McAllen about the Edison Electric Light Company. Why was I keeping this secret? I had told Castle. Then a thought struck me. The Schmidts had warned Castle not to involve Winslow in his defense case for Sharp. Could he have told them about the certificate? If he had, the Schmidts discovered that someone else knew about Campbell's possession of the certificate. They might view me as a threat, as someone who could ascribe motive for them to kill Campbell. Then I shook off the thought, because if these men came from Wickenburg, the arrangements would have taken days.

I finally spoke. "Jeff and I came to Prescott to get a stock certificate from Elisha Campbell." With that opening, I told the whole story. At first, McAllen looked intrigued and then increasingly angry.

"Damn it, Steve, you've done this to me before.

You don't share your plans." The voice was quiet, scary quiet.

"This isn't a plan. I don't see a connection to Campbell's murder. Listen, I didn't want to start a gold rush. If word got out, people would tear this town apart looking for that piece of paper."

"No connection? You tell me this "piece of paper" could be extremely valuable, but you see no connection. You aren't that dumb, Steve." He waved his arm. "Now, you listen, these people don't believe electricity can be harnessed. Hell, I'm not sure I do. Puttin' lightnin' down a mineshaft? Bullshit. Now, what's the real reason you didn't tell me?"

"Because I wanted to find the certificate first. The papers at Castle's office say that certificate has no value, but people unaware of all the facts may think it's worth a lot of money. All I need to do is destroy it to avoid court challenges. I've been planning this for months. It's business. I don't believe it has anything to do with Campbell's murder. On our first day, Jeff slugged and threatened Campbell, and then he was framed that very same night. Somebody already pissed as hell took advantage of an opportunity."

McAllen stared at me for a long moment before saying, "Did it ever occur to you that the murderer got hold of that certificate and used Sharp as a way to get rid of Campbell? The killer didn't know you knew about the damn thing. The

Schmidts are experts at turning an incident like Sharp's threat to their advantage. Even if it was a coincidence, it connects the stock certificate and the murder."

"Did it occur to you that those men were dumb as timber? We both have reputations of being good with a gun, yet they came at us like we were a couple of dry goods clerks. They approached when we were with Maggie and then warned us by telling her to step aside."

"What are you suggesting?"

"Not to jump onto the Schmidts too fast. They're smarter than that."

"They're out of their element. They do things with finesse, not brutality."

"You make my point," I replied.

McAllen snapped his coffee mug down with more force than necessary. "After you talk to Castle, find us at the newspaper office," McAllen said. "I want to know what you learn. All of it."

"I presume you don't want me to tell you in front of the editor."

"Steve, I'm not in the mood for your sarcasm."

"Yes, sir." Before he could respond, I scurried out of the café.

Something didn't feel right. If the Schmidts had the real stock certificate, how much could they gain by my being dead? They would still need to sue to challenge ownership of the shares. I didn't see how my being alive or dead would affect their chances of prevailing in court. More important, what could they possibly gain by killing McAllen? Neither of us had the slightest evidence that pointed to the Schmidts, and at the moment, Sharp would likely be convicted for the murder. The only clue we had that the Schmidts might be involved was Carl's volunteering to travel to Wickenburg. Weak. As I entered the building where Castle kept his office, I reminded myself that there was one other indicator of the Schmidts' guilt—McAllen's instincts. Betting against McAllen was never a good idea.

When Castle answered my knock, he didn't look any more pleased to see me than he had on my previous visits. He immediately returned to one of his leather chairs and tossed aside some handwritten documents. I sat opposite him.

"You confirmed your tendency for violence this morning."

"Four bad men tried to kill me and a Pinkerton officer. We defended ourselves."

"Very skillfully, I hear. I understand none of the four got off a single shot."

"My preferred outcome in a gunfight."

Castle lit a cigar while striving to appear disinterested. "Why are you here?"

"You do remember that I'm a friend of your client."

"I've suggested to him that he needs better friends."

"It must have disappointed you when he declined."

For the next long moment, we sat in our opposing leather chairs, daring each other to blink. I won.

Castle said, "I repeat, why are you here?"

Without preamble, I took Castle through all of our investigations since I had last seen him, omitting mention of the Schmidts. By the time I finished, his cigar was half smoked, and his posture had become more relaxed. He seemed genuinely interested. At the end, I asked if he could add any insights to what we had found out.

"Nothing initially comes to mind. That old barn has been abandoned for about two years. To my knowledge, only kids go there, especially at night. I think you're on the wrong track, pursuing this horse idea. It's not far enough to warrant saddling a horse. By the way, did you see Campbell standing up on his own two feet?"

"Uh, yes. Before Sharp hit him. Why?"

"Well, I can assure you, it would not be difficult for Mr. Sharp to send him down with a single punch. The man was skinny as a rail and probably only about five foot five or six. A strong man could have used that halter to manually pull the body away from the barn."

"That doesn't bode well for Jeff."

"No, he's a large man. So is Lew Davis. The rest of your suspects are of normal stature. Except for yourself, of course. You're not thick like Mr. Sharp, but you're tall and appear strong."

"Still on your list, am I?"

He laughed. "Not really. At least, not at the moment. You received a strong character reference from my client."

"Then whom do you suspect?"

"Lew Davis is capable of this type of action, but he's a gambler, and he's lost more in a bad night at the tables than Campbell ever took from him. I don't see him holding a grudge for several months. Like all gamblers, he would just move on. Jonathon Winslow would think it, want to do it, but in the end probably doesn't have the nerve. He'd also be afraid to hire someone because of blackmail. Herb—"

"What about Winslow's parents in Boston? The wealthy have long arms. They could have hired someone to do the deed."

"Who would have been their agent to hire someone? Murderers don't advertise in the newspaper. I don't believe they would ask their son."

I immediately realized that the Schmidts were the only possibility. Could they have accepted a clandestine fee to take care of the problem? Damn. The possibility that they could be doing side work for Winslow's parents meant that they might be involved independent of the stock certificate. This new suspicion made more sense, especially if they feared that McAllen was going to discover their unauthorized activities.

"You met with the Schmidts," I said. "Was that today?"

"Yesterday."

"What did they want?"

"Do you want me to tell others about our conversations?"

"The Schmidts are agents of the Pinkerton Detective Agency."

The information was not a surprise, so I continued.

"Their supervisor is Captain Joseph McAllen, the man in the gunfight with me this morning. They were in Prescott to investigate Campbell. You'll be able to read all about it in tomorrow's newspaper, but you already know the highlights from Mr. Goldwater."

"My conversations are confidential, whether with a visitor to this office or a lodge brother."

"Fine. All I want to know is if you told the Schmidts about Campbell holding a stock certificate for the Edison Electric Light Company. The real company."

"I just told you, I don't discuss my conversations with others."

"I'm sorry. I need a yes or no."

"No."

He was on the verge of throwing me out of his office, so I said, "I'm sorry to have interrupted you before. What were you going to say about Herb Locklear?"

"I was going to say that Herb is too much of a gentleman to do such a grotesque deed or deal with the type of element that would."

"Morris Goldwater shares your high opinion."

"We're all lodge brothers."

"Are Masons incapable of wrongdoing?"

"I meant that both Morris and I know Locklear. He's not the vengeful type."

"I asked who you suspected. So far you've told me who you don't suspect."

"You're too impatient. Lawyers have a tendency to go after a thing sideways. May I continue?"

"Yes. Please tell me who else you don't suspect."

"Young man, sarcasm is not an admirable trait."

"I apologize. Proceed."

He puffed his cigar a moment to show he was in control. "Since you told me about the body being moved, I have mentally eliminated the women, but they were never high on my list anyway."

"That leaves only George Blanchet."

Castle took one more puff and then stubbed out the cigar. "Let me ask you a question. When a man of bad character is murdered, is it usually his victim or his partner that does the deed?"

"I don't know. I've never encountered a murder of this sort before."

"Unfortunately, I have. For the most part, victims remain victims. Scoundrels that escape the law for any period of time usually find themselves dead at the hands of one of their own. Perhaps it's God's way of keeping bad men from overrunning us all."

I considered what he had said and then asked the obvious question. "What did you find that tied Blanchet and Campbell together as partners?"

"Before Campbell's arrival, George Blanchet had a very large unpaid account at Goldwater's. He has not only paid it in full but has also bought a new wardrobe."

"Can you tie the newfound cash to the timing of the swindles?"

"Practically to the day."

Chapter 36

Instead of going directly to the newspaper office, I decided to walk around the courthouse square to think. Castle was unconcerned that he had no hard evidence against Blanchet. He needed only to establish reasonable doubt. He wouldn't tell me exactly how he would use this information, but had said that he wouldn't make a motion to have Blanchet disqualified as prosecutor. I could guess the rest. He would let the trial go through the prosecution phase, then lay the series of swindles in front of the jury. Next, he'd show that the prosecutor was Campbell's partner in these swindles. I could imagine the gasp from the courtroom when Castle called the prosecutor as a witness for the defense. Castle was only concerned with getting an acquittal for his client, and he had enough to achieve this goal. My friend would be free, but was that enough? Not for me. After all this turmoil, I wanted the real murderer brought to trial.

But who really murdered Campbell? Blanchet or the Schmidts? They were all my prime suspects. So which? I still thought the barn was the key. Could Blanchet or the Schmidts be tied to the abandoned livery?

I was so lost in my thoughts that before I knew it, I had twice made the circuit around the square.

Suddenly, I had an idea and charged into the courthouse. I asked directions from the watchman in the foyer and easily found County Records in another part of the basement. It cost me fifty cents and ten minutes to get the answer to my question. In another couple of minutes, I was at the newspaper office.

The McAllens were having a very cheerful conversation with the editor of the *Arizona Daily Miner*. It didn't take but a minute to see that Maggie had thoroughly charmed the heavily bearded man behind the desk. After the captain introduced me, I leaned against the back wall.

"Well, young lady, are you going to marry a Pinkerton agent one day?"

"Never. It would be unfair, because I would always be measuring him against my father, a standard no man could reach." Maggie smiled engagingly. "Perhaps I'll marry a Wells Fargo agent."

That got a good laugh from the editor. I realized I was laughing as well. It seemed that Maggie had learned a lot from Mrs. Schmidt. It made me hope that Blanchet was the guilty party. The thought reminded me that I wanted to talk to McAllen privately.

After clearing my throat, I said, "Captain, I was wondering if I could have a word?"

McAllen nodded and then tried unsuccessfully to smile. "Do you have any further questions?"

The editor stood up behind his desk and extended his hand. "No, I think I have enough. If a question comes up, I'll find you. Right now, I'd better get busy writing this article, or I'll miss the morning edition."

After everyone, including Maggie, shook again, we left the office. Once outside, McAllen pulled up on the boardwalk and looked in both directions for eavesdroppers before saying, "You have an answer to my question?"

"Not one you'll like." I paused to take a full breath. "I can see no reason that the Schmidts would want me dead. On the other hand, I discovered two bits of information that raise Blanchet to the top of my list." When McAllen merely continued to stare at me, I added, "Mac Castle has indications that Campbell and Blanchet were partners in all of the swindles. Also . . . George Blanchet was the legal owner of that old barn and the property around it. A month ago, he sold the property to Elisha Campbell. That means they're both connected to that old livery."

"Why would Campbell buy property in Prescott?" McAllen asked.

"I believe it was meant to put a legitimate shroud around the money that Campbell gave to Blanchet. Castle says it's the money transfers that tie Blanchet and Campbell together. Blanchet's a lawyer. It's his kind of solution to disguise the source of his newfound wealth."

"That's interesting, Steve, but it doesn't help with my two questions. Why would Campbell's murderer want you dead, and why is Carl scared of what I might find in Wickenburg?"

"I have a better question for you. Why would the Schmidts want their supervisor dead?" I paused a beat. "Do you have evidence implicating the Schmidts that I'm unaware of?"

McAllen looked ready to explode but said only, "Maggie?" in a quiet voice.

"Two weeks before Campbell's murder, I walked with Mrs. Schmidt to the telegraph office. She made me stand outside on the boardwalk while she collected two messages. Later, when we were changing to go riding with Pa, the telegrams fell out of her dress pocket. I picked them up, and she snatched them out of my hands like they were hot coals. She yelled at me to never snoop into her affairs." Maggie lifted her chin. "I wasn't snooping. I was just picking up some dropped papers. There was no reason for her to show temper with me."

I looked at McAllen, knowing what was coming next.

"After Maggie told me this, I made a visit to Western Union. With a little persuasion, I was told one of the telegrams came from Denver and the other from Boston. The first, of course, was from our own office. The second message was a single word: *Proceed*."

"Did you ask about any other telegrams?"

"No prior telegrams from Boston, but they might have used the mail. It's more secure and you can write long letters."

"Joseph, they were under contract to the Winslows. *Proceed* could mean any number of things. Besides, it doesn't answer why they would want you killed."

"Because after I left, Mary bribed the Western Union man to find out what I was doing in the office. She discovered that I had been asking questions about her." McAllen sounded very frustrated with my stubbornness. "To please you, let me rephrase the question: Why did someone want us both killed?"

"I don't—"

Maybe I did have an idea. What were we doing? McAllen and I were working to get our friend out of jail. If Sharp ended up convicted, the matter would fade away, but if we turned up enough evidence to set him free, the whole affair would be investigated anew.

"They don't want us to exonerate their scapegoat."

McAllen's expression looked like that of a schoolmaster who had finally gotten a dunderheaded student to correctly answer a question. "We're a thorn in their side. I told you there were no prior telegraphs, but there was a telegraph from Boston afterwards. It said, *Ten additional if convicted*. I took it to mean the Winslows would pay Blanchet ten thousand dollars if Sharp was convicted. Ten thousand dollars makes us a very big thorn."

I took my time responding. Finally, I said, "Earlier, I was trying to figure out if it was Blanchet or the Schmidts. I think I know the answer. It's got to be Blanchet *and* Carl Schmidt. They must be working together."

"What makes you think so?" McAllen asked.

I could tell by his tone of voice that he thought so as well, but wanted to hear my reasoning. "I know how rich people think, and Jonathon's parents would have done everything they could to protect their son. So my guess is that they sought out political and legal protection, as well as Pinkerton detective services. With his connections with the governor, Blanchet would be a natural for political protection. In fact, Blanchet could have been the one who had extensive communication with the Winslows back in Boston. After gaining some confidence, the Winslows could have subtly suggested a more permanent solution. At some point, Blanchet discovered that the Schmidts were Pinkertons—probably from Jonathon because he can't keep a secret. Blanchet isn't dumb. He knew he'd have a hard time getting away with the murder with two Pinkerton agents close by. He could have approached the Schmidts, got their measure, and eventually broached a deal with them."

"I heard from Omaha. Blanchet's an escaped prisoner," McAllen said. "He was convicted of extortion, bribery, and attempted murder in Omaha. Different name, of course, but it's him. That kind of information wouldn't be missed by an operator like Campbell, and I suspect he was threatening Blanchet with it. That means Blanchet might have a motive beyond being hired by the Winslows."

I walked to the end of the building and then turned around. "All of this makes sense, except for one thing. Why would the Schmidts get involved in murder with Blanchet as an accomplice? Don't tell me it's for the money. I may not know them well, but I've watched them enough to know they love their work, live well on client money, and disdain men like Blanchet. It's not their nature." When McAllen's expression didn't change, I added, "Joseph, you've entrusted your daughter to this couple twice."

"They're not afraid of working with Blanchet. They surely know he's an escaped prisoner with a thousand-dollar reward on his head. What you say sounds logical, but it's emotion. Four men tried to kill us. There's no chance the attack was not connected to this case. The killers came from Wickenburg. Mary and Carl don't want me to go there. What are they afraid I'll find?"

"Something feels wrong," I said.

The three of us stood there looking at the street traffic.

"I know how to find out," Maggie said.

"How?" McAllen asked his daughter.

"Mr. Dancy should leave for Wickenburg first thing in the morning. He can be there before tomorrow's stage arrives and follow Mr. Schmidt."

"I'm not a detective. Besides, Wickenburg is small; he'd be sure to spot me."

"You can wear a disguise." Maggie was getting excited.

"Not necessary," McAllen said. "If Carl investigates, he'll see the marshal and visit all the saloons. But he won't. If he hired those killers, he'll stay around the hotel, catch the next day's stage back to Prescott, and then give me some cock-and-bull story when he gets back. You only need to see if he stays put or really investigates. The hotel's two front rooms have windows facing onto the town. If you can't get one of those, bribe the innkeeper to knock on your door if Carl leaves the hotel. Observe him from the lobby window."

"How far?" I asked.

"Sixty miles. You'll need to leave before light. That stage moves fast and picks up fresh horses in Yarnell, so it'll be a hard ride."

"The judge?"

"Taken care of. There will be no inquest. Virg Earp gathered up a few more witnesses, and the judge ruled it self-defense."

A swift ride on Liberty might be fun, but I wasn't confident about pretending to be a detective. It seemed like Schmidt would easily spot me. Even if I got one of the front rooms, I'd need to bribe the innkeeper to bring me food and drink. I hated to use chamber pots but would have no choice if I was stuck in the room.

McAllen's voice intruded on my thoughts. "After Carl leaves, see the marshal and learn what you can about those killers."

"Do you want me to talk to other people in town?"

"Only if you can't learn anything from the marshal."

"What am I trying to find out?"

"Who hired those men."

Chapter 37

I wanted get well ahead of the stage, so I left before dawn. At first, I rode slowly by nascent light. Once I could see clearly, I let Liberty run at his own pace, which was pretty quick. Chestnut, my previous horse, could outrun any horse for distance but wasn't speedy. Liberty ran as smooth as oiled pistons in a steam engine. Except that he wasn't an engine, and we had a long trip ahead of us, so after an hour I dismounted and walked alongside him so he could rest.

Wickenburg was another mining camp, only this time it was gold instead of silver. I had learned about Wickenburg from Comstock miners while I was still in Carson City. Henry Wickenburg had discovered gold in the area and named his claim the Vulture Mine, and the town grew up as a supply center twelve miles away. It was a remote camp in a young territory. Only nine years previously, Henry Loring and his companions were brutally slain by Indians in what came to be known as the Wickenburg Massacre. As I remounted Liberty, I hoped the area was more civilized today.

About mid-morning I arrived in Yarnell. It was no more than a stage stop, with a scattering of rough-hewn buildings. I paid a boy to water, groom, and feed Liberty while I did the same for myself. Outside the stage line building, I found a pump delivering surprisingly cool water that felt refreshing in my mouth and on my face. The operator for the stop appeared to be in his mid-twenties and talkative. He served up endless coffee, biscuits, and baconed beans for four bits. I learned I was nearly two hours ahead of the stage but ate hurriedly anyway. I wanted to arrive in Wickenburg with enough time to survey the town before having to hide in my room.

The morning had been cold, but about noon I pulled off my heavy coat and tied it across my saddlebags. Despite my remaining four layers, the air felt refreshingly crisp and clean as I let Liberty race down the easy slope. We were making exceptional time. The road was really two parallel ruts carved by the hoofs and wheels of countless stages, but all I had to do was pick one and give Liberty free rein. About four in the afternoon, I saw a cluster of buildings nestled between small rises barren of anything taller than a man's waist. I had descended three thousand feet. Prescott had been green, but now everything was desert brown. All I could see was dirt, rock, and sagebrush, with a scattering of cacti.

There wasn't much to Wickenburg. The biggest building was the hotel, and it looked like a strong gust would blow its wood planks around the surrounding hills. As usual, I found the livery at the edge of town, where the odor wouldn't overwhelm the already smelly residents. I had begun to think of the ramshackle camp as penniless until the liveryman insisted on two dollars to board Liberty for a day. I forgot that mining camps made New York City appear reasonably priced.

The hotel wasn't any better on the inside. Everything was unfinished. The floors were worn smooth by boot leather along general pathways, but the outside edges had never seen a lick of sandpaper or even a plane. The walls were raw lumber, the burlap curtains hung lopsided, and the lobby furniture was beaten and threadbare. I had expected more, because the Vulture Mine had been producing at high yields for over fifteen years. A grisly man behind a makeshift counter was lost in a book and didn't look up until I spoke.

"A room, please."

"How long?"

"One night."

"Two dollars . . . in advance."

The same price as Liberty, except my horse got food and drink too.

"Do you have a front room available?"

"All our rooms is available 'cuz the stage ain't arrived yet. But a front room'll cost you four dollars."

Since I had no choice, I laid four silver certificates on the counter. Now I understood the shoddy appearance. Stage stops were notoriously bad. The stage delivered bone-weary passengers who just wanted a quick meal and a bed. Innkeepers never expected to see them again. I had previously stayed in one only in inclement weather. I found my bedroll more comfortable, a can of beans more digestible, and dirt cleaner.

"I'll put ya in room twelve, top of stairs to the front. Recently done up nice." He slid a key across the counter. "Entertainment?"

"Excuse me?"

He pointed at a framed photograph behind him on the wall. "Either one, ten dollars. She can be in your room in ten minutes."

The photograph showed two women in dresses that would be appropriate for Easter services. They were young and pretty—very young and demurely pretty. They would have to be pretty to charge ten dollars.

Since I hadn't responded, the innkeeper said, "Men come from all over the territory for a taste of one of those." I must have looked puzzled because he added, "The men who ask for room twelve usually partake."

I grabbed the key. "Thank you, just the room."

At the top of the stairs was a central hall with the same unfinished look. I found my room and opened the door to a surprise: It was nice. The clean yellow bed cover showed no visible lumps, the dark brown Roman shades looked like they would keep the morning light out, and the furniture looked substantial and new. I immediately went over to the window and was pleased that I could see most of the small town. Perfect.

I had almost two hours before the stage arrived, so I walked around Wickenburg. I discovered that the only buildings outside my hotel view were private homes. I ate a meal and drank beer in one saloon and peeked inside two others. They were all fairly empty at this time of day. I spotted the tiny marshal's office next to the livery. Most of my time was spent in the sole general store. I bought a saw, hardtack, jerky, hard candy, a tin cup, and a used set of *Gulliver's Travels* by Jonathan Swift. I had read the four books before but had no books with me, so I considered them a great find. Returning to the hotel, I had one more task before the stage arrived. I ran up to my room, grabbed the pitcher of water, and took it outside. I poured it out and then rinsed it thoroughly at the town pump before refilling it. I wasn't sure the water had been done up as recently as the room.

I bought a bucket of cool beer and carried it along with the fresh water to my room. When I got back, I adjusted the Roman shades down to four inches above the sill. Pulling a chair over, I tested the view. As I had suspected, the chair was too high. I was staring right into the dark brown material. I flipped the chair upside down and sawed about four inches off the legs. Now it was perfect. Except the window wouldn't open. My plan had been to lie on the bed reading until I heard the ruckus of the arriving stage through the open window.

I poured beer into my new tin cup and contemplated the window. It had been painted shut. In about fifteen minutes, I had the window open by using my knife to scratch through the paint. Just as I was congratulating myself, I heard the stage. Damn.

The stage pulled directly below my window. Schmidt was the last passenger to disembark. Clutching a small valise, he didn't wait for any bags to be thrown down from the top of the stage. After he disappeared inside the hotel, I used the opportunity to pour another cup of beer and then settled onto my truncated chair to watch the other passengers collect their belongings and disappear into the hotel as well. After the driver climbed back aboard and drove off, dusk settled over the brown hills and clapboard buildings. The street grew quiet, but I heard muffled voices through the floorboards as passengers jostled for room.

Now was the part I dreaded. In the dark, I might not recognize Schmidt. Suddenly, I saw a spill of light as a lantern was lit at the front desk. I'd have to watch carefully, because the light was weak and didn't extend beyond the narrow boardwalk.

Three hours later, I was sure Schmidt had either

decided to stay in his room or do his drinking in the small bar in the lobby. Besides, if he went out this late, I'd have no idea whether he was investigating or carousing. Jonathan Swift beckoned, so I went to bed.

I rose early. I couldn't leave the room, so I had hardtack and water for breakfast as I sat in my Lilliputian chair, watching the street. About nine o'clock, Schmidt left the hotel and walked over to the general store. He was in there almost an hour. Next he visited the livery. I hoped he didn't nose around the stalls, but the only time he had seen Liberty was the first time we had ridden out to meet McAllen. Since Schmidt didn't seem to care about horseflesh, I didn't worry too much. After no more than ten minutes, he walked over to the marshal's office. Schmidt stayed inside for a while, and then he and someone I assumed was the marshal walked over to one of the three saloons. When the two of them came out, they proceeded directly to another saloon. There was no doubt about it, Schmidt was investigating. He was talking to all the business owners, and he had sought the marshal's help. I was more relieved than I had expected. Blanchet was our man.

In another hour, Schmidt and the marshal had completed the rounds. I watched as they energetically shook hands, and Schmidt lazily walked back across the street to the hotel. I was feeling good, when I saw something that gave me pause. It was quick, but I was sure I saw Schmidt glance up at my window. I was sitting well back in the shadows, so I didn't believe he saw me, but I had seen a tiny smirk on his face. Damn.

Chapter 38

The next morning, I stayed cooped up in my room until Schmidt boarded the stage, and I saw it leave. I bounded down the stairs while the sound of the driver's snapping whip still reverberated in the cool morning air. I was hungry and desperately needed a cup of hot coffee.

The innkeeper was still slouching behind his counter. "Where can I get a good breakfast?"

He pointed across the room. "Right there."

"I want a better meal than you serve the stage passengers. Where do the locals eat?"

He pointed across the room. "Right there. Food's better after the stage departs. Folks'll get here soon."

"Did any of the passengers ask about me?"

"Who're you?"

This was frustrating. "Do you remember the last man off yesterday's stage, a sharply dressed gent?"

"What if I do?"

Obviously, the man was asking me to jog his memory. I slid a silver dollar across the counter. He didn't even look at it, so I took out a five-dollar certificate, folded it neatly and laid it on the counter. When I went to slide the silver dollar back, the innkeeper said, "Leave it."

"How's your memory now."

" 'Bout like it was. What'd you want to know?"

"Do you remember him?"

"I do."

"What did he say when he first came to the counter?"

"Howdy."

"What next?"

He scratched his head like it was a difficult question. Before he answered, he put the six dollars in his vest pocket. "Asked for the room you was in."

That told me a lot. "What happened after you told him it was taken?"

He scratched his head again and then laid both hands flat on the counter.

"No more money," I said as I also laid both of my hands flat on the counter and stared across at him.

Eventually, he said, "Asked when you arrived. What kind a' horse you had."

"Next."

"Asked how you looked."

"And?"

"Asked how long you was stayin'."

"And?"

"And nothing." This time he scratched more private parts. "At least nothing for six dollars."

My frustration grew to anger. Reminding myself to remain calm, I pulled out my wallet and threw another five dollars onto the counter. It seemed to disappear faster than I could draw my gun.

"He asked about your doin's in town. I told him you bought some goods, ate, and drank a bit. Said I heard you sawin'. If you harmed something in that room, it'll be an added charge."

"Anything else?"

"Naw. Coffee?"

"How much?"

"Two bits. Full breakfast six bits. Dollar total."

"You have a customer."

He smiled for the first time. "Had one for several minutes."

I sat at one of the rough plank tables and had no sooner received a mug of coffee when several men entered the hotel and took seats around me. As the minutes went by, a few couples came in as well. Everyone knew each other. The innkeeper had not lied. The locals came here for breakfast.

A man I wished looked cleaner plopped a plate down in front of me. It smelled great and looked appetizing. There were fried eggs with dark yellow yolks; thick, crispy bacon; beans; and steaming biscuits. The previous day, I hadn't eaten a solid meal, so I dug in with gusto.

After I wolfed down the entire plate, a thin, middle-aged man came in wearing a badge. I stood. "Marshal, may I buy you breakfast?"

He looked at me oddly and then asked, "Mr. Steve Dancy?"

"Yes, sir."

He took a seat across from me. Before he could scoot his chair up to the table, the not-so-clean cook placed a steaming cup of coffee in front of him. He extended his hand. "Marshal Lewis."

After shaking, I said, "Did Captain McAllen wire you about my coming to Wickenburg?"

"No. Carl Schmidt told me to expect you at breakfast this morning."

I shook off the surprise. But this confirmed that he had glanced up at my room yesterday. If Schmidt knew I was watching him, I learned nothing except that he was a better detective than me. He either came down here to do an honest investigation, or he mimicked one for my benefit.

"Good. Carl and I are working together on this."

"Why'd you hole up in your room yesterday?"

"What did Carl tell you?"

"Nothing. He laughed and said you'd explain."

I tried to act embarrassed. "I couldn't be far from a chamber pot. He thought it was funny."

"Yep. Had that problem. Ain't funny."

"I presume Carl told you that two days ago, four men stopped McAllen and me on the street and tried to gun us down. Constable Earp said they came from Wickenburg."

"Mr. Schmidt only saw the men dead . . . and he said he didn't take a good look. What'd they look like?"

"Rough. About normal height and stout. Not bearded so much as unshaven. In need of haircuts. One wore a plaid wool coat, the other three sheepskin. All carried Winchester '73 carbines."

"Sounds like the Cody bunch, just like I told the other gent. Two brothers and a couple friends. Suspected of killing on occasion, but mostly they just scare people off claims. If they got dead in Prescott, they won't be missed 'round here."

The marshal sipped his coffee as the cook laid a breakfast plate in front of him. Without my asking, the cook placed a plate of hotcakes in front of me. I was going to say I was full, but they looked too good to turn back.

As we began eating again, I said, "We're here to find out who hired them."

"No telling. Stage comes and goes, and it's always filled with strangers."

"Would they be expensive?"

"Those boys? Hell, no. Might even do it for the fun of it." The marshal cut a big piece of fried egg with his fork edge and laid it on top of the biscuit he held in his other hand. He bit it quick, before the egg slipped into his lap. After he swallowed, he asked, "You and McAllen killed all four?"

"We did."

"They're a dangerous bunch. You must be good."

"Lucky. They made a mistake and gave us

warning." I poured more syrup onto my hotcakes. Surprisingly, the syrup was pure maple. I couldn't believe it had been shipped all the way from New England to this wilderness. There was a lot of money in mining camps, and merchants were always thinking about ways to get it away from the miners and into their own pockets. I might use this nifty trick if I ever got back to Leadville. It was a taste of home and I ate slow to savor it.

After swallowing, I asked, "What did you and Carl do yesterday? I saw you wander the town together."

"Asked townsfolk if anyone had seen a stranger talking to the Cody brothers. No luck. The miners come in on weekends. Told Schmidt I'd ask around and send a telegram if I learned anything." Lewis shoved his plate away. "Schmidt didn't tell you anything before he climbed onto that stage this morning?"

"No, still sick. Yelled at him to go away."

"If you two are working together, why are you on horseback while he rides the stage?"

"I don't ride stages. The rocking makes me sick."

"Seems you got sick anyway."

"I sure did, but I'm sure it was from eating something in Yarnell. I don't travel well." I sopped up the last of the syrup with my final bite. With my fork halfway to my mouth, I asked, "Have you met Carl Schmidt before?"

"Of course." He looked puzzled by my question. "He was here about a month ago. Visited Henry—Henry Wickenburg. Henry sold the Vulture Mine years ago and now owns a large ranch. He got swindled by some dude from New York, and Schmidt said he was investigating for the Pinkertons."

"He was. I didn't know if he announced himself at your office or just went out to the ranch."

"I took him to Henry's. That tenderfoot would never have found the ranch house." He looked at me oddly. "You're not telling the whole truth. You ain't a Pinkerton, are you?"

"No, sir. I'm a friend of Captain McAllen, Schmidt's supervisor."

"What're you doing here? Don't take two men to ask a couple simple questions."

If I was going to learn anything, I would have to trust the marshal. "I'm here for the same reason as Carl Schmidt: to find out who hired the Codys. Captain McAllen asked me to come separately to find out if there was any possibility that it was Schmidt that hired those boys."

"Don't trust his own man?"

"McAllen's cautious."

"I can't help ya. I got my own spread, so I'm mostly in town only on the weekends. Schmidt coulda come in and out any time."

"Could he have met the Codys when he was here a month ago?"

"Unlikely. Henry hates them boys, so they wouldn't be anywhere about that ranch. And if the Codys saw a dude like that in town, they'd steal his pants or shave his head. Those boys did things like that to strangers who wandered away from the hotel. If it don't get rough, I leave those boys alone, but I'd still hear 'bout it. No, nothing like that when your friend was in town."

I had one last question. "Did he stay at this hotel?"

"No, at the ranch."

So Schmidt had been to Wickenburg more than once. On the visit a month ago, he had stayed at the Wickenburg ranch. He must have been here again because he knew to ask for the room that the manager had said was "recently done up nice."

Chapter 39

I left Wickenburg right after my breakfast with the marshal. My return ride was tougher because, instead of dropping three thousand feet, we had to climb as many. Even pushing Liberty a bit more than I should have, we arrived in Prescott after dark.

I found McAllen and Carl Schmidt at a back table in the Palace. I ordered a beer from the barkeep and started drinking it as I walked to their table. After a long, dusty ride, the beer was unbelievably refreshing. So refreshing, I reversed course before I got to McAllen and ordered another. The first was gone before the barkeep had drawn my second.

When I arrived at their table, McAllen looked impatient. Never one to waste words, he jumped right in without a greeting.

"What did you find in Wickenburg?"

The question was directed at me, so Schmidt must have already told him that he knew I was down there.

"I found out that Carl is a fine detective." I sipped my beer and let McAllen take the lead in the conversation.

"Yep, he spotted you right off."

"Is that what he said?" I looked at Carl. "You never spotted me. You found out someone was in the room you wanted, so you questioned the innkeeper about the boarder's horse, appearance, and length of stay. That was odd. Why did you ask about the occupant in room twelve? What made you fearful that McAllen would send someone to watch you?"

Schmidt sat upright. "*Fear* is a strong word . . . and incorrect. The captain and I go back a long way. It was obvious that he was nervous about me going to Wickenburg. Guessing what he would do about it was easy."

McAllen raised his hand. "It's okay, Steve. We've talked this all out."

"If you don't mind, Captain, I'd like to talk out a few things."

They glanced at each other, and McAllen said, "I think we can leave this alone now."

"I'm not ready to leave it alone. Carl either answers my questions, or I keep investigating."

"You're not an investigator," Schmidt said. "You need to—"

"Go ahead, Steve." McAllen cut him off. "Ask your questions."

"If you knew I was upstairs, why did you pretend I wasn't there?"

He chuckled unpleasantly. "I wanted you to think you had outsmarted me . . . at least until you ran into the marshal."

His smirk irritated me, but I tried to ignore it. "We ate breakfast together . . . he said you gave him my name."

"I did." The smirk became an unfriendly smile.

"Had you ever met any of the Cody bunch?"

"No."

"Did you discover who hired them?"

"No."

I watched McAllen out of the corner of my eye. Since he showed no interest in the questions or answers, I assumed that Schmidt had already told him all about the Codys and his otherwise unsuccessful trip. Maybe I knew something that Schmidt had failed to tell McAllen.

"How did you know about room twelve?"

"What?"

"How did you know that room twelve was the best in the house?"

"I've stayed in the room. So what? I always stay in the best room."

"When you were there a month ago, you stayed at Henry Wickenburg's ranch." I let that sink in before asking, "How many times have you been to Wickenburg?"

McAllen leaned into the conversation, started to say something, and then apparently changed his mind. Instead, he took a sip of whiskey from the glass in front of him. Was this studied disinterest, or did he already know that Schmidt had been to Wickenburg more than once?

"This is none of your business, but I've been down there several times."

"And in all of those visits, you never ran into one of the Cody bunch?"

"You can ask that question as many ways as you want, but the answer will always be that I never met the Codys."

Now I was becoming convinced that McAllen knew everything. But apparently, there were things I didn't know. I hated being in the dark. "Were you always on Pinkerton business?"

"Captain?"

McAllen took another sip before responding. "I think it would be better if Steve knew the whole story. Otherwise, he'll just be a pest."

"Not if you tell him to back off this line of inquiry."

"Is that true, Steve? Would you back off if I told you to?"

"I might drop it for now, but I'd never trust Carl. It would always be in the back of my mind."

"Bullshit," McAllen said, but he wore his funny closed-mouth smile to let me know he wasn't angry. "The honest answer is hell no, I won't back off." He directed his next comment at Schmidt. "Steve always goes his own way. He won't let this be. You might as well tell him. Come on, it's only embarrassing."

"Embarrassing? Captain, it can ruin my life."

"I said that Steve goes his own way, but he keeps his word. I know from experience. If he promises to keep it at this table, he'll never mention it to another soul."

What could have happened in Wickenburg that could ruin his life? Why would McAllen accept it? What was Schmidt's life? He was a Pinkerton agent. Could he have violated some policy that would get him fired? Wait. His life was as half a Pinkerton team. Breaking up his marriage would ruin his private life and his professional life.

"Carl, you have my word. I'll never say a word to anyone after I get up from this table. Not even to you or the captain. It dies right here."

His lips quivered like he was about to speak, but then he closed his mouth. I might as well let him know I had already figured it out. "Carl, I know about the entertainment available in room twelve."

"Shit." He put his face in his hands.

"Other men have wandered," I offered weakly.

"Other men aren't married to Mary," McAllen said. "She'll put up with a lot, but not that."

"Carl, I can't guarantee that Mary will never find out, but I can guarantee she won't find out from me."

"Nor me," McAllen said.

"I know you don't want advice," I said. "But stop right now, because if you don't, sooner or later she'll find out. The captain and I just gave you a stay of execution, not a pardon."

Schmidt pulled a handkerchief from his pocket

and blew his nose as he looked around the saloon. No one was paying any attention to us. To emphasize that we had changed subjects, I got up and ordered whiskey for McAllen and Schmidt. The barkeep said he'd bring them over, so I went back to the table to find everything relatively normal.

"Steve, we had a development while you were away," McAllen said. "Mary uncovered letters that prove Blanchet was independently workin' for the Winslows."

"Do they tie him to the murder?" I asked.

"No. Nothing that clear. But you were right. The Winslows hired us to get evidence on Campbell and used Blanchet for political cover. It looks like they took the third step and hired Blanchet to get rid of him permanent."

"How did Mary get hold of these letters?" I asked.

"She's very good with locks. But I won't talk about this one any further. An agent doing her job is different from what we were discussing before."

"I forget," I said. "What were we discussing before?"

Chapter 40

The next morning after breakfast, McAllen and Maggie knocked on Mrs. Cunningham's door. I had no plan for the day, so I was happy to see McAllen. With the trial only a couple of days away, we had to make good use of our time. I escorted them to the sitting room and closed the sliding doors with a rather loud clap.

After we sat down, McAllen said, "I believe Blanchet's our man, and the Winslows paid him to get rid of Campbell. He probably didn't murder anyone himself, but we can't be sure because of his Omaha conviction for attempted murder. Steve, that night you got shot at, the supposed highwayman was probably a hired killer. He was ham-handed, just like the Cody bunch that accosted us in front of the Palace. Someone is hiring second-rate bad men, and that sounds like Blanchet."

"I take it you no longer believe the Schmidts are part of this."

"Carl was stupid, not criminal."

Maggie leaned forward to ask a question but McAllen stopped it with a raised hand.

"Steve, do you have a problem with Blanchet as the key suspect?"

"Not at all. The evidence points to him, but in a way, I wish it had turned out to be Winslow. If he lives his life dream, he'll probably harm a lot more people."

"I take your point," McAllen said. "But if it's not Winslow, it'll just be some other damn politician ruining what's already workin'. Any coffee around?"

"I'll check."

I jumped up and heard Maggie's footfall behind me. In a loud voice, she said, "I'll help you carry." Then in a whisper she added, "Mr. Dancy, I need to talk with you. Private. It's personal."

"Too personal for your pa?"

"Oh, yes."

I stopped in the dining room. "Will it be a quick conversation?"

"A moment." She studied her feet and then lifted her chin. "Mr. Dancy, I need you to talk to Mr. Winslow. Tell him to leave me alone or you'll kill him."

"What happened?"

"Two days ago, Pa and I went to the jail to see Mr. Sharp. They were bathing prisoners, so Pa told me to stay upstairs. I sat on a chair in the lobby, and Mr. Winslow saw me. His behavior was inappropriate and rude."

I felt a sense of relief that he had only been rude. "Maggie, I normally need a better reason to kill a man."

"He asked me to help carry a few boxes and then led me into a storage room. He closed the door and then unbuttoned. I want him to leave me alone."

"Did he, uh—?"

"Of course not. While he was occupied unbuttoning, I shoved him against the shelves and left. He yelped, and stuff fell all over. It made a terrible racket, and everyone in the lobby stared at me. I want you to stop him. Please."

"He'll never bother you again. Let's get the coffee and return before your pa wonders what's become of us."

We soon returned with the coffee. McAllen and I drank it black, but Maggie put enough cream and sugar in hers for the three of us.

McAllen continued as if there had been no interruption. "Everythin' points at Blanchet. He wants us dead or gone at least, so Jeff swings for this murder. He's too much of a coward to try it himself and too cheap to hire men that know what they're doin'."

"Why doesn't he attack the Schmidts? He knows they're Pinkertons."

"He does now, but I'm not sure about before. He's certainly known since that newspaper article. But if Winslow told him they were Pinkertons, he also told him they still work for him. That means they're not a threat to Blanchet because they aren't tryin' to free Jeff."

That made sense. "When is the trial going to start?" I asked.

"Two days. Castle and I have talked about the defense. He says he's ready. He believes he can get Jeff off, but indicting Blanchet is a whole different matter. All the evidence is circumstantial."

"What about those letters that Mary found in his room?"

"Too vague. Mary had to return them anyway."

"Why?"

"Steve, our best chance is to surprise Blanchet in court. If the letters weren't returned, he'd know we were on to him. The most important task is to get Jeff free. Worst case, we return Blanchet to Omaha to serve the rest of his sentence. Maggie and I are gonna tie up a few loose strings with Castle. I want you to see Sharp and keep him calm. He doesn't know about Blanchet. Tell him, but do it calmly. Act confident and tell him he'll be free in two days. We'll meet at Mrs. Potter's at one—after most of the traffic."

I stood up. Maggie looked at me with pleading eyes. "I need to go. I have another errand at the courthouse. Did you see Jeff this morning?"

"We did. The jailers are taken care of through the trial."

"Anything else before I go?"

"Yes. I'm dropping Maggie at Mrs. Cunningham's after we leave Castle's office. Pick her up for our lunch date."

"Where are you going?"

"Castle wants me to check Winslow's alibi. I

don't doubt it, but he wants no stone left unturned by trial date."

This meant he was going to interview the high-priced whore. No wonder he didn't want Maggie with him.

I gave Maggie a smile and started to leave. "Mr. Dancy?"

"Yes."

"I need to go to Goldwater's, so if I'm not at Mrs. Cunningham's, don't worry. I'll be there by a quarter of one, latest."

I left the house wondering why Maggie's comment made me uneasy.

Chapter 41

As I approached Jonathon Winslow, he leaped to his feet and raised both hands, palms out.

"Stop. The governor will not see you. I have strict orders to keep you out."

"To hell with the governor. I came to see you."

"Guard!"

I almost punched him right there. He looked as scared as any man I had ever seen. Either he knew why I wanted to see him, or the gunfight with the Cody bunch had unnerved him. In a moment, a burly watchman approached me like a charging bull. I put my hands in my pockets, striking a casual pose. He stopped about four feet away and looked to Winslow for instructions.

"Throw him out of the building!"

I brushed the watchman's arm off before it reached my shoulder. He looked like he was going to get forceful but calmed down when I started sauntering toward the staircase.

Without looking back, I said, "Since you won't speak to me, Jonathon, I'm going to write to Mrs. Anna Cabot Lodge."

"Who?"

I slowly turned and looked at him. "I'm sorry. I thought the Winslows were part of the social register in Boston. Perhaps I've been misled by your previous remarks."

"The Winslows are one of the most prominent families in Boston. The oldest family, I might add."

"Yes, I know. Your ancestors came over on the *Mayflower*."

The guard allowed me to take a step toward him.

"Have you been fibbing? How can you not know Mrs. Lodge?"

"I know who Anna Lodge is. Do you?"

"She's the wife of John Ellerton Lodge. They're the parents of Slim . . . I'm sorry, Henry Cabot Lodge. John Lodge was a good friend of my father. Slim and I were friendly rivals during our sculling days."

"You expect me to believe this, after the governor failed to remember your fantasies?"

"I do. Surely you know Anna is a bastion of the social set in Boston. She loves gossip, especially gossip about secrets others would prefer remained in the closet."

His belligerence continued, but then slowly recognition of the meaning of my reference came into his eyes, and he wobbled badly. Gripping the edge of the desk, he waved the guard away.

"How do I know you didn't look her up at the *Arizona Daily Miner*?"

"Evidently you haven't been to the *Arizona Daily Miner*. It's not the *Boston Herald*. But don't take my word for it. Go to Western Union and ask your parents to check my references with Anna Lodge or her husband. That is, if they know the Lodges well enough to call on them."

"You overbearing upstart. The Winslows are accepted in the homes of the Cabots and the Lodges."

"Then you'll have no difficulty checking my references." I walked to the edge of his desk and, leaning in to within inches of his face, spoke barely above a whisper. "Don't be a fool. Have your folks check me out. Because I want to be clear, if you so much as look at Maggie McAllen again, I will destroy your reputation in Boston. I will make you the laughingstock of Beacon Hill. Forget your congressional run, you won't even be accepted in polite society. But if you touch her . . . I'll geld you like a rogue animal."

When I left, the man was shaking.

Chapter 42

Sharp was not his normal jovial self. In fact, he was cranky. While I told him everything that had happened in the last few days, he constantly interrupted me with questions, many impolite. It seemed that while I was away in Wickenburg, McAllen had given Sharp only terse explanations of events. Sharp was starved for information and company. After I finished, he went back to his bed and sat with his back against the wall.

"Two days." He shook his head. "Is Castle sure about lettin' Blanchet act as prosecutor?"

"I haven't talked to Castle since I got back. When did you see him last?"

"Yesterday."

"What did he say?"

"He didn't say a damn word 'bout Blanchet. Just told me to relax. Said he was confident an' ready. Puffed his damn chest out. Hell, the way he talked, I ought to be lookin' forward to the trial like some great adventure. Let me think, if this goes bad, who goes to the gallows? Will Mac Castle say he's sorry an' volunteer to take my place? More likely, he'll want to make sure he collects all his fees before I join the dearly departed."

"Tell you what: If Castle loses, I'll shoot your

way out, and we'll hightail it back to the United States."

"Always good to have a second plan." He pounded the bed with his fist. "Damn it. I'm used to takin' charge. Ain't nothin' I can do in here."

I didn't know how to respond, so I didn't.

After a few silent moments, Sharp asked, "Anythin' on that stock certificate?"

"No. I searched that room top to bottom. Checked for loose floorboards, fake drawers, sewed up mattresses. Nothing. Looked outside the room and couldn't find anywhere else in the house or grounds to hide a piece of paper. Practically ripped that Saratoga trunk to shreds and cut apart everything I found inside it. I've only found the materials he used to forge certificates." I shook my head. "I'm beginning to think he left it in New York."

"Why wouldn't he?"

"First, he was running away from the law, but more important, he wouldn't want Vanderbilt to get his hands on it. That sort always believes they're going to find the money to set everything right."

On the floor opposite the bed, Sharp had stacked all the old newspapers I had brought to keep him occupied. He went to a short stack and held them out between the bars. I took them and fanned them out. There were four issues.

"What's in these that makes them special?"

"Stories on Edison an' his marvelous inventions. Just the thing to whet the appetite of local investors."

I perused them quickly. "These are reprints from eastern newspapers." I let them drop against my leg. "Could be innocent. Papers do that all the time."

"Read them."

"I'll take them with me and read them later. What's significant?"

"All four stories mention the Edison Electric Light Company."

I bounced away from the wall I had been leaning against. "How prominent?"

"Inside page, closing paragraph. But a discernin' reader might pick it up."

"And that discerning reader might ask Campbell about the difference in names." I paced back and forth along the corridor wall. "Jeff, I don't think this means anything. Campbell was good at swindling. He'd create some cock-and-bull story about two companies, but he'd say the Illumination Company owned the prize inventions. If we concentrate on this, we'll just muddy up your defense. Blanchet is the murderer, and he did it for money, not a stock certificate."

"A Pinkerton might put things together. Don't underestimate the Schmidts."

I paced some more. "I don't want to underestimate McAllen's instincts either. He's

316

satisfied with Carl's story. Why are you dubious about Blanchet?"

"Wishful thinkin', I suppose. Not particularly comfortable with the murderer prosecutin' me. But . . . Blanchet partnered up with Campbell. He sold Campbell that old barn to disguise his cut from the swindles. Those letters Mary found prove he also worked for the Winslows. An' he's an escaped prisoner. Don't look good for him. Just hope Castle knows what he's doin'. By the way, ya searched that barn, didn't ya?"

I was stunned. I thought I had searched everywhere for that damn document, and it never occurred to me to search the barn and grounds. How stupid could I be? Where would I put it if I were hiding it out there? It would have to be someplace safe from the elements. Inside the barn would be risky because young people supposedly rendezvoused out there. I'd wrap it in oil cloth and bury it deep in an area of the barn that still had a good roof. I'd also make sure there was good water drainage in case a downpour seeped into the barn.

"Steve?"

"Yes."

"The barn?"

"I forgot. I've got to go. I'm sorry, I'll be back as soon as I can."

I rushed out as Sharp yelled after me, "Hell, Steve, do I gotta do all the thinkin' for ya?"

It was embarrassing enough, but what if I actually found the certificate? Then Sharp would never let me forget how dumb I had been. As I scrambled out of the courthouse, a thought struck me: What if Blanchet weren't done hiring assassins? Everything in Prescott surrounded the courthouse square, so Mrs. Cunningham's was just across the street. I decided I wanted my rifle with me when I walked to the abandoned barn. A six-shooter is fine for close work, but for distances of more than a few yards, I preferred my Winchester '76.

When I came through the front door, the house was still. Mrs. Cunningham was probably doing the shopping for the day's meals. I was thinking hard as I climbed the stairs. The trial was less than two days away. Blanchet had to be busy getting ready. My guess was that he probably hadn't hired any more bad men. Besides, the Cody episode made us waste time in Wickenburg, which, for Blanchet, was almost as good as if they had killed us. Despite my reasoning, I still wanted my rifle with me as I walked along a road that would take me into the woods.

I threw open my door and was so shocked I couldn't move or speak. There was a couple on my bed. Finally, I regained my senses.

"Maggie!"

Chapter 43

Maggie and John were sitting on my bed—fully clothed, thankfully. But they had been kissing, and John's cupped hand had jerked away from Maggie. My first response was anger, not at the invasion of my room but at Maggie's putting me in this position. She had no right to make it difficult for me with her father. Damn it. I knew this was natural, but it was something for a parent to deal with, not me. Should I tell McAllen? What would I want if I were a parent?

"John, get out of here."

Both kids jumped to their feet.

"No!" Maggie yelled. "You can't make him leave. We weren't doing anything wrong."

"Perhaps he'd like to tell his mother that I want my rent back for the day because he used my room without my permission."

That did it. He literally ran out of the room. I gently closed the door after he left. Maggie sat back on the bed and jutted out her lower lip. This whole situation had me bamboozled. I didn't want to be complicit in a deceit with Maggie, and I sure didn't want to be the messenger of this type of news to McAllen. He might be more mature and worldly than me, but this was far too close to home. How would he handle discovering them together? I had no idea. Which meant I had no idea how I should handle it. I wasn't a parent and didn't know how to be one. An odd thought struck me. If I got married and had a baby right away, I'd be as old as McAllen by the time my kid was fifteen. I was thirty-one. Did I need to start thinking about this? I pushed the thought from my mind and sat on the bed next to Maggie.

"What do you think I should do?"

She didn't answer.

"Maggie?"

"I don't know."

"Your father is a friend of mine. You've put me in an awkward position. If I tattle, I'll make an enemy of you and suffer your father's wrath for being the bearer of bad news. If I don't tell, you'll take advantage of me in the future."

"I won't."

"You will. Perhaps I should tell both John and Jonathon to stay away from you or I'll kill them."

"That's not the same thing! Mr. Winslow doesn't care a whit for me. He's old, and he wants to do vile things. John and I were just kissing. It wasn't going any further."

"I'm sorry, you're right. It's not the same thing. Thank you for telling me about Mr. Winslow. I can assure you he'll never bother you again. I should tell you, however, that I did not kill him."

As soon as the words left my mouth, I knew it was not an appropriate time for humor. The problem was that I didn't know what to say or do.

I was still trying to make up my mind when Maggie said something that shocked me.

"I want to go further, but I won't. I'm not sure I'm ready." She looked at me with pleading eyes. "It's hard living in the room next to the Schmidts. Mary is so loud. I know what it's about; I just want to feel what it's about."

This conversation was getting uncomfortable for me. Was I the only man she could talk to? McAllen was too off-putting and her stepfather was a fire-and-brimstone preacher. She spent a lot of time on the ranch of her uncle and aunt, but I had never met them. What about her mother? That's who she should be talking to: someone of the same sex who could give her advice based on similar experience. How did I get into this situation? How much responsibility did I have because I threw a door open at an inappropriate moment?

"Listen, I'm no good at this, but I'm the only one in the room, so I guess I'm the one who's got to talk to you. The Schmidts are different. They're married. That's what husbands and wives do. At your age, it will only get you in trouble. I remember you told me you would never get pregnant and need to get married because you were a McAllen. I liked that, and you should always remember it."

"I wasn't going to get pregnant. Do you think every time a girl kisses a boy, she's telling him that whatever else he wants to do is okay? I can take care of myself in that regard. And for your information, Mary still made her noises when Carl was out of town."

Her retort was so angry that I actually moved an inch away from her. Obviously, I was no good at fatherly advice. Then I stopped. What did she say? Mary still made her noises? Was Mary unfaithful? If she was, it was none of my business. But still, I wanted to know.

"Maggie, when Carl was out of town, what noises did Mary make?"

Now she pouted. "I don't want to talk about this any longer. You know what kind of noises."

"And Carl was gone?"

"Yes! He was gone. Gone to that Wickenburg place. It made Mary furious. She'd stomp around for hours and then disappear and come back with a man. I don't want to talk about this."

"Then we won't. I'm sorry you had to experience that." I stood up and faced Maggie. "I've decided what I'm going to do about you and John."

"What?" There was a hint of fear.

"Nothing."

"Nothing?" Now hope.

"That's right. I'm going to do nothing. I won't talk to your pa, and I won't mention it to Mrs. Cunningham." I watched a smile appear on her face for the briefest second, but she quickly changed her expression to show seriousness. "However, if I ever catch you like that again or catch you lying about John or any other boy, I will immediately tell your pa, and I'll write your stepfather as well. You know he will keep you close to home in Durango. You won't be visiting your aunt on her ranch, so you won't get to see or ride your horse." The smile was completely gone. "Do you understand?"

"Yes, sir." She sounded sincere and a little bit frightened.

"Okay, come on, we're going treasure hunting at that old barn. First, we're going to Hill Hardware to buy two shovels, and then we're walking to the barn. Hurry. We've got to get back to meet your pa at Mrs. Potter's."

Maggie beamed as she jumped off the bed, obviously relieved to change the subject and get out of my room. I had no idea whether I had handled the situation correctly. Maggie was headstrong. I didn't want to punish her, nor was it my place. I just wanted to change her behavior—at least until we went our separate ways again.

Since she was happy, or at least relieved, I hated to spoil it. Unfortunately, I had one more question. Just before I opened the door, I said, "Maggie, do you know who the man was who visited Mary when Carl was away?"

"Please, Mr. Dancy. I don't want to talk about

it. I wish I had never told you." She looked embarrassed.

"It's important."

"If I tell you, will you never speak of this again?"

"Promise."

"It was that Campbell man. The one who got killed."

Chapter 44

The walk should have taken about fifteen minutes, but I walked slowly. My mind was so occupied with Maggie's revelation that I never said a word. The Schmidts' job was to catch swindlers and confidence men. They were experts at fooling people. Had they fooled Captain McAllen?

"Mr. Dancy?"

I became aware of my surroundings and realized we were standing in front of the barn.

"Sorry, I was distracted. We're looking for a piece of paper. It will be wrapped in something to protect it, but it'll still be delicate, so dig very carefully. Yell out if you find anything."

"Where do you want to start?"

"Inside. Let's take a look."

I pulled both doors open and filled the barn with light. The sunlight also cascaded through holes in the roof. The obvious place to dig was under the hayloft that ran down the left side of the structure. It was fairly intact and would provide protection against rain and snow. The floor was hard pack, with no signs of recent digging. If there was any slope, it appeared to go front to back, so I decided we'd start by the door. Maggie took the inside by the wall, and I intended to dig a lane along the centerline of the barn. In less than ten minutes, I hit something very hard about six inches below the surface. At first I thought it was a rock, but after a couple of thrusts using the shovel like a posthole digger, I definitely heard metal against metal.

"What is it?" Maggie asked.

"Let's see." I used the shovel to pry hard-packed dirt away from the object. "It's a strong box."

"Darn," she said.

"Darn?"

"A treasure hunt is supposed to be an adventure. I didn't even get my dress dirty."

"Let's not count our chickens." I got down on the ground and jerked the box out with both hands. A puff of dust covered the lower part of Maggie's dress. The box had a small outside lock that came apart with a single strike from the shovel. When I opened it, I said, "You may count the chickens."

"What is it?"

"A stock certificate. A real one." I pulled out the rolled piece of paper and gave it to her to examine.

After a moment, she said, "One thousand shares of Edison Electric Light Company. Why was it buried here?"

"Because Elisha Campbell didn't want anyone to see that piece of paper. It would ruin his swindles."

"Is it valuable?"

"Only troublesome." I always carried a tube of matches to light my pipe, and soon I was holding the burning certificate over the metal box. When my hand got hot, I dropped it and blew on it to keep it burning until there were only ashes left. I should have been ecstatic to dispose of this troubling document, but instead I was worried.

"Let's get back," I said. "We've got enough time to see Jeff before we need to meet your pa."

"I'm not moving until you tell me what this was all about."

"I'll tell you, but on the way. Leave the shovels."

"You don't want them?"

"No."

"Can I have them?"

"For what?"

"I'm going to sell them back to Mr. Hill for half price."

I laughed. "They're yours."

We walked at a brisk pace. Maggie already knew about Edison and his inventions, and got all excited to learn that I owned a piece of his company. She didn't know about stocks and Wall Street, but asked endless questions all the way to Hill's Hardware. She ran in and came out in less than five minutes, showing off two silver dollars. Perhaps she had a future as a capitalist.

When we got to the jail, I had to leave Maggie

with the guard because only one person at a time was allowed down the corridor. Sharp had been napping, but my footsteps woke him.

"Did ya find it?"

"I did. Buried inside the barn in a small strong box. Dug it out and then burned it."

"What d'ya think?"

"It means the real Edison stock never had anything to do with this murder. No one knew it existed except Campbell and me."

"Yep, Blanchet's gotta be the one. Just hope Castle's got it figured out so it comes out right at the trial."

After a few more minutes of discussion, I thought I should send Maggie down to say hello. Maybe Sharp should have been the one to deal with her and John. She seemed to like him better than me, and he certainly had a way with women. That thought prodded me to ask a few more questions.

"Do you remember Mary Schmidt?" I asked.

"Yep, attractive woman in a matronly sorta way."

"Do you think she and Carl have a good marriage?"

"She's wrong for you, Steve. That's a hard, possessive woman."

"You think she's possessive of Carl?"

"Hell, yes. That woman would terrorize a cheatin' husband. If I remember correctly, she always carries a pocket pistol an' a derringer. Some woman ya don't mess with."

"What about Carl? Is he the jealous type?"

"Those two been cheatin' on each other?"

"Maybe. What about Carl?"

"Hell, I don't know. He's number two in that partnership, but I can't tell how he'd act. Hardly knew him."

"You hardly knew Mary."

"I always understood women right off. 'Sides, she ain't hard to read. Puts it right out there for everyone to see. Leastways, when she ain't workin'."

"I'd better send Maggie down. She'll lift your spirits."

"Better than ya yammerin' 'bout women. Remember, I've been locked up here near a week."

I sent Maggie down the corridor to Sharp's cell. As they talked and laughed, I leaned against the wall and thought. I suddenly pushed myself away from the wall. I needed to see Virgil Earp.

Chapter 45

I had planned to drop Maggie with her father at Mrs. Potter's and go find Earp, but Morris Goldwater was walking out as we arrived. I hurriedly left Maggie with McAllen and walked Goldwater back to his store.

"Your suit is ready," he said. "I've been wondering when you'd come by. You were in such a hurry."

"I apologize for not informing you, but I had to take a trip to Wickenburg. I'll pick up the suit this afternoon. By the way, I hope I'm not imposing, but you offered to help me with the community."

"If I can. I know everyone, but I won't disclose their darkest secrets." He smiled to show he wasn't entirely serious.

"I won't bother you about the fine citizens of Prescott. In fact, you may not be able to help at all because my questions are about Wickenburg."

"Actually, I go to Wickenburg frequently. I supply the general store there."

"Then you know Marshal Lewis?"

"You mean Deputy Lewis. The marshal's name is Malcolm Henry. Lewis just helps out on weekends."

That made sense. Lewis didn't seem particularly capable. The Cody bunch weren't tough enough to cow a real lawman, and Lewis said he left them alone. So that meant that Schmidt had gone around town with a deputy.

"Have you heard of the Cody brothers?"

"Those men you killed outside the Palace? Sure, everybody that has spent any time in Wickenburg ran into that bunch. They were always in the saloon or the hotel café. Bad men, but they behaved in town. Had to, or Henry would have locked them up straightaway."

This was more information than I had expected. Since my conversation with Maggie, I had become convinced that the Schmidts were playing us. And if they were, Carl might have misled us about his activities in Wickenburg. My hope had been that Earp would tell me if the person I thought was Marshal Lewis was reliable. Now I knew how a prospector felt when he discovered a mother lode.

"Do you know the Schmidts? The Pinkertons staying at Prescott House?"

"You mean the ones pretending to be Maggie's parents. I'm acquainted with them as customers. She's an odd shopper."

"What do you mean?"

"Well, she doesn't shop the dresses, shoes, or hats like other women. Seems more interested in undergarments. Expensive undergarments." He laughed. "She also buys handkerchiefs by the dozen. Says she throws them away instead of washing them." He rubbed his chin. "She had an odd request lately. Wanted expensive stationery embossed with initials. When I told her it would take a month, she said never mind."

"Perhaps it was a gift."

"That's what I thought, so I tried to direct her to our silver gifts. We have an engraver who can do work in less than a day. But she said no, she wasn't interested in a gift. She said the stationery had been for her."

"What was odd about that?"

"They weren't her initials."

"Did you address her by name?"

"I address all my customers by name, Mr. Dancy. But she may have forgotten. Many people don't notice their names in conversation."

"Do you remember the initials?"

"No . . . possibly E L W, but I could be mistaken."

This vein of information ran deep. It struck me that shopkeepers knew a great deal about the local people who frequented their store. I had part ownership in a general store in Leadville, but my real shopkeeper experience was in our family-owned gun shop in New York City. It was a high-end affair, selling mostly European shotguns to rich bird hunters. When I thought about it, men did tell us more in the store than they would ever disclose at my father's club. If you repeatedly buy items from someone, you develop a level of trust uncommon in purely social situations.

We had reached the front of the store, but I had one more question. "Did you ever run into Carl Schmidt in Wickenburg?"

Goldwater looked up and down the street before responding. "Yes. I'd rather not talk about it."

"I know he hired those girls who have their picture behind the innkeeper's counter. Anything else you don't want to talk about?"

"He was like a man suddenly unshackled. He drank, caroused with those girls, gambled, and generally raised a ruckus. He became friendly with the ruffians about town. Always buying drinks. Got arrested once. Schmidt and Henry don't speak anymore. Schmidt thought his Pinkerton badge gave him free rein. Henry had other ideas. Don't blame the marshal, though. Henry's a good man . . . a lodge brother."

I was no longer standing steady. "Any rumors about Mrs. Schmidt?"

"Only the ones that came from Campbell's mouth. He claimed to have bedded every unattached woman in town, and a few of those who were attached, like Mrs. Schmidt. He was the worst sort of braggart. I guess he had his charms, but I failed to see them."

"Thank you. I'll see you later in the day to pick up my suit and the other items. You've been most helpful."

Without waiting for a reply, I practically ran back to Mrs. Potter's. Before entering, I decided to calm down first, so I slowed my pace and walked around the courthouse square. To McAllen, honor was everything. When I told him Carl Schmidt had lied to him, he would go into a rage. I needed to be careful how I told him. I didn't want to trade one friend in jail for another. I thought about having Virgil Earp present but decided that Maggie would be a greater restraint.

By the time I walked around the square, I had regained my composure and my appetite. McAllen and his daughter were almost through with their meal, so I ordered a piece of cake. Depending on how the day played out, I'd probably get a sandwich at the Palace later in the afternoon.

"Are you going riding this afternoon?" I asked.

"As soon as you satisfy that sweet tooth," McAllen said.

"I need to talk . . . before you go. It's about the case, and confidential. Perhaps we could spend a few minutes in Mrs. Cunningham's parlor." He looked uncertain, so I added, "It's important, Joseph."

"Steve, in a few days Maggie will be on her way to Durango. It better be more important than spendin' time with my daughter."

"I assumed she'd join us."

"She needs to change clothes."

"She can help."

"Sittin' in a parlor ain't the same as bein' out on the trail."

That sounded like an odd statement for a father, but it was probably true for Maggie. She wasn't much for parlors. Maggie loved the outdoors, horses, riding, and being with her father.

"I'll make it short."

"You will. Let's go." He got up.

"My cake?" It had just arrived.

"You can eat your cake in the parlor. Bring the plate back when we walk Maggie to Prescott House to change."

I paid for all three meals and promised to have the plate back shortly. I was a fifth wheel as we made the short walk over to my boardinghouse. Maggie jabbered away, while McAllen looked on proudly and made an occasional affirmative grunt. McAllen was a man of his word, and in a few minutes I would break two promises—one I had made to him and another to his daughter. I decided I'd better get this over as quickly as possible.

As soon as we settled into chairs, I set the cake aside. I didn't want to talk around a mouthful of food.

"Carl lied about Wickenburg," I said. "He knew the Cody brothers, and the man he sent to reassure me at breakfast wasn't the marshal, he was a deputy."

The room was dead silent.

"How do you know he knew the Cody brothers?"

"Goldwater told me." I relayed the entire conversation, including the portion about Mary's shopping habits. When I finished, McAllen stood and paced the tiny room.

"Why did you keep looking into this? I told you to drop it." His tone was not angry.

I studied the pattern in the rug. When I looked up, I caught Maggie's eyes. "I know. I'm about to break another promise, one I made to Maggie."

She shook her head no.

"This is embarrassing for you, Maggie, but it's important."

I turned to McAllen. "Maggie told me she heard Carl and Mary at night through the bedroom wall. She also heard Mary with another man when Carl was in Wickenburg. Whenever Carl went south, Mary got very angry. I think she brought this other man to her room to get even." McAllen had quit pacing, and was staring at me. "Joseph, that other man was Elisha Campbell."

McAllen seemed to have no physical reaction— he just resumed pacing. I had often said foolish things in front of him, but this time I was smart enough to remain quiet. I was surprised how calm he seemed. The Schmidts had lied to him, behaved inappropriately when his daughter was nearby, and had possibly committed serious crimes.

"This plays out only one way," McAllen said. "Let me take it one step at a time and tell me if you see it different."

I remained silent.

"Carl made periodic trips to Wickenburg. Mary figures out what he's doin' there and gets even by cavortin' with the target of their investigation. One of the two of them murders Campbell. They frame Sharp for the murder, but we're workin' to prove him innocent. They get concerned. Carl does a poor job of tryin' to kill you as a highwayman, so he hires the Cody bunch to get rid of us both. When we plan a trip to Wickenburg to investigate, Carl panics. But Carl works under pressure all the time, so in short order, he hides his emotions and contrives a plan. He plays it just right, both down there and when he gets back. That about it?"

"Yes, but I assumed it was Carl. You said *they*. Do you think it was both of them?"

"They're a team," Maggie said.

"Correct, Maggie." McAllen beamed. "Also because Mary forged those letters while you were in Wickenburg. That means they were workin' together. Those two always have a second plan. If Sharp got freed, they had another culprit set up."

"You sure Mary forged those letters?"

"She only let me see them briefly. Said she had to get them back before they were missed. They were written on quality paper, but not stationery like a Boston Winslow would use. Yep, they're still workin' as a team. A damn good one. They hunt confidence men and they know all the tricks." He paced a bit more before adding, "We need to work this in two steps. First, we get Jeff free, and then we convict Carl and Mary. Maggie, do you have a key to the Schmidts' room?"

"No. They need to answer my knock before I'm allowed into their room."

"It doesn't matter. I can still get in. Steve, go tell Castle everythin'. Maggie and I are goin' to search their room. Those letters are the only piece of hard evidence. Maybe she didn't destroy them."

"If she destroyed the letters, how do you intend to put them behind bars?"

"No choice," McAllen said. "We're goin' to have to con them."

Chapter 46

I grabbed my lapels and snapped my new suit coat taut. The tailor at Goldwater's had done a fine job. When dressed in a suit, I carried a Remington .38 pistol under my arm in a shoulder holster of my own design. The tailor had done a nice alteration that almost completely hid the gun. As I looked at myself in the mirror, I felt I would be welcome in the toniest establishment in New York City. My hair was neatly trimmed, my shirt was so white it almost sparkled, and my maroon silk tie went perfectly with the dark brown suit.

I was ready. I hoped *we* were.

McAllen, Castle, and I had worked feverishly over the last two days to prepare for the trial. McAllen, of course, could find no trace of the letters. In fact, he couldn't find any blank stationery in the room. Mary had evidently destroyed everything. With no physical evidence, we were dependent on Mac Castle's skill.

When I came downstairs, Mrs. Cunningham smiled before saying, "Mr. Dancy, you cut a handsome figure in that suit. This is the big day for your friend. I wish you luck."

"Thank you, Mrs. Cunningham." I looked at John, who was studying the floor. "Do you have that room ready, John?"

"Yes, sir. Ma, I gotta get over to the livery to fetch Mr. Nelson's horse."

"Go then." After John had run out the door, she asked, "What's going on with you and John?"

"Nothing, as far as I know. He's a fine boy."

As I turned to leave, she said, "Mr. Dancy, I apologize, but if your friend is convicted, I'm still going to charge you for that extra room."

I turned back. "Thank you for reminding me." I handed her five dollars. "Please prepare the finest meal you can—for the entire house. It's a celebratory supper, and my friend, Mr. Jeffery Sharp, will be occupying that room this evening. Now, if you'll excuse me, I want to hear the opening arguments."

As I walked across the square to the courthouse, I noticed new leaves sprouting from the trees. There was a special green in spring, a lighter, more iridescent color that seemed to darken in only a few weeks. I loved the color as a boy because it meant summer was near, and that meant playing outdoors with friends all day long. Even as an adult, I felt good spotting the fresh green of spring on the trees.

My reverie was broken in the courthouse lobby.

"Mr. Dancy?"

It was Jonathon Winslow.

"Yes, Mr. Winslow?"

"I didn't recognize you."

"Nor were you meant to; I'm in disguise."

"Is that a joke?"

"Not if it didn't make you laugh. Are you coming to the trial?"

"Later, after I finish a couple errands for the governor." He waited until some men passed us on the stairs. "You are going to restrain yourself from writing that letter?"

"I will . . . unless your parents had anything whatsoever to do with the murder of Campbell."

"What? That's a terrible thing to say. I can assure you, they did not."

"I'm not as sure as you appear to be."

"What does that mean?"

"It means they had reason to want Campbell out of the way of your grand career in our nation's capital. Now, if you'll excuse me, I need to get upstairs, and you have errands."

I left before he could reply.

I sat next to McAllen, Maggie on his other side. Carl and Mary Schmidt sat directly behind us. The courtroom was packed, with people standing along the back wall. A murder trial was free entertainment, and this one promised to end with a hanging. Sharp looked at us from the defense table and gave us a wink. Exactly on the hour, we all stood as Judge Carter entered the courtroom.

The opening statements were as expected. Blanchet droned on, explaining that the evidence was extensive and irrefutable. Castle had warned us that he was going to be bland because he didn't want to give away his strategy in the opening act.

Blanchet called six witnesses to testify that Sharp went into a rage that afternoon, not only knocking Campbell to the floor, but also hitting two other customers who were trying to break up the fight. Each testified that Sharp threatened to kill Campbell if he ever saw him again. From the testimony, it sounded like an all-night brawl instead of two punches that lasted only a few seconds.

The next prosecution witness was Captain McAllen. He testified about where he and Earp had found the body and the position of the rifle. Next, Constable Earp repeated McAllen's testimony and then described Sharp's arrest. He also told about the pine needles found on the stairs and stuck to Sharp's boots.

What came next was somewhat of a surprise. Blanchet had hired a lawyer in New York to take depositions from several of Sharp's business associates. Blanchet submitted them into evidence and then read them with a bit of dramatic flair. The business associates meant to defend Sharp by painting Campbell as the offending party, but instead of helping, they established motive by showing that Sharp's anger was probably justified in his mind. Blanchet also had depositions from people in Nevada and Colorado. They painted Jeffery Sharp as a violent man.

The prosecution rested just before the noon break. The jurors filed out quickly. I guessed that they thought Sharp was guilty and the trial would be over before supper. I hoped that only the second supposition was correct.

Sharp was returned to his cell, and the three of us went over to Castle's office for lunch. Sandwiches, nuts, beer, and a root beer had been brought over from the Palace. Before long, we were all eating.

"Do the Schmidts have any inkling of what's to come this afternoon?" Castle asked.

"Maggie?" McAllen gave the question to his daughter.

"Pa gave me a stethoscope to listen to their conversations through the wall. I can hear everything they say. Unless they know I'm listening, they still believe you will present Blanchet as the murderer. They sound cocksure."

"You gave her a doctor's stethoscope?" Castle asked incredulously.

"She has the room next door, and she's a reliable observer."

"But you turned your daughter into a spy."

"She's a darn good detective, not a spy."

"The difference?"

"A detective finds criminals. Spies pry into the business of people they don't like."

"What do we do if Carl or Mary leave the courtroom?" I asked.

"A constable will take care of that. If they try to leave the building, they will be detained in the judge's quarters." McAllen took a large swig of beer. "Relax, Steve. The trial's the easy part. If you want to worry, worry about what comes after."

Chapter 47

"As my first witness, I call Captain Joseph McAllen, of the Pinkerton National Detective Agency."

McAllen sat in the witness chair. His stoic expression and relaxed posture said he was at ease being in court.

"Mr. McAllen, you testified about finding the body of Elisha Campbell. Was that the end of your investigation?"

"No, sir."

"Explain to the court what you discovered in your further investigations."

"The lack of blood indicated that Campbell had not been shot at the location where the body was found. I searched the grounds along the trail back toward town and found a bloody horse harness that had been used to drag the body from another location."

Castle entered the harness into evidence and allowed the jury to examine it.

"Did you find the actual location of the murder?"

"I did. The abandoned barn outside of town. It's about halfway between town and where the body was found. There was a bullet embedded in the back wall of the barn that matched the caliber of Mr. Sharp's Winchester."

"Drawing on your investigative experience, can you recreate the scene for us?"

"It appears that when Campbell entered the barn, someone was behind the door. When Campbell moved into the barn, that person shot him in the back of the head. This would keep the blood spray and pooling in the dirt, where it could be covered up."

"What does that indicate to you?"

"That the murderer understood investigative procedures."

"If Mr. Sharp murdered Mr. Campbell, can you think of any reason why he would want to move the dead body?"

"No."

"How many shots had been fired from the rifle?"

"Two. The evidence indicates that one shot killed Campbell at the barn, and the other shot drew Constable Earp and me to the site, where we found the body."

"Why might the murderer fire that second shot?"

"So the body would be found immediately. The murderer probably knew that Constable Earp lived a short distance away."

"If Mr. Sharp murdered Mr. Campbell, can you think of any reason why the defendant, Mr. Sharp, would want the body found that night?"

"No."

"To your knowledge, did Mr. Sharp know where Constable Earp lived?"

"No. He had just arrived in town that afternoon."

"Can you think of a reason why someone else might want the body found that night?"

"Yes. If someone framed the defendant, then they would want the body discovered right away to connect the fistfight to the murder."

"Objection!" Blanchet had leaped out of his seat. "That's unsubstantiated speculation."

"Sustained," Judge Carter ruled.

"Why are you in Prescott?"

McAllen told the court about his team's being hired to investigate the series of swindles perpetuated by Campbell. He then described the methods used by Carl and Mary Schmidt.

"Did both of the Schmidts remain in Prescott all the time?"

"No. Carl Schmidt made frequent trips to Wickenburg."

I sensed rather than saw movement behind me. Then I heard Mary Schmidt's harsh whisper.

Castle asked, "For what purpose?"

"Originally, to interview Henry Wickenburg, who had been defrauded as well. Later, he went to Wickenburg for recreational purposes."

"Could you tell the court about the four men who tried to kill you in the shooting across the street?"

"Two of them were the Cody brothers. The other two were their friends. They came from Wickenburg, where they were known as the Cody bunch."

"Had you ever seen or heard of them before?"

"No. To my knowledge, they had no reason to threaten us. They were apparently hired to kill us."

"Did you investigate Carl Schmidt's activities in Wickenburg?"

"I did, through an associate. Carl Schmidt did his best to throw our investigation off course."

For ten minutes, McAllen explained the entire sequence of events surrounding Carl Schmidt and Wickenburg. During his testimony, I twice heard Carl try to get up to leave, but Mary kept him in place with a stern whisper. Since I didn't want to turn around, I watched the jury. Both times, the sudden motion drew their attention.

Castle resumed his questioning.

"Captain, what do you make of all that?"

"You mean you want my opinion?"

"Yes. As an experienced investigator, what might Carl Schmidt's actions mean?"

"First and foremost, Mr. Schmidt is hiding something. He went to elaborate extremes to mislead my associate. In my opinion, Mr. Schmidt was trying to hide the fact that he hired the Cody bunch to gun us down."

Although the conclusion was obvious, there was an audible gasp in the courtroom.

"What motive could he have to take such heinous action?"

"To cover up that he had killed Elisha Campbell and set up Jeffery Sharp to hang for the crime."

"What reason could he have for killing Campbell?"

"He had a reason, but I am not directly privy to that information."

"Who is?"

"Constable Earp."

"Very well. Previously, you said that Carl Schmidt went to Wickenburg for recreational purposes. Can you elaborate?"

McAllen made a show of scanning the audience. "My meaning should be obvious. Must I elaborate? There are women and children present."

Castle looked over at the jury with a contemplative expression. "No. I believe the jury understands your meaning. I may call you again if the need arises." He made a bow toward Blanchet. "Your witness."

"Mr. McAllen, do you have any physical evidence that supports this *story* of yours?"

"No, sir. But I have a witness who can corroborate that Carl Schmidt obstructed my investigation."

"Would that be your associate, Mr. Dancy?"

"He can confirm it as well, but I was referring to Malcolm Henry, Wickenburg's town marshal."

"No further questions." Blanchet scrambled back to his table.

"In that case, I call Constable Virgil Earp."

After Earp took a seat in the witness chair, Castle asked, "Did you know Mr. Campbell?"

"I did. I had a number of complaints about his business dealings, but although his actions were unethical, I found no laws were broken."

"Are you familiar with the barn that Captain McAllen believes was the murder site?"

"I am. I pass it every day on my way into town. I also went over the site with the captain, and I agree that it was the murder site."

"Why would the murderer haul the body out to Thumb Butte?"

"Only one reason that I can think of . . . the barn must link Campbell and the murderer, so the murderer would want to conceal that fact."

"How could it connect them?"

"Probably as a rendezvous point for the two."

"I see. On your daily trips to town, did you have occasion to stop at the barn on official business?"

Earp laughed. "I'm not sure it's within my official duties, but I frequently stopped to chase away youngsters. That barn is a notorious spot for young couples."

"Did you ever happen on adults?"

"Once. I heard some activity, so I stopped and knocked. Finally, I had to bang pretty hard to get a response. Mr. Campbell came out. He asked me not to embarrass his partner. He said if I would ride on down the road, they would leave."

"Did you?"

"I did, but not before checking behind the barn. I found two tethered horses. I recognized one as belonging to Mrs. Mary Schmidt."

Until the prior afternoon, we had assumed that we would have to use Maggie to confirm an illicit relationship between Mary Schmidt and Elisha Campbell, but when McAllen explained the defense strategy to Earp, the constable informed us that he could give testimony that would reveal that something untoward was going on between them.

I wished I had taken a seat behind the Schmidts instead of in front. I heard no more whispers and sensed no sudden movements.

Castle called several witnesses to testify that Sharp was in a playful mood that night and not angry at all. By the time he left the saloon, he was falling-down drunk and unlikely to haul himself, much less a dead body, out to Thumb Butte.

I testified next. I said that the door to his room had been unlocked, and that Jeffery Sharp was a man of sterling character. He might punch someone he hated, but he would never back-shoot even his worst enemy. I also testified that his rifle was an extension of his arm, and he would never leave it behind, even if he were drunk.

Blanchet's closing remarks remained consistent with his opening argument. It was as if Castle had presented no revelations that he needed to explain away. The jury must have noticed that he spoke with little enthusiasm.

Castle opened with an accurate description of the short fight and reminded the jury that Jeff had given five dollars and an apology to the innocent party he had hit. Castle described Sharp as a solid businessman newly arrived in town to invest in the community. He asked the jury if they believed a man incontestably drunk could have the wits to lure a victim to a barn he had never seen, or possess the control needed to shoot straight or the unwavering strength to haul a body half a mile.

He reminded the jury that infidelity was one of the oldest and most common motives for murder. Then he asked if it were more believable that Carl Schmidt, in an angry rage, used Sharp's threat to kill Campbell as a cover to revenge being cuckolded. He reviewed Carl Schmidt's shenanigans in Wickenburg and ended with a graphic description of the gunplay across the street from the courthouse. Carl Schmidt had motive, had obstructed the investigation, and had apparently hired killers to stop an independent investigation.

I thought it was a skillful summation. The jury must have thought so as well, because they came back after deliberating only twenty minutes.

When called upon, the jury foreman read the verdict—not guilty.

Chapter 48

"What the hell are you doing?"

I was bent over a bureau drawer when Mary Schmidt entered her room and yelled at me. I had congratulated Sharp on his acquittal and then raced over to Prescott House. I wanted to search the room before they returned. I obviously had not been quick enough.

I straightened and slowly turned to face her. "Looking for the original letters."

"What letters?"

"The original letters from the Boston Winslows. The ones written to you, not George Blanchet. The letters you used to forge the ones you showed to McAllen."

She reached her hand into the folds of her dress. I knew what that meant, so I took a step closer.

"I don't believe Carl killed Campbell because of your infidelity," I said. "McAllen may think you're a happy couple shocked at each other's indiscretions, but I believe you're just a couple of hard-hearted killers for hire."

She started to pull her hand out of her dress, and I took another step toward her, but she was quicker than I expected. I pulled up short in the face of a .41 caliber derringer.

She looked smug. "Did you find any letters?"

"Not yet."

She laughed. "You think you're going to have additional opportunity? I can assure you, you're done rummaging through my things."

"What are you going to do, shoot me?"

"If you turn toward the bureau again, I will. I'll shoot you in the back, and say I was startled by an intruder and shot before realizing it was you." She smiled. "Don't be disappointed. There are no letters."

"Because you destroyed them?"

"Does Captain McAllen know you're snooping around my room?"

"No. He and Earp are discussing Carl's arrest." I took another step toward her. "I may not have found the letters, but I found something else that proves the captain is wrong about Carl doing this on his own."

She remained smug. "What did you find?"

I pulled a lady's handkerchief from my left pocket and then dramatically drew a soiled one from my right pocket. "I believe these are both yours."

She looked perplexed. "So what?"

I held up the neatly folded handkerchief in my left hand. "I found this one in your drawer." I held up the soiled handkerchief in my right hand, stepping forward as if to hand it to her. "This one I found off the trail to Thumb Butte. Morris Goldwater says he has only sold this particular handkerchief to you."

"I rode that trail every day."

"Yes, you did . . . with Maggie. She says you not only never threw anything from your horse but scolded her harshly when she threw away a wadded-up piece of wax paper she had used for her peppermint stick." I again held up the soiled hankie and again moved closer to her. "This proves you were there when Campbell was murdered and helped Carl drag the body away from the barn. It'll change McAllen's mind."

"Those hankies only prove that you're a pest . . . a dangerous pest."

I could read her thoughts on her face, and I didn't like what I was reading.

"You're right and wrong," she said. "There were letters, but they're ashes now. But I didn't kill Elisha for money. That was just an additional benefit to something already good. After Carl whimpered for forgiveness, I couldn't allow Elisha to walk around blabbering away about me. It was too unseemly."

She raised the gun slightly but kept it aimed at me. "These derringers are terrible for any distance over a couple feet. Thank you for moving closer."

I knew she was squeezing the trigger, and I was just a bit too far away to lunge at her. I heard a terrific pounding on the wall as I jumped to the side.

"Mary, we heard everything!" It was McAllen yelling from Maggie's room.

I thought nothing could be louder, but then I heard two earsplitting reports from the tiny derringer. When I threw myself, I hit the bed and bounced back up. Mary had fired two blind shots through the wall into the next room. She dropped the derringer and reached inside her blouse for her pocket pistol. Her second gun was proving harder to retrieve. She never made it. I hit her with a closed-fist punch, using every bit of strength I could muster. She banged against the wall and slid into a sitting position. Her head flopped to the side, and I knew she was knocked out. I reached inside her blouse and found her small-caliber revolver cleverly holstered in the middle of her chest so her bosom helped to hide it. As I stood, I unloaded it and flipped the small pistol onto the bed. I grabbed her chin and straightened her head, but when I let go, it just flopped to the side again. I could see that her jaw would never work smoothly again.

I raced into the hall only to find McAllen and Earp racing to Mary's room.

"Anyone hit?" I asked.

"No," Earp said. "The captain suggested we listen low to the floor. I guess he knew she was a hothead."

"What'd you do to her?" McAllen asked.

"Laid a Jeff Sharp roundhouse into her jaw. She's out, but where's Carl?"

"You bastard! You had no right!" Carl sounded frantic.

I whirled around as a hand on my shoulder shoved me down. I immediately went to one knee and drew my Remington from my shoulder holster. Carl fired first—and second. Then a barrage of bullets from three guns drove him backward down the hall until he hit the window casing and broke the window with the back of his head. As I watched him bend backwards, my vision was obscured by so much gun smoke that I slid forward and lay down to see better and get a breath.

The smoke was taking a long time to clear the narrow hallway, so I kept my aim where I thought Carl should be. Soon I felt someone step over me, and then I heard the door to Maggie's room open. It was McAllen—and he had dripped blood on me.

"That should help clear the smoke," McAllen said.

It did. And what it revealed was grotesque. Carl hung partially out the window. His head was bent so far back that he looked headless, his torso was riddled with holes, and blood pooled around his feet.

I scrambled to my feet and glanced at Earp to see if he had been shot. He looked whole, so I went to McAllen, who was wincing as he held his arm.

"Where did he hit you?"

"Just the arm, but it hurts like hell. Damned

easterner was never very good with a handgun. Hell, we were only eight feet away."

"I can't believe you're complaining about his marksmanship."

"Gotta sit."

He went into Maggie's room and sat on a chair. I stood there perplexed, but Earp knew what to do. He ripped apart one of the stethoscopes on the floor and used the rubber tubing as a tourniquet. When he got McAllen a glass of water, I finally figured out what I ought to be doing and went to the next room to check on Mary. She was still knocked out cold. I picked her up, dragged her by the armpits into Maggie's room, and dropped her unceremoniously onto the bare floor.

"How is he?" I asked Earp.

"Hell, Steve, I'm right here. Ask me."

"How are you, Captain?"

"In a lot of pain and happy as can be."

Chapter 49

Mrs. Cunningham's dining room rang with laughter. Sharp's ribald quips, facial antics, and really bad accents had put everyone in a gay mood. Mrs. Cunningham laughed heartily and put a hand on Sharp's forearm. Then Sharp covered her hand with his. The entire time I had been a boarder in her house, Mrs. Cunningham and I had remained barely civil. Yet Sharp had bounced in from jail, capturing her attention in mere minutes. Seating herself next to him, she had been flirtatious all evening. I had watched the entire episode and still couldn't tell what he had done that was so special.

The guests included all of the boarders, as well as McAllen, Earp, and Maggie. Mrs. Cunningham had prepared a pot roast with all the fixings, including fresh vegetables brought up from Mexico. She was a fine cook and everything tasted delicious.

The bullet had passed through McAllen's upper left arm. The doctor had said he was lucky the bullet had glanced off the humerus and passed right through his biceps brachii. He had cleaned and wrapped the wound, put the arm in a sling, and told McAllen the wound would require lots of alcohol—administered both externally and internally. With the meal only half over, McAllen had already done a manly job on a bottle of Jameson.

At the other end of the table, Maggie and John sat next to each other in an entirely different world. I could not care less. With her father present, I felt relieved of any responsibility. Besides, I was sharing the bottle of Jameson.

It was a merry party, as it ought to have been. Sharp was a free man, Mary sat in his cell, and the stock certificate that might have challenged my ownership had been destroyed. While McAllen was getting doctored, I wrote a letter to Anna Cabot Lodge that hopefully would ruin Jonathon Winslow's career. I had enjoyed posting that letter. Everything was finished off nicely, so there was good reason to enjoy this celebratory supper.

Then I remembered an unfinished item.

"Captain, in the morning we need to see Judge Carter about Blanchet."

"Already taken care of," Earp said. "He's keeping Mrs. Schmidt company in jail."

"How did that happen?" I asked.

"I was informed that he was a fugitive from Nebraska. I was able to verify the allegation with a quick series of telegrams and arrested him just prior to coming over here for dinner."

"There was a reward on his head," I said.

"A substantial one . . . a thousand dollars. Yes, sir. Somebody earned a nice grubstake."

I looked at McAllen, but he was looking at Earp with a perplexed expression. Our end of the table suddenly grew quiet.

"Who is this someone who *informed* you?" McAllen demanded.

"Listen, Joseph, I understand that you knew about this for a while, but you didn't officially inform me, and you didn't fill out the paperwork. You know how this is supposed to work. The first person to bring a fugitive to the attention of an officer of the court is the acknowledged claimant for the reward. I'm sorry."

"I didn't ask for a lecture; I asked who this someone was."

"Don't get hot. This is a good person. Might even be a detective one day. Her name is Maggie McAllen."

"Maggie!"

Now the entire table grew quiet. At the other end, Maggie and John had been talking with their heads bent together.

With the shout of her name, she straightened, and said, "Yes, Pa."

McAllen just stared down the table at her. Everyone's gaze alternated between McAllen's bewildered look and Maggie's contrived expression of pure innocence. I glanced at Sharp, and he gave me a big, broad wink. I immediately knew he had tipped her to be quick about turning Blanchet in to Constable Earp. I bet she'd done it with relish. Soon I was laughing. Sharp joined me, and then the whole table laughed, except for father and daughter. Someone leaned over and told Maggie what the fuss was about. Finally, she stood and waited for the ruckus to settle down.

When all eyes were on her, she did a perfect curtsy and said, "I'm flattered by the attention, but it's no more than any of you would have done. By the way, Mr. Earp, I would appreciate it if the money was deposited in my name at Durango First Bank."

Now McAllen joined in the laughter.

Chapter 50

The next morning, I knocked on Sharp's door, but he didn't answer. I followed the giggling conversation and found him in the forbidden kitchen with our landlady.

Standing at the door, I said, "Good morning."

I got a return greeting from both and was told breakfast would be a little late. Mrs. Cunningham giggled again and threw me an orange. I caught it and went out to the front porch to eat it. I didn't want my orange spoiled by their merriment. In a few minutes, Sharp came out with two china mugs of coffee. I said thanks and gave him a quizzical look. He just smiled contentedly, staring into the middle distance.

"The last time you walked out onto a porch with two mugs of coffee was at the St. Charles Hotel in Carson City . . . just before we started this adventure."

"Are ya suggestin' we oughta start a new adventure?"

"After breakfast."

"After breakfast," he repeated.

We sat a few minutes watching the street traffic. Most of it was heading for Mrs. Potter's Café.

"Are you free to depart?" I asked.

"Except for the last week, I've always been free

to depart." He took a sip. "Maybe a day or two more. Like ya said, Leadville's still frozen solid."

I glanced toward the house, but Sharp declined to satisfy my curiosity.

"It's a pleasant little town," he said. "Haven't seen much beyond the Palace an' that jail in the courthouse." He used his mug to point out the building, as if I would be confused by another courthouse in the vicinity. "Yep, now that I'm free, think I'd like to look 'round a bit."

"McAllen is leaving on tomorrow's stage. Escorting Maggie back to Durango."

"Hate stage travel, but if ya gotta do it, now's the time of year. Hell, those stages sure get ripe when it's hot."

I pulled out a folded piece of paper and handed it to Sharp. He read the letter and whistled. The wire was from Richard in Carson City. He begged Sharp and me to return because Jenny Bolton was taking over the state. She had the governor in her pocket, was the de facto leader of the cattlemen's association, and had just purchased the second biggest mine in Virginia City. Richard wanted help because she was also building a little army composed of cutthroat lawyers and gunmen.

He handed the letter back. "You promised to go to Leadville."

"I did . . . and we shall."

"Now?"

"Maybe a day or two more. Like you said,

Leadville's still frozen solid," I responded, badly imitating Sharp's accent.

We both laughed.

"I'm done with Nevada," I said. "I've helped my friends over and over, but they just keep needing help. You were right: knock down one crook, and another just pops up."

"So, it's on to Leadville?"

"Yes, but first snow, I want to go somewhere else."

"Where ya thinkin' 'bout goin'?"

"Menlo Park."

Center Point Publishing
600 Brooks Road ● PO Box 1
Thorndike ME 04986-0001 USA

(207) 568-3717

US & Canada:
1 800 929-9108
www.centerpointlargeprint.com